The Mountain of Light

The Mountain of Light

Claire Allen

review

Copyright © 2004 Claire Allen

The right of Claire Allen to be identified as the Author of
the Work has been asserted by her in accordance with the
Copyright, Designs and Patents Act 1988.

First published in Great Britain in 2004
by REVIEW

An imprint of Headline Book Publishing

10   9   8   7   6   5   4   3   2   1

All characters in this publication are fictitious
and any resemblance to real persons, living or dead,
is purely coincidental.

Cataloguing in Publication Data is available from the British Library

ISBN 0 7553 0740 2

Typeset in Minion by Palimpsest Book Production Limited,
Polmont, Stirlingshire
Printed and bound in Great Britain by
Mackays of Chatham Ltd, Chatham, Kent

Headline's policy is to use papers that are natural, renewable and
recyclable products and made from wood grown in sustainable forests.
The logging and manufacturing processes are expected to conform to the
environmental regulations of the country of origin.

Headline Book Publishing
A division of Hodder Headline
338 Euston Road
London NW1 3BH

www.reviewbooks.co.uk
www.hodderheadline.com

For Paul

Acknowledgements

Thank you to Susannah and Mary-Anne, and to everyone else who gave me help and encouragement. I would also like to acknowledge Jan Ciepliński's book, *The History of Polish Ballet 1518–1945*.

The Mountain of Light

Balu moves sedately; careful and ponderous, he is like a bear on a tightrope. When he walks he holds his head and shoulders well back, as if there were a pendulum weight somehow attached to the back of his head, threatening to pull him over backwards. This posture throws his belly out to the front, so that it appears to lead him as he glides up and down the central aisle of his demesne, beaming radiance and welcome, confetti-like, on all who enter.

He is at his happiest between seven and eight o'clock. He perches on a high stool in a mirrored grotto from where he distributes chilled bottles of wine, beer and mineral water from beneath a counter. Behind his head the wall is tiled entirely with a mosaic of tiny silver mirrored squares which make the neatly arranged shelves of beer and wine glasses appear twice as laden.

Running wide and low around the restaurant walls, a band of these same reflecting tiles throws the diners' smiles and red-shining faces back at them each time they cast furtive glances around the restaurant. The worn red velveteen covering the chairs is warmly welcoming, the heavy chairs clumsy yet comfortable. Balu favours candles and muted lights; he has a dimmer switch which he can sometimes be seen turning minutely, anxious to get everything just right. No diner would ever suspect such attention, yet plenty agree that it is a restaurant to linger in even when the food is gone.

Balu started here as a waiter, more than twenty years ago.

He had been in Britain for one winter and was beginning to wish he hadn't come at all. But he was given this job and so he had stayed. Ten years later, and an unidentified number of stones heavier, the restaurant was his. Well, truthfully, it belonged to his brother, Jayesh, as well. When the elderly owner finally died, the two brothers took it over with the agreement that if Jayesh paid for the business and dealt with the money side of things – he had, by then, been working as an accountant for ten years in the City – and Balu dealt with the day-to-day running of the restaurant, the hiring and firing of staff and all the kitchen side of things, any profit or loss would be shared equally between them. And so, to all outward appearances, Balu was the sole proprietor, because Jayesh had made it clear from the outset that he wasn't really interested in food or the magic that could be conjured by the mixing of one spice with another, nor the pleasure that could be taken in the rituals and repeated processes of preparing ingredients. The comfort in the thud, thud, thud of dough against wood, or the precise, twisting wrist action which ground spices into a fine powder. Jayesh was really just interested in it as a business. And so every morning he would leave the flat upstairs in his spruce suit, and Balu would watch him (looking increasingly nervous, as the years went by, probably in case he was seen leaving what was, after all, only a flat above a shop) walking smartly along the road to the tube station to catch the Underground to Liverpool Street. Balu would have been up at five thirty and already out to buy fresh meat and vegetables from the market by then, and he would stand at the front window with his mug of coffee, watching his brother's diminishing figure.

In the hour between seven and eight the evening is young.

All the food that can be has been prepared. Stainless steel vats, tightly lidded, hold dishes which have been cooking slowly all day, and every inch of shelf space in the fridges is filled. Bowls of peeled and chopped potatoes, topped and tailed okra, chopped coriander, lime juice, skinned tomatoes, yoghurt and shredded cucumber stand on the surfaces, covered with cling film or clean tea towels, and there is, all of a sudden, nothing to do but wait. Balu, for a time, leaves the kitchen and squeezes himself behind the counter, watching the tables gradually fill up.

Before, when he lived in the flat upstairs, he would have used this time to return there, going out the back way, through the kitchen and up the fire escape. He would unlock the door into the flat and untwine his cat, Sita, from around his ankles, bending down to scratch her under the chin, feeling the motor purring under her skin, her throaty pleasure thrumming loudly in the silence. He would uncover the plate of meat scraps he had accumulated from the kitchen and carefully carried up for her, and scrape them into her bowl which he first rinsed out in the sink. All the while Sita would be rubbing and twirling round his ankles as he waited for the trickle of water to give off steam, twiddling his fingers in it, hearing the tink of it against the metal sides of the sink.

Whilst she ate he would escape to the bathroom and diligently roll up his sleeves, humming quietly sometimes, before preparing his implements, lining up his brush and soap and checking for rogue hairs still clinging to the razor from the morning, for a clean shave. He had always shaved twice a day when he lived in the flat. Afterwards he would splash his face with cold water and rinse out the basin and, again, check the razor, carefully separating the head and holding it firmly between chubby thumb and forefinger beneath the full-flowing tap, watching the short black bristles, like a fall of tiny fine dashes drawn in Indian ink, gradually diminish in number and disappear down the plughole.

At some point, as he pulled a comb through his dampened hair, watching the teeth channel deep, evenly spaced furrows like a plough turning over rich, black earth, Sita would appear in the doorway and he would watch her in the mirror, first licking round and round her chops and then alternately glancing up at him with round, questioning marble eyes and bending briskly backwards and sideways, washing every inch of her already impeccable ebony sheen. As he dibbed his finger-tips into a pot of hair cream and ran them across his head, spotting, here and there, single, defiantly grey hairs, she would clasp her tail tip between her two front paws, pinning it against the floor, and show it the round ridiculous pinkness of her tongue.

 confused

'Look,' he said to Sarah, the first time they met, after he had shown her round the flat. 'I don't know if you want it or not, but let me give you something to eat. And a drink. A coffee.'

She nodded. All day she had been going in and out of houses and flats, up and down stale-smelling stairs, shivering in miserably small rooms with shabby curtains and depressing, yellowed wallpaper. This was certainly the best she had seen so far. It was above an Indian restaurant called the Mountain of Light. It had a living room with doors which opened onto the protruding rooftop of the front of the restaurant below. The rooftop was safe to walk on, he said. You could put chairs out in the summer.

She doubted that. She could hear the traffic from the busy road the restaurant stood on, even with the doors closed. She certainly couldn't imagine herself sitting out there. And anyway, right in the centre of it was a peculiar dome-shaped skylight, like an ornate, miniature palm house. She saw herself tripping and falling through it, crashing down into the busy restaurant beneath. He must have seen her looking at it because he rushed to open the doors, gesturing her out onto the roof so that she could get a better view. He followed her out and stood eagerly beside her as she struggled to find the right words with which to frame her doubtful admiration. He was evidently enormously pleased with it. He had designed it himself, he told her, in confidential tones, leaning closer to her so that she felt the plump outer edge of his arm press softly against her shoulder. She had the feeling that he was trying to keep her there. Almost as though he had decided that she was the right person for his flat and was working on the assumption that the longer he kept her there the more likely she was to decide to stay indefinitely. He had had the skylight installed two years ago, he said, nodding enthusiastically as he spoke, as much to himself as to her, as if to confirm, to underline his achievement. She found herself nodding along with him as they stood side by side on the roof of his restaurant.

Back inside, he demonstrated the wooden shutters which closed across the doors instead of curtains, and again she got the feeling he was keen for her to stay longer. He shut out the watery March daylight then let it in again after a silent couple of seconds standing there together in the dark. Well, they, at least, were a plus point, she thought.

The kitchen, smelling faintly of old cooking, had a table and chairs there already. He was leaving most of the furniture, he said. And the back door opened onto a fire escape which took you down to the huge metal wheelie bins outside the kitchen door at the back of the restaurant.

Only two weeks before, Balu had finally moved out of the flat where he had lived for more than ten years. His health wasn't getting any better. He had been having pains down his left arm and had felt funny, fluttering sensations in his chest and stomach which had eventually, with Sharmila, his sister-in-law's constant nagging, taken him along to register with a GP's surgery and see a doctor. Once the doctor had got over her initial shock at his never once having been to see a doctor in twenty years, she examined him, pushing a cold stethoscope through the gap he had coyly allowed her in his shirt by unbuttoning two buttons; asked him lots of questions about his diet, whether he exercised, and whether he smoked or drank, and wrote out an appointment slip for him to go and see a specialist at the Royal London Hospital. Just to rule out any problems there might be with your heart, she said, as delicately as she could. And so he had caught the bus to Whitechapel Road with the appointment card tucked carefully into the inside pocket of his too-tight jacket, had found his way through the labyrinthine sprawl of buildings and back streets and, after a good deal of patient waiting, had been told that he had angina. Now he had pills which he took every evening, and he dissolved a daily soluble aspirin on his tongue as he performed his morning ablutions.

Sadly, regretfully, he had packed his belongings into cardboard boxes brought by Sharmila from the supermarket in the boot of her car, and had unpacked them in the little room in their new house in Enfield. From now on he was to live with

Jayesh, Sharmila and the baby. It distressed him greatly that some stranger would be living in the flat and he had placed the advert in *Loot* with a heavy heart. He'd had about five phone messages about it so far and he had returned only two of the calls. Something about them, either the tone of voice or the words they used, had put him off and he had known they wouldn't do. When Sarah phoned that morning he had been standing by the phone and had picked it up. He had liked the sound of her voice, perhaps the unsureness he could detect, and he had invited her to visit the flat the same afternoon. He was acting impulsively now, a habit neither customary nor comfortable, but he felt, in an indefinable way he sometimes had which he could only put down to instinct, that she was the right person. As he pointed out every last detail of the place he hoped she didn't mind too much, but he wanted his tour to win enough of her heart to persuade her to stay.

Sarah followed him out of the flat, down the fire escape and into his restaurant through the kitchen at the back. Proudly, he extended his arm to indicate, in a broad, upward angled sweep, the ordered tables; the mirrored walls, quietly spangling away unnoticed; the clouded glass shades muting the wall lights; the newly painted ceiling, a deep, warm red, gridded into metre squares with bold, turmeric-coloured lines running the length and breadth of the restaurant along raised channels of beading which gave a panelled effect; and, finally, the soaring edifice of glass, which drowned the front half of the long, narrow room in pallid, rain-filled light.

She sat in this gloomy brightness at an empty table near the huge, plate-glass window at the front of the restaurant and waited for the coffee she felt she had not been allowed to refuse. Outside, a spare-looking woman with a double pushchair marched across the window, her blank face fixed at some point in the distance invisible to Sarah, her arms stretched out straight as rods as she leaned into the combined weight of two stolid toddlers and the bulging shopping bags which hung heavily from the handles. Sarah had already decided that, all in all, she had better take the place, was already readjusting her impressions of it until, by the time the fat Indian man reappeared with the steaming cup rattling in its saucer, they were almost favourable. Yes, OK, so you had to go along a dark, narrow passageway and up those steep, narrow stairs before you even got to the flat. And yes, the wallpaper was foul, and there was a nauseating range of swirly-patterned carpets that could drive you insane, really, if you spent too long cooped up in there, staring at them. And there was the oblig-atory mahogany-coloured bedroom furniture, with the heavy wardrobe leaning at a dangerous looking tilt into the room, and that hideous dressing table with adjustable side mirrors so you could see your face from every conceivable angle. Her grandmother had had one of those when she was a child and she remembered spending hours upstairs in the unheated bedroom with her sisters, playing make-up and hairdressers in front of it. But in the flat's favour were those wooden shutters. For some reason they had escaped adornment, and were completely unpainted. On either side of the window was a tidy little niche which they folded neatly into. And that little scrap of rooftop outside. Wouldn't she be able to do something with that? Was there any reason why she shouldn't fill it with plants and have her own little garden? It looked like nothing now, with the ugly grey roofing stuff it was covered in, and that ridiculous glass dome thing in the middle. She peered up at it from where she was sitting, wondering whether anybody eating down here would be able to see her if she were on the roof.

The Indian man returned and placed the steaming cup of coffee on the table in front of her and stood uncertainly for a moment or two before pulling out another chair and lowering himself into it. She noticed he didn't choose the one directly opposite her. He seemed awkward, in a vulnerable, almost innocent way, she thought, sipping carefully at the coffee. His geniality was genuine, but it masked something – perhaps shyness, or loneliness – which made him appear slightly over-eager. She decided she liked him and told him she would take the flat.

ॐ

Balu's ideas for the skylight had fermented slowly, like a plump pat of dough rising over a period of months. Once the notion had seeded itself and taken tentative root he had started to sketch out spidery little drawings on the backs of old envelopes at odd moments in the restaurant, tucking them hurriedly into the deep pocket at the front of his apron if anyone should walk into the kitchen and disturb him.

By the time his plan had taken firmer root, and was sending out nervous green tendrils to sniff above ground, Balu had condensed his bundle of scrappy doodles into one much bolder plan, drawn carefully to scale with a ruler on a sheet of graph paper, bought especially for this purpose from a cramped little stationery shop he had spotted underneath the railway bridge. Out on the flat roof above the front of the restaurant one morning he carefully measured and marked out

9

a rectangle in chalk. Then, following closely a scaled-down version of the same shape on another piece of graph paper, which he kept extracting from his apron, consulting, and then carefully replacing, he drew a short diagonal line across each of the corners of the rectangle, and then scuffed out the original corners with the toe of his shoe. Once this was done he sat down briefly, puffing slightly at the exertion, on the single deckchair which, apart from a mop and bucket in the corner, was all that there was on the little square of rooftop, and admired his work. So far so good.

The next step had been to find someone to make the skylight. This wasn't the kind of thing you could just go and buy from B&Q, he realised, rather self-importantly. It would need a craftsman. He did his initial research by telephone, working his way through the Glaziers, Leaded Lights, Joiners and Window Manufacturers – Special Purpose sections of the Yellow Pages and repeating his request down the phone so many times that it became almost mantra-like and started to sound faintly ridiculous. Eventually he had found a couple of places that might be willing to do the work. Then began the surreptitious ferrying of strange men in overalls up the back fire escape – for he wanted no one to know about his plans just yet – to measure up for quotations. Only after all this, armed with details of the cost, timescale, disruption to the business, *et cetera*, did he lay his scheme in front of Jayesh.

ॐ

Balu gave Sarah free rein in the flat. When she said she would like to take it, she tentatively asked if he very much wanted the decor to stay as it was, and he said no, he was sure her tastes were for something a little more modern. There was something rather wistful about the way he said this, and she was tempted to say she didn't really mind it the way it was after all, just to save his feelings. But standing in the middle of the living room, surrounded by the boxes and black bin bags one of the waiters from downstairs had helped her bring up, she knew she would drown if the wallpaper, at the very least, wasn't silenced.

She bought four large tins of white emulsion, left her stuff in the boxes piled up in the middle of the living room, and covered the floor in newspaper. She went down the fire escape and knocked on the kitchen door, hoping there was a ladder somewhere around that she could borrow. The door was propped open with an enormous yellow tub of ghee, and she could see a man she hadn't yet met inside, stirring one of the huge steaming pans on the stove. She knocked again and cleared her throat; there was loud disco music playing on the radio, and the stirring man was jigging his hip in time with it. Eventually, the waiter who had helped her with the boxes came in through the door dividing the kitchen from the restaurant and saw her standing there, half in the room and half out. He shoved the other man playfully aside and reached over to the radio to lower the volume.

'You'll never get Colin's attention,' he said, laughing, and began to sing: 'He's lost in music. La la lalala.' She smiled, and the aproned man finally turned round, a little bewildered, and smiled too. 'This is Colin, Balu's second-in-command,' he said, with theatrical gravity, and Colin smiled again nervously as he extended his hand. His voice, when he spoke, was softly Irish, his face a little like a cherub's.

The waiter fooled with the tea towel he was holding, flicking it a couple of times with a practised snap of the wrist so that it cracked neatly in the air. Sarah asked about a ladder, feeling suddenly self-conscious, but he willingly scampered off to find one and with his help she carried it up the fire escape and into the newspapered flat.

'Looks better already' he said, glancing round the living room, with the sofa and chair pushed up against her pile of boxes and covered with some sheets she had found on the wardrobe shelf. He was good-looking, she thought. She hadn't really noticed the day before, she'd been so intent on bringing her things up the stairs and getting rid of him. Carelessly pristine. His hair looked freshly cut and was shiny and black. He was dressed in his waiter's outfit – black trousers and a white shirt – and there was something so perfect, just for a moment, about him, standing there in the mess of the room and the debris of the past few days, that she didn't reply immediately, but looked at him in slightly breath-held silence.

'Oh, Balu said to ask you down to the restaurant tonight,' he said. He had noticed her silence and wasn't especially troubled by it. He forked his fingers through his hair. 'I think he wants to welcome you.' He placed the tiniest emphasis on the 'welcome', so that, after he had gone and she was alone with the ladder and the tins of paint, she wondered whether he disapproved of her.

She had a feeling Balu was rather old-fashioned and courteous, and intended this meal to be a rather formal affair, and so she made an effort, scrubbing the dried paint off her hands and elbows in the bath and pinning up her hair. For the most inexplicable reason, she felt nervously excited. As if this meal were somehow important. Silly really; she'd only moved house. But it was more than that, she supposed. She had got a flat of her own, away from the communal existence of student houses and, before that, the tumble and din of life with her mother and younger sister, Joan, both with their endless processions of boyfriends and arguments. She fumbled in one of the black bin bags for her black skirt and found, instead, a dark red dress she had worn only once before and had forgotten she had. Lucky dip, she thought, and stepped into it, zipping it up and adjusting it over her bra straps in the wardrobe mirror. It was chilly in the bedroom and she felt the prickle of goose pimples up and down her arms as she looked at herself. Too severe, she thought, and loosened a few wisps of hair so that they hung down on either side of her face, softening the effect. She dug around for a bit until she found a tiny black cardigan, and pulled this on, knotting the ends together at the front so that it looked like one of the crossover type of cardigans dancers wear. She put her shoes on and checked again in the mirror, then sang her way down the stairs and fire escape to the door at the back of the restaurant.

She was feeling buoyant. For a while after finishing university she had felt as if she was drifting and had feared a slide into the kind of locked-away inertia that she dreaded. One by one, people she had grown used to had moved away, finding jobs, moving in with boyfriends, and she had decided, in the end, that if she didn't take the opportunity the freedom of her rootlessness offered her, something would happen and she would end up staying for ever in the safe, unexciting little town she had fetched up in. And so she had decided to move to London. She had planned to stay for a couple of weeks with someone she knew vaguely, someone she had lived next door to in halls in the first year and had kept in sporadic contact with. She would camp in a sleeping bag on their living room floor by night and trawl the streets by day, flat-hunting. By the end of the first week, though, after poking her head round the door of every damp-smelling poky room for rent north of the river, she had worked her way down to Balu's advert in *Loot*.

It was eight o'clock, the restaurant was already buzzing with conversation and heavy with the mingled smells of frying garlic, seared meat and hot spices. The sleek-haired waiter, whose name she realised she didn't yet know despite their having met twice already, led her a little too ceremoniously to a table at the back, smaller than the rest and slightly apart from them, where Balu was waiting. He stood up immediately when he saw her, knocking the side of the table slightly and dragging at the tablecloth as he sidled out from his place to welcome her. He looked at her strangely, and she wondered whether she had misjudged the occasion and was over-dressed. The waiter, too, had had to conceal something in his expression when he saw her. Oh well, what the hell. It wasn't as if she was teetering on six-inch heels and wearing a boob tube; they'd only ever seen her in jeans and a holey jumper before, anyway.

'What can I say?' said Balu, having managed to squeeze himself from between chair and table and regain some of his composure. She noticed there were beads of moisture on his temples. 'You look absolutely beautiful. I couldn't wish for anyone more delightful to live in my flat and look after my Sita!'

Now here was another thing. When she had come to see the flat nothing had been said about Sita although there had been plenty of opportunity. Not until she had moved in yesterday had Balu confessed that, yes, the cat on the kitchen table which was looking quizzically at her was a sitting tenant, and that, yes, if she didn't mind very much, he would like her to look after Sita. He had been deeply apologetic in his admission, as if he felt she might think him guilty of fraud and consider taking legal action. He would provide money for Sita's food and any necessary expenditure, of course. And really, she was not a troublesome creature. But if Sarah objected, of course he would make alternative arrangements.

Balu was shameless in his bowing and scraping apologies. But the cat was not a problem; it was delightful and sleek and beautiful. 'Well,' she had said out loud to it that afternoon, as she rolled the first band of pure white across the hideous, screaming wallpaper, 'it's just you and me now,' and it had chirruped appreciatively as it settled itself down at the foot of the ladder to watch.

Balu had prepared something special, something not on the usual menu, for her tonight, and the waiter served them as if they were real customers. It was all very friendly. Balu introduced them quite formally, forgetting they had already met.

'Hari, this is Sarah, our new tenant. Sarah, this is Hari, one of my marvellous waiters, without whom,' he said, with a glance in the young man's direction, 'we could not manage. He has impeccable manners,' he added, turning back to her, as if this were something in particular to know about him. They shook hands. There was a sharpness, a curl of animosity, she thought, in Hari's smile. She found it odd, considering how friendly he had been earlier. Maybe it was the falseness of this situation or having to wait on her that he didn't like.

As they ate, she listened to Balu's enthusiastic answers to her polite questions, and discovered that the busiest hour was between nine and ten. Later, when the last group of diners were on their coffees, Hari joined them, and Sarah began to realise the depth of the relationship between the two. Balu wasn't just an employer; the two were friends, were almost like father and son. They shared jokes and memories of customers. They interrupted each other. At one point Hari corrected Balu when he was listing the essential ingredients of a *dansak*. Balu waved away the younger man's interjection as if it were so much fluff or thistledown.

She had felt rather awkward at first when Hari joined them, sitting opposite her at the small table, and she had to stop herself from looking at him too intently. The conversation shifted away from her, as conversations do when two people know each other better than they know the third person, and she felt easier again. He saw that her glass was empty and filled it deftly without pausing in what he was saying to Balu or breaking eye contact with him beyond a quick glance at her wine glass. He was practised with people, she thought. He had a physical fluency which neither she nor Balu possessed.

When the last group had paid and put on their coats, Hari showed them out, thanking them for their comments about the food, wishing them goodnight, and locking the door behind them. She felt the first pang of attraction then, as he closed the blinds and tidied away the last of their meal, carrying the stacked plates and dishes back into the kitchen. What she liked was the way he seemed so comfortable in himself, within the space he occupied. There was a self-sufficient ease in his movements, his way of dealing with things. He seemed the kind of person who sorted things out, got things done. She couldn't imagine him ever being short-tempered or weary of customers, or at least ever showing it. He could keep up an appearance without any awkwardness, almost as if he was protected by it. And he was beautiful. When he came back to the table and sat in the chair opposite again she felt herself blush at his glance.

Back in the flat, she found herself reviewing the evening in terms of how much of it had been Hari. Already, she was searching for a way in, wondering whether there was anything that went beyond politeness in the way he acted towards her, looking for evidence in glances or comments. She dwelt on the minutes they had been alone at the table when Balu had gone to fetch more wine. A slightly awkward silence and his sudden, blurted offer to help with the painting on his day off. He wouldn't have done that, would he, if there hadn't been a flicker of something?

She hung the red dress on a hanger and put it in the empty wardrobe, her movement disturbing all the other hangers, making them clang together mournfully in the echoey darkness, and left the rest of her clothes on the floor before climbing into the strange bed.

He arrived unexpectedly early at her door. And so, while she rather shamefacedly got dressed, Hari set to work. By the time she was washed and dressed, he had already covered half a wall in fresh, white paint, and the smell of newness filled the room and was creeping into the hall.

While they waited for the first coat to dry they sat on the floor and smoked. Sarah still felt a little awkward with him and sensed his restraint more than ever. She felt she couldn't ask him anything about himself, and was horrified at the thought that he might think her rude for not doing so, because he had asked her. But it seemed like politeness rather than interest, the expected questions you ask when you meet someone new. And, because she was nervous, she found herself chattering on, spilling out silly anecdotes, filling the dreaded silence while he sat and listened.

They finished painting the room, but she had a vaguely uncomfortable feeling all day, and by the end of it she had deflatedly accepted that he didn't much like her. After he had gone she stood for a long time in the middle of the shrouded, white room, unable to make herself uncover the furniture and the floor, and then she went to bed.

She certainly wasn't expecting him the following afternoon. His voice on the entryphone was noncommittal and brief.

'I'm outside. Are you busy?'

When he came in he seemed agitated, anxious. She wondered fleetingly if he was angry with her. He wouldn't sit down and his face had lost some of its brittle perfection; he looked exposed and jagged. It was raining quite heavily; spring was slow in starting this year and March had so far been nothing but wetness and gloom. He had been caught briefly in it and had sheltered in the doorway before ringing the bell. Now he looked forlornly out of the open shutters at the rain pinging off the skylight on the flat roof outside, wondering whether he should just leave. He didn't know why he had come.

'What's wrong?' Sarah dared herself to ask. He massaged the side of his face with one hand and looked at her as if he had been stung. 'You don't have to tell me,' she added quickly, with a nervous smile.

'I thought . . . well. I thought you might need some more help.' It sounded excruciatingly lame.

Afterwards, she couldn't remember the precise choreography that led them from opposite sides of the room into each

18

other's arms. The memory of it was all tumbled together in a curious mixture of sympathy, awkward embarrassment and a sudden surge of fumbling desire. They made love on the sofa which was still covered with one of the old sheets she had found in the wardrobe, pulling urgently at each other's clothes, kissing deeply, hungrily. She felt his fingers in her hair, his fists clenching handfuls of it, anchoring her head as if she were chained down. It was a wordless, almost soundless act, without eye contact. When it was over they lay in silence as their breathing slowed and stilled. She wanted to kiss his neck, to stroke the pale brown chest her cheek was resting against, but she feared he might pull away from such familiarity and so she lay still.

After the first time, he came up to the flat often. From the restaurant he came up the fire escape at the end of a long night and tapped on the door. If Balu knew anything about it he never let on, and neither of them mentioned it to anyone. It was an unspoken agreement that it need concern only themselves and something about it always seemed temporary. He never stayed the night, and they never made love in the bedroom. Somehow this was significant. As if they both knew it was an arrangement of convenience. He never said he loved her.

She enjoyed the attention of his body, his sexual confidence, although even this seemed to be a guard against anything further. Theirs was not an intimate lovemaking, she realised later, after she had met Jude; it was sexual acrobatics. Even after weeks, she had no idea of his feelings for her, and she didn't ask. She wondered at times whether he might be in love with her but dismissed the idea almost as soon as it shaped itself. Sometimes she prayed for him to appear, her appetite for him suddenly enormous, and when he tapped at the kitchen door she flung it open and they would start undressing each other, crashing against the table, knocking things over and laughing.

She made the rooftop into a garden, filling it with red geraniums. Her mother and stepfather came to visit and brought with them a miniature Japanese maple which she put in the far corner. In the April breezes the serrated burgundy leaves stirred gently, silhouetted against the orange glow from the street light.

The garden quickly became a passion. She bought a book about herbs and filled innumerable little pots with lavender, savory, mint and thyme. As spring moved into summer and the rain stopped she took to lying outside on a pile of blankets and cushions, reading voraciously, devouring all the books she had meant to read at university but had never had enough time for. Now, her time at home was free, was hers to do with as she liked. She had signed on and had put cards in a few shop windows offering cleaning, ironing, babysitting. For the time being that was enough. There was nothing she particularly wanted to do. At the end of a chapter she would pause, placing her open book face down, and stretch luxuriously, looking up at the sun filtering through the spindly, fine as lace leaves of a fennel plant.

At night the ornamental skylight glowed like a huge, halved honeydew melon in the centre of the flat rooftop, sitting like a smug fruit amongst the muddle of flower pots. When she picked mint, or snapped off a mauve lavender flower to crumble in her fingers and release the sweet, rosemaryish scent, she peered down onto the heads of people dining in the restaurant below and saw forks raised to mouths, and the flatness of round plates, oval serving dishes, square, white-clothed tables. Empty plates were whisked away by disembodied arms, people suddenly stood up to leave and their heads disappeared from view. Tablecloths were refreshed, and knives and forks rapidly set again. Often she would catch a glimpse of Hari and would watch him moving around below her, like a figure in a silent film, his movements always so assured and graceful. She crumbled her lavender flower and let the pieces fall against the glass. She stood in darkness, looking down, rubbed her fingers together and then smelt the smell out of them. When she was a child she thought it was possible to do this; to smell something so much that you smelt it away, like the sun leeching out colour from flowered wallpaper or curtains.

During a summer thunderstorm one night, sticky with sweat, they lay naked on the rooftop, grateful for the huge drops which exploded against their skin. Hari lifted his head and peered down into the restaurant. She shivered. She had already met Jude, already knew that something was going to happen. She pulled Hari towards her again, felt the rain dripping from his wet hair onto her face, and kissed him.

෨෧

Of course Jayesh had thought he was mad at first. Had asked, 'Why would we want to make a huge, great hole in the roof? Imagine the mess, Balu. Just for a skylight nobody'd notice.'

'But of course they'll notice!' Balu insisted, incredulous, tilting his head back and staring at the low ceiling, covered entirely in the same tired polystyrene tiles that had been there when he first started working at the restaurant. By now, his head was swimming with the majesty of his grand scheme. He could see it perfectly in his mind, exactly as he wanted it. On summer evenings light would pour into the restaurant, making it feel spacious and airy, and as the sun began to weaken and set, the fading purples and oranges would be there, right over their heads, and then, when it grew dark enough, he would light the delicate little lights he was envisaging hanging inside it and it would shimmer like a jewel.

For once, he was determined to have his way. What did Jayesh know about what people wanted, anyway? When did he ever talk to customers, or spend time in the restaurant? For the first time in his life he knew, with an absolute and calm certainty, that Jayesh was wrong.

ॐ

'When we're finished down here,' Balu says, puffing at the top of the fire escape steps outside Sarah's kitchen door, 'come down for *kulfi*.' He means much later, once the restaurant is closed. She watches his retreating back as he walks down the clangy metal steps, reaching out her hand to feel the vibrations in the hand rail. He looks up when he reaches the half-landing and grins. Balu is never in a hurry, she thinks. He is just the same when he thinks; he paces a thought out, it has stages, half-landings too. There is something of a tragic grandeur about Balu. His happiness; his acceptance of anything. He is too good-natured.

As he waits for the simmering milk to reduce, he grinds spices for garam masala. He remembers his mother doing this. He remembers sitting on a stool at the kitchen table watching her for what seemed like hours. When he was old enough she would crack cardamom pods and ask him to separate out the seeds for her. He learnt to count this way, learnt tidiness and order as he arranged the seeds into separate piles. As long as it was below ten, he could count how many pods, and how many seeds in each. Sometimes she would give him dough to play with. As she shaped bread, flouring and slapping against the table top, she sang. He remembers all this as a time of softness and serenity, of endlessness. After Jayesh was born things were a little different; his grandmother was in the kitchen more often and the special quietness he had shared with his mother was lost in their chatter and the new baby's crying.

With the cold stone weight of his large *himam-dasta* on the table in front of him, he carefully begins to unpick the small, neat pile of cardamom pods he has placed just to his right. They leak their dark, plush aroma into the cool kitchen stillness. He has cracked the dry skins already, spreading the handful out on the flat stone bed of the *sil*, and working the *batta* roughly, gently over them, first in one direction and then the other, picking them up and returning them as they roll off the edge of the stone, away from the roller. Both of these tools, the huge mortar and pestle, and the stone slab, heavy as rocks, brought back from the first visit home by his brother, a year after arriving in London, have ingested the life of every piece of bark, seed and bud ground against them. Holding his face fleetingly above the smooth cold rim of the mortar, nosing into the circumference, breaking the meniscus of bowl-held air, Balu locates cinnamon, cloves, mace, aniseed.

In the silence the pick and pull of his fingers' tiny movements is like the tear of paper tickets, the embarrassed muffled rustle of cellophane sweet-wrappers at the cinema. Into the mortar he drops each small dark seed separately; almost too small for sound, the pleasing tap against stone, they fall silently against the surface. A couple stick to his fingers and he brushes them off.

The pestle corrugates the silence, tatters the skin of air enfolding him in his concentration. He stands over the bowl, one hand at its rim, the other gripping the stone handle, directing his force downwards to fracture the denuded seeds.

He loves the slowness of preparation, the need for time. Reducing the milk will take the rest of the morning. Wisps of cardamom-infused steam rise lazily from the pot and the kitchen is filled with the comforting baby smell of heated milk. He likes to measure out and grind each spice individually, as his mother still does. When the cardamom seeds are broken open and the pods are ground to a powder, he gently brushes out the mortar with his fingertips and introduces cinnamon.

His mother told him stories as she ground and mixed, standing at the table as wisps of black hair stuck to her fore-head in the relentless heat of Indian summers. A story for each spice. In Arabia, she told him, cinnamon was stolen by the phoenix and carried off to its vast nest, high up in the highest trees. The desperate gatherers, hungry for the wealth the rare, rust-coloured bark would bring them, put out huge chunks of raw meat for the bird and then waited. The phoenix would come. Always it would come, although they might wait for hours, sometimes days. It would come, and it would drag away the hunks of meat, so heavy that even this huge, strong bird, feathered entirely in gold, was scarcely able to lift away from the ground and swing upwards into the sky. The bird would always drag off one piece too many into its overladen nest, and the whole thing – meat, twigs, golden feathers, cinnamon quills, everything – would come plummeting to the ground and the gatherers would go away happy. Balu had no idea where his mother's stories came from. They were part of the ritual and secret of the garam masala. She always told him a family's recipe belonged singularly to that family, that no other family would do it exactly the same. It was like a signature, a fingerprint. And then she would pull out his tiny hand, sticky with dough, uncurl it and walk him over to the window to show him the tiny swirls and whorls that made each of his fingers unique.

When the milk is slow and thick he weighs out sugar and slides it into the steam. Slowly it submerges, dissolves. He stirs until the wooden spoon meets no grittiness at the bottom of the pan. Then he turns off the heat and waits for it to cool.

As his mother rasped half nutmegs against the rough surface of the nutmeg grater she would tell him of the wars that had been fought over the spice islands in the name of this precious seed. How the island of Banda was captured by the Dutch and only a few of its inhabitants survived the slaughter, escaping in boats under cover of darkness to take their know-ledge, their lore, elsewhere. In other parts of the world, she told him, rich people used to carry their own nutmeg graters on their persons and pulled them out of tiny, velvet bags embroidered with patterns and decorative initials in rich, gold thread. Tiny gold and silver graters with handles made of horn and ivory, or deep yellow amber, carved into stems or intricate buds and hanging from thick cords of silk. As she spoke he would look at the grater against which she pressed the tiny nubs, watching them grow smaller and smaller, the bunched tips of her fingers white from the pressure. The concentration in her tight lips and taut brow. He had seen the damage the grater could do to her knuckles, had heard the wince of pain, the suck of breath. He couldn't imagine these foreign women, with their delicate fingers and fine silks, doing what his mother did.

When the sweetened milk is cool he sieves it to remove the softened pods of cardamom, and stirs in chopped pistachio and cashew nuts. He soaks threads of saffron in a small amount of hot water in a tiny, eggcup-sized glass, and carefully adds these, swirling the yellow colour into the mixture. The almost red threads which he has carefully crushed will, he knows, stain an area around them like a golden bruise, a halo glow of sunset, and so he makes sure they are evenly distributed. When all this is done he spoons the mixture into aluminium cones, covers each one, and stands them in the freezer.

Every spice is valuable. Every spice has a cost in lives. A spice can be used as medicine; it can keep away infection, hold off sickness, calm a bilious stomach. Many are said to be aphrodisiacs. Yet the same spices can kill if taken in large quantities. Nutmeg. Saffron. His mother always said it was to do with balance. That people lost their lives, in all things, when the scales were tipped too heavily in one direction.

ৈ

Sarah throws down her bag in the hallway, stands on the heels of her trainers to pull out her feet and goes into the living room. She flings open the shuttered doors and steps out gladly, freely, into her garden, Sita at her heels, and arranges the blankets and cushions in the sunniest corner. Then she sits down with her back against the wall, feeling the smooth, warm brick through the thin fabric of her T-shirt. With her eyes closed she breathes in deeply and feels for the black nose nuzzling her hand. Cold and wet, it dots itself against her skin. She feels the points of contact, little smears of moisture, collect on the warm back of her hand. Still unseeing, she finds the warm, guarded throat beneath the sharp little chin and outstretches two fingers against it, feeling the cat's deep rattling purr. She bends down to the furry body and presses her ear against it, a flank, a resonant bellows, and the sound comes loud and warm.

She exhales a long, slow breath. She has spent the day in Islington, doing housework in other people's houses. In a very short time she has come to realise that there are, essentially, two types of people where cleaning is concerned. There are the ones who like to be in when you go round, and you have to shimmy round them with mops and Hoovers, and be respectful as you pick up clothes in their bedrooms in case they are watching. And then there are the ones who prefer you to come when they are out at work. She finds these people much more fascinating, imagining them coming home on the days she's been there, walking through their front doors and remembering with a surge of gladness that their homes have been magically cleared of all the muck and grime, that temporarily all the evidence of their physical, biological, day-to-day existence is banished.

It isn't to do with lack of trust, the ones who like to be there. Because they have all given her keys. And often they go out while she's there, or they're out when she arrives and she has to let herself in. She thinks it's more to do with the steadfastly absent ones not being entirely at ease with the idea of somebody else clearing up after them. They're just a different sort of people, less chaotic, less at ease with themselves. Their houses are often nearly spotless before she even begins, whereas with the stay-at-homes she is pulled, welcomed, into the mêlée of grouchy toddlers and spilt Ribena, toast crumbs and soggy, towel-strewn bathrooms. They chat to her, ask her what she's been doing, make her cups of tea and tell her about their lives. Sometimes she feels like a confidante, a confessor. She goes home wearily, after having listened to what's been worrying them, sitting down on the closed toilet seat and peeling off her Marigolds to comfort a young mother perching palely, desperately on the edge of the bath clutching a plate of biscuits.

If she's honest, though, she prefers the silent, empty homes. She likes being at the nub of other people's lives unobserved, invisible. Alone, she can scour their bookshelves and try to glean something about the kind of people they are. In their kitchens she can imagine the smell of dinner cooking. She can make herself tea and hear the unfamiliar whistle of someone else's kettle, see the half-eaten jars of olives and anchovies in the fridge as she fetches the milk, the bowls of cold pasta covered in cling film, and imagine the meals they make. In babies' nurseries she straightens the covers in cots and folds tiny, clean-smelling cardigans and T-shirts before placing them carefully in the drawers of pastel-painted furniture.

She finds other people's lives fascinating precisely because they are not her own. The framed photographs which she carefully polishes intrigue her; she studies them minutely, memorising the tiny holiday faces, the wrinkle-faced newborn surrounded by smiling family, the wedding photographs, the posed school portraits. She picks up the dropped petals and staining pollen from vases of, waxy lilies. The stillness, the fragility of these frozen lives is strangely comforting some-times. In bedrooms, nurseries, the most private of spaces, she will sometimes switch off the Hoover and inhale the stasis, sitting fleetingly on the edge of the bed in a room that has grown familiar, and which a practical stranger will come home to and go to sleep in in a few hours' time.

She thinks. She met Jude through a friend from university who, like her, had found himself drifting and let the current carry him to London. One night, in search of drugs, this friend dragged her to Streatham and she found herself on Jude's doorstep. 'Meet my dealer,' her friend said, his face breaking into a wide grin as she and Jude politely shook hands. He was barefoot, she remembers that, and the hand she shook was so warm and soft that she felt instantly covetous of it, wanting it not to be the hand of a stranger but one that she could reach out and touch whenever she wanted to.

He lived in one room on the ground floor of a shared house – the room which should have been the front room – and his bed was a mattress on the floor. There was a dodgy-looking gas fire which was on full blast and the room was heavy with airless heat. The three of them sat on the mattress passing round a joint, intending to go to the pub, but it got later and later and nobody moved. Sarah felt Jude's eyes resting on her as he spoke and did not feel in the least bit uncomfortable. She was glad her friend had convinced her to come out, and soon, with the warmth, and the calmness of Jude's soft, low voice, she felt safe enough to curl up on the bed beside him, and eventually fell asleep, drowned by the heat and lulled by the slow, meandering conversation which wove itself into a dream in which Jude was stroking her hair and kissing her forehead with lips that were as soft and warm as his hand was.

She woke up to find her friend gone. A grey dawn was showing round the edges and along the top of the drawn curtains and Jude was asleep on the bed beside her, fully clothed. He had doubled the limp duvet over so that she was folded inside it and he lay uncovered. Carefully she folded it over him and crawled underneath herself.

When they made love it felt easier than it had ever felt with anyone else; she was able to look him in the eye. It was only when they got dressed that she felt suddenly self-conscious. 'With our clothes on,' she said, 'you're just my mate's mate again.' They were sitting facing each other in his grimy kitchen, and he had pulled her foot up onto his lap. He squeezed it tightly and looked at her. 'I'm Jude,' he said, smiling curiously, as if he were laughing at her a little, and the awkwardness seeped away.

She didn't feel as if she was betraying Hari. If anything, she felt worse that she had told Jude nothing about the relationship she was already in. She didn't know, specifically, why this was. It just felt uncomfortable and so she avoided it. And really, when she told Hari about Jude, what exactly was it she was telling him? She wasn't sure she was clear even about that. Was she ending their strange, unacknowledged relationship, or was she merely informing him of a peripheral change in her circumstances? She can remember the moment with distressing clarity; she had been reading in the garden and had not heard him until he appeared beside her, making her jump.

'Sorry. The kitchen door was open.' He stepped out of the room and eased himself into the green and red striped deckchair on the roof. Sarah had never taken to it but Balu liked to sit in it sometimes.

'So. How's Sarah?'

'I'm OK,' she said. And then, boldly, her palms suddenly damp with fear, 'I think I'm in love.' He stiffened, and although his body scarcely moved she saw his sudden tension. 'With . . . with someone . . .' she faltered, the thought suddenly hitting her that he might think she meant with him. 'Will it be all right?' He put his head on one side, the corner of his mouth pulling down slightly. She didn't know herself what she was asking. Would what be all right? There was a long pause before he spoke.

'I don't know,' he said. His brief loss of composure was over. His face betrayed nothing. She stood up and led him back inside the room and he followed her woodenly. Her heart was beating wildly, close to the surface, as she pulled him closer, fixing his arms round her. As they kissed she wondered, briefly, if it might be wiser not to do this, but his hand was already between her legs, rubbing gently through the layers of her clothes as she unbuttoned his jeans and whispered against his shoulder, 'I'm sorry.'

He was hunting for an entrance as they moved towards the sofa. She felt his fingers and widened her legs, letting the feeling fill her as he knelt before her, pulling her closer to the edge of the seat. Almost lying down, with only her head and shoulders against the back of the sofa, she felt his breath on her. His tongue. She wrapped her legs round his neck and lifted herself against him. When they kissed she could taste herself in his mouth, and she felt the coldness of his saliva slide between her buttocks.

ৡ

'What's your first memory?'

Jude reaches for the cigarette he has left slowly burning away in the ashtray, and brings it to his mouth in slow motion. For a moment Sarah thinks he hasn't heard, or is ignoring her. He stares concentratedly at the tip of the cigarette, then drags on it, inhaling the smoke deeply, holding it in his lungs before breathing out and answering.

'It's not really any one thing, I don't think. Any one memory, I mean. It's more a period of time. A certain time when things were a certain way, before the time was gone and things changed. D'you know what I mean?'

She looks at him, opens her mouth as if to speak, but doesn't. In many ways, although less noticeably at first, Jude is as guarded as Hari is, and she knows that he will clam up within a ten-mile radius of anything that is too personal. When he told her that his father had been killed in a road accident when he was a child he mentioned nothing of what it had been like. She wanted to know how a four-year-old understood these things. But he had managed to steer her away and into something else. She wonders whether there is something in her that is only attracted to closed-up people.

He sits up suddenly and scrambles out of bed.

'Out of tobacco,' he says. 'I think there's some in my coat.' Subject closed. She smiles. Jude's bare feet thump irregularly down the stairs.

They eat in the restaurant, to the sound of clanking pots and rattling cutlery from the kitchen.

Balu has turned out each *kulfi* mould onto a white dessert plate and the perfect, yellow-tinged cones are speckled with green and spots of reddish-gold, the top of each one flaked with fine silver *vark*. They are fine and rather festive puddings and Balu is delighted with the oohs and aahs they draw.

Balu has been telling them about his latest project: a literature course which he has just enrolled on for a term at Birkbeck College. He has always loved reading, would always pick up the books his mother borrowed from the library when he was a child and read them too. Sometimes they were great thick books with difficult language and he would have to get his mother to renew them because he couldn't finish them by the return date stamped on the ticket inside. Sometimes he didn't understand what he was reading and would swim his way through the books half blind, ending up with an impression of the story which was like a half-lost series of snapshots. His mother was a voracious reader; she still is. She would read anything and everything, giving the same degree of concentration to trashy novels she bought from market stalls as she gave to the more serious volumes she found in the library. Often friends passed books on to her, always with a recommendation. Whether she liked it or not she would read it to the end, put it down when she had finished and pick up something new. When Balu was a child she would always have a book in the front pocket of her apron and would fish it out at odd moments during the day, while she waited for dough to rise or for a few minutes on the roof if there was a breeze, after pegging out the washing.

Balu left school when he was fourteen years old, and by then his reading habit was as entrenched as his mother's. As he got older he drew her out more and she no longer digested her books in silence. He would ask her what she thought about this writer or that, would quiz her about a book's ending: did she think it would really happen like that? Did she agree with the way the writer had made this character or that character behave?

Since the completion of the skylight he has been itching to start something new, and the course seemed like just the thing. The first text they are going to study is *Othello*; he has borrowed a copy from the library and has been reading it sedulously. He has just finished it and is eager to hear what his new young friends have to say about it. The three of them are slouching around a table at the back of the restaurant, punctuating their speech with sweet, cold mouthfuls of the rich, golden ice cream he has made.

'What I don't understand,' Balu says, his loaded spoon pausing in mid-air, halfway to his mouth, 'is that Othello almost seems to want to believe his wife has been unfaithful.'

'Well, yes. Once the seed's been planted I suppose he does.'

'But why would he want to do that? Wouldn't he just *know* that it wasn't true?' He finds it easier sometimes to work problems like this out with real people rather than with the characters on the page and he sets a comparative scene amongst themselves. 'Just say, Jude, that I tell you Sarah is having it away with, I don't know ...' Hari comes through from the kitchen with an armful of clean tablecloths '. . . with Hari,' he concludes, innocently. 'Would you really believe my word against hers?'

Jude puts his spoon soundlessly onto his empty plate and leans forward, resting his elbows on the table and looking sideways at Sarah before he speaks. He half notices the sudden flush that deepens the colour of her cheeks at his glance.

'It doesn't work if you put it into our situation,' he says finally, his voice so quiet that Balu has to lean in closer across the table to hear him clearly. 'Othello is in an alien country –

he's very vulnerable. He has to place his trust somewhere. He is just unfortunate in trusting the wrong person.'

'Hmm.' Balu leans back, pursing his lips, and pinches his chin thoughtfully. He isn't convinced.

'You don't lose all your sense just because you are in a different country. I can't see that at all,' he says.

'It *is* frustrating,' Sarah agrees. 'My feeling is always, you fucking *idiot*. I can't feel much sympathy for him.'

'Exactly,' Balu says, wiping his moist forehead with the back of his sleeve and then reaching forward to start clearing the bowls.

'I'll do that,' Sarah says, and so he leans back again, leaving his hands on the table in front of him. Jude notices the small forestations of black hairs sprouting unashamedly from the fleshy back of each of his plump fingers. Balu isn't fully attuned to the tides, the sudden ebbs and unexpected revivals of conversation, and the tightenings and relaxations of tension between his young friends, and sometimes he feels they are being carried on completely different currents. He sits silently for a few moments as Sarah clears the table and his mind drifts back to the *kulfi*. It has been a particularly successful experiment and he would like to introduce it onto the menu now that it has met with the approval of what he sometimes jokingly calls his 'tasting panel'.

Balu has fallen into the habit, in recent months, of experimenting with new ideas. This is another of his projects; he seems, suddenly, to have a lot more time on his hands and he needs more than one project to keep him fully occupied. Since moving out of the flat, his sister-in-law has taken over many of the daily chores which used to fill much of his time. Now his clothes appear in a neatly ironed pile on the end of his bed every few days, and fortnightly trips to the supermarket in Jayesh's Range Rover style car obviate the need for daily excursions to local shops for this or that. And there are no shops within walking distance anyway.

Balu is not someone who can sit idle for very long and, in these sudden expanses of free time spent cocooned in his new, immaculate home, he has begun to think about his approach to food. He has been toying with the idea of combining the traditions of Indian cookery with western tastes and he has brought the ideas that have been fermenting in his mind to the restaurant to try out. So far he has concentrated on desserts. He does not hurl ingredients together without thought, though; he teases out complements, uses opposites to lighten a heaviness or sweeten a sharpness. He thinks it is better to do this than to do as some prefer, trotting out the same old recipes as everybody else, never thinking, never changing anything. For him cooking evolves, it is a constant and gradual amalgamation, an assimilation. It is a process which has no completion, and this, perhaps, is the source of his particular brand of calmness: with no destination urgent in the back of his mind he explores slowly, gently probing into inlets which look interesting and then paddling carefully away.

Othello. It would be impossible, he supposes, for the three of them not to see parallels, to think that perhaps he might possess some insight into the confusion of being an outsider in a foreign country. Even Hari, because he is as English as they are. He has never been to India, has never had the faintest desire to go there, and, disappointingly really, never shown any great talent in the kitchen.

And they are right in a way; they themselves have no conception of it – such enormous, irreversible leaving. The

36

world *is* different in this country, this city, which is so self-contained and self-serving.

He remembers first arriving in England; there were more immediate differences then, of course. He was cold, for one thing. England was cold. He and Jayesh had shivered in their newly bought wardrobes of western clothes, had worn mismatching jumpers in pairs. But he knew English. Knew *the* English. He cannot remember a shock of the kind of strangeness Othello seems to suffer. It was only things at the surface, like the cold, and all the different sounds, and the long, dark winter evenings. Beneath that he had always felt some kindred seam in those early days.

Sarah reappears from the kitchen, holding the door for Hari. Jude watches her as she sits down and Hari pulls out the chair beside her, jabbing her a couple of times teasingly with his elbow, as if they have shared some joke together out of earshot. They've forgotten all about what we've just been talking about, he thinks. But he hasn't. While they have been in the kitchen he has been sitting at the table with Balu in silence and has been wondering how he would be if Balu *did* tell him for real that Sarah was sleeping with Hari. Not that Balu would betray her, of course. He is far too fond of her. But what if he did?

The conversation is over, has run its course, and he should just leave it, but somehow, seeing Sarah and Hari so giggly makes him want to return to it, to drag them back.

'What it comes down to,' he says matter-of-factly, as if there had not been any break in the conversation at all, 'is that he can't stand not knowing. That's fair enough, isn't it? Once your suspicions have been aroused?' He looks up. Sarah and Hari are looking at him a little quizzically, as if they aren't quite sure what he is talking about. He can't help letting this annoy him but it makes him feel a bit superior at the same time.

Eventually Balu manages to muster up his thoughts sufficiently to reply. 'But he is wrong,' he says simply, an edge of weariness creeping into his voice. He releases a long, loud breath and leans back in his chair, slowly shaking his head. The chair back squeaks gently as it takes his weight. 'I can't understand a man like that,' he says.

ॐ

Back in his small, tidy bedroom, Balu pauses at the desk he has arranged in the corner, neatly fitted in at the end of the bed. In his rush to leave for the restaurant earlier in the evening, he had left his copy of the play open, the well-thumbed pages splaying comfortably, needing nothing to weight them down at the corners.

He has enjoyed his evening but he is exhausted. He wishes he still had the energy he had when he was in his early twenties, back in the days when all he knew of London was the photographs he had seen in magazines, and the engravings in an ancient history book his mother had kept on her shelf. He is excited by the world folded between pages of print, and the different interpretations people have of them. Jude especially, tonight, said some interesting things which he would not really have thought of on his own.

He can't think of a time when he was not curious about stories, about the telling of stories which were written down. When he was a child he was surrounded by stories; he grew up amongst their wisps of colour and fragrance. But they were stories which were listened to, not read. Their magic resided partly in his mother's voice, the silk and pulse of her body, her patterns, her activity. He watches, sometimes, his brother's wife sitting with her baby daughter in her arms, speaking in the well-spaced, sing-song voice reserved for children's stories. The child is nearly eighteen months old, and starting to have an attention span which can make sense and shape of them. He remembers how his mother's mixture of tales was always told as an accompaniment to something else. Her voice was underlaid with the thud of dough against wood or marble, the *grit grit* of spices being ground to powder, or breathless from the sweaty plunge then plunge then plunge, the rhythmic, repeated action of washing clothes in steaming, soapy water. There were always books in the house and he remembers a time before he could read, flicking them open and running his eyes wonderingly along the lines of curly symbols. Feeling the texture of the pages as he turned them one after another after another. He knew that they could be stories too, but he didn't yet know how, other than that they came from the repeated turning of pages, one by one.

The evening has set him thinking. Apart from his mother, he has never been really close to anyone. Has never known, loved, doubted, been let down by anyone. Well, not apart from that one, solitary venture into the realm of human relationships which was such a spectacular, dismal failure. And even then he had lost the love before it had bloomed. Had seen it nipped, as it were, in its infancy. He has never grown an emotional dependence to supercede his innocent bond with his mother when he was a child. He has become an entirely self-sufficient unit, a one-man band. For the first time in a long while he wonders whether he mightn't have missed out a little in life.

In bed, he ponders some more, going through the rarely sifted memories of his own failed attempt at love. His wedding: that great non-event that brought him, cowed and ashamed, to London. Well, again, that was decided for him, wasn't it? The new start which would help him to forget – and he'd gone along with it as readily as he'd gone along with the wedding plans, knowing that the beautiful, dark-eyed girl could never feel anything but revulsion for him. He had never understood why no one else could see that; he had known it so surely. So when his mother had come and knocked carefully on his bedroom door, in the house in Mangalore where he had always lived, which he and his new wife would at some point in the future inherit, he had known. Sniffing and red-eyed, she told him that Maya, their jewel of a future daughter-in-law, was to be a daughter-in-law no longer. He hadn't been in the least bit surprised. And when it was decided that, as a tonic, a restorative, he should accompany his younger brother, who had been accepted on an accountancy course in London, halfway across the world, he hadn't demurred. He had gone, trailing in his lumbering wake the dull ache of uprootedness and a niggling sense that the failure was all, somehow, his own fault.

൭

Sarah steps down into the road as a bus is passing, at just the right moment for one moving pane of glass to glance the whole of the sun's bare white glare into her eyes, searing her vision so that her step becomes a stumble. She moves blindly backwards, away from the road, feeling for the kerb with the back of her foot and stands blinking, mole-like, waiting for sight to return.

40

When she crosses she enters a pool of shade and sees huge blue spots hanging ominously, like pregnant balloons. Again she stops, and screws up her eyes, tries to blink her sight back, reminding herself of a horse trying to shake its head free of flies.

Someone just behind her touches her elbow.

'Excuse me. Are you all right?'

She swings round. There's a silhouetted person there. The voice is a man's.

'I was just blinded,' she begins. She cannot see the owner of the voice, and she narrows her eyes a little as she tries to pick his features from the gloom. 'It's so bright today. The sun in a bus window . . .' she says, trailing off, hoping he'll understand and go away. Whatever she looks at directly evades her, covered by one of the balloons, a large bobbing blue disc which moves with her eyes as if it is floating on their surface.

The voice's owner hasn't gone. 'You look unsteady,' he persists. 'Let me buy you a cup of tea.'

The offer is excessively polite, as if whoever it is is terribly afraid of sounding presumptuous. Nonetheless, it is sudden. Unexpected. Completely unnecessary.

She hovers, embarrassed, unsure, as slowly a colour-filtered face emerges in front of her, earnest and birdlike, a thin rubberband neck outstretched in keen solicitude. The stranger seems to be fashioned from something lighter, more fragile than bone and weighty flesh. She feels a peculiar sensation that, as he stands before her, his true colour gradually increasing, he might at any moment lift from the ground like a helium balloon. The narrow bridge of his nose, the cliffed brow and deeply sunken eye cavities seem shaped of stiff, folded paper. His arms fail to fill the loose sleeves of his twill overcoat and end in long, fleshless fingers which, for all their bony, clawlike appearance, touch her arm for that brief moment softly enough.

It isn't something she would normally do. She is by nature neither gullible nor persuasible. But he is an old man, not some would-be Lothario. And she is inexplicably curious. After a moment she nods agreement and feels again his light, dry touch against her elbow as he indicates the direction of a café he knows.

The National Gallery

He first saw Ewa as she rushed from behind the stage door of the Warsaw Grand Theatre and down the steps into bright sunshine, almost colliding with him before she ran off up the street, trailing her scarf out behind her as she tried to wrap it round her neck.

The look on the face of this girl, stumbling as she tried to cross the road, was painfully reminiscent for some reason. It was as if, for just a flutter, a half-moment, Ewa had been standing there, unchanged and ageless, before him. It was nonsense of course, just a trick of his stupid, old mind. He knew better than to dwell on it.

Yet he continued to watch; all at once he had felt compelled to see her safely across to the shady side where he was standing. He saw her blink and shake her head slightly, then rummage, cursing, in her bag.

Knowing he ought not, he approached her, touched her elbow, and watched as she tried to see him through her momentary blindness. Before he knew what he was saying he had suggested he buy her a cup of tea, and crossed over the square with her towards a café he knew.

Sitting opposite her at a plastic table, in one of the orange, moulded chairs which are bolted to it, he now realises the extent of his madness. This girl looks nothing like Ewa. She is pale and thin; her colouring is all wrong. She has on a shabby coat – a man's coat – with the excess of the too-long sleeves turned under. A knitted hat of an indeterminate colour and style is crammed onto her head, pulled down over her ears, and loose wisps and twists of hair straggle about her face and shoulders. Ewa would never have worn such a hat. He looks at her eyes, shyly, not wanting to appear to be looking. She says she will have a cup of tea. Strong. No sugar.

Yet still, there is something in the expression of those wrong-coloured eyes, and in the way she clasps and unclasps her fingers around the polystyrene cup of tea, when it arrives, that drags at him. That knobbly bone at her wrist. Her ill-concealed puzzlement. He feels a sudden stab of remorse as he realises he has intruded into someone else's delicate life.

'Don't think, please don't think,' he begins, 'that I make a habit of inviting young women for cups of tea.' He pauses for breath. 'I am an old man.' He gestures inwardly to himself, mimics his own crabbed hands. 'I . . .' He shrugs. 'Well, I don't do such things. Not usually.' He flickers a smile, ingenuous, yet knowing that 'old man' is not sufficient excuse or explanation. He smiles at her again, anxious not to appear in any way sinister. He doesn't want to frighten her off – suddenly this is important.

'I don't think that.' Her voice is level, expressionless. He will lose her, he thinks. He will lose her because she doesn't want to be here. She wants to leave. Why have I come here with this old man? she is thinking.

And what is it, exactly, that he will lose if she leaves? What is the matter with him? He shakes the thoughts away and makes a more solid attempt to explain himself, illustrating his genuineness, his humbleness as he clears his throat, by showing her his credentials. He fetches out a wallet and extracts a library card for the university. She blows on her tea; she doesn't seem impressed.

'I am translating the written works of an unimportant painter from German into English,' he says, rather stiltedly. 'It is taking me years. Seven so far. I stopped you because you reminded me of someone. I'm so sorry to presume upon your time, you're probably desperate to leave.'

She sips tentatively. 'No.'

It is one of those sharp spring mornings that are colder than they look. He is wearing a woollen scarf wrapped round his neck several times and he pulls at it as if to take it off, and then hesitates and leaves it where it is. The weather has given him a heightened colour, so that he looks a little feverish; a rosy flush has crept into the creased cheeks and his eyes are watery and bright. A slight hint of moisture glistens at the tip of his nose. He is one of those old men who in many ways don't seem as old as they are; he has a quickness which gives him a kind of youthfulness. He tells her he has only stopped smoking in the last four years. He must be in his eighties, she thinks, surprised. Why give up now?

The pale eyes quizzing her face have curious, dark-edged irises which make them seem rather startling at first, and they are hooded like a chameleon's. The fine skin around them is almost translucent and there is a fragile blueness at either side of the bridge of his nose. His lips, though, are full and dark, the creases and lines continuing into them from the surrounding skin, like bled ink on absorbent paper, following along the grain of individual fibres. They are unusual lips for an old man, seeming to have half a mind to shout vitality, virility. When he speaks they give his words definition, although he might seem to be fishing for expression. Each word comes out firmly shaped, curiously un-English.

As they sit opposite each other she notices his fingers twitching a little on the tabletop and wonders whether they still crave the occupation smoking gave them.

When she asks, he tells her he is from Poland, that he once lectured at Warsaw University, but that he has not been there since the war. He has adopted London as his home and it has accepted him into its fold – another of the thousands of casualties from elsewhere. He is an art historian, he says, and he tells her how he spent his younger days crossing and re-crossing Europe, travelling to America, lecturing at universities, advising on exhibitions.

He asks about her and listens intently to what she tells him about her own life, as if unconscious of the smallness of a garden on a London rooftop compared with a lifetime of travelling the world. She tells him about her friends, a boyfriend. Silly details, but he watches her carefully, leaning forward slightly, as if he is a little deaf and fears he might miss something. When they leave he realises an hour has passed.

'Well,' he says, as they stand outside. 'I have thoroughly enjoyed meeting you. I hope we shall meet again.' He holds his hand out to her and she takes it. He feels the pressure of her hand through the leather glove he has pulled back on. How awful, he thinks. How awful to spend an hour with someone and then just walk away. He hesitates for a moment, undecided, and then reaches inside his coat and fetches out a card which has been folded in half to fit into his pocket, and hands it to her.

'Here,' he says. 'I don't know if you are at all interested in painting, but . . .' The card is an invitation to the private view of an exhibition of someone he once taught. 'I get invited to lots of these,' he explains. 'It would be interesting to have a fresh eye. I find myself always, nowadays, running out of things to think.' He gives her a shy half-smile. 'Perhaps I am too old to understand art.' He pulls on his other glove and steps away from her. 'So, don't feel obliged. But if you would like to come, it is next Wednesday.'

ᕙᐤ

Jude is stretched out on the bed when she returns. She sidles past the skylight and sits down by his feet. He is reading a book which she hasn't yet finished – her bus ticket bookmark is poking out just less than halfway through.

She grabs hold of his bare foot and squeezes it, then lies down beside him, propping her head on his shoulder and lazily reads half a dozen lines out loud.

Jude breathes deeply and puts the book down. He is glad and not glad that she is here and that he has stopped reading because of her. He has already watched her face as she absorbed the pages he himself has just been reading, undisturbed, all afternoon. Part of him had wanted to read quickly, to overtake her bus-ticket marker, but somehow he felt that this would be underhand, like playing a record bought as a present for someone else. Getting there first and somehow soiling the pristine newness. He doesn't like it when certain people have read a book before he has. Something in the knowledge that they have already been there makes the preciousness seem second-hand; the idea of their already knowing what he himself is new to spoils it for him. But it is only certain people. Sarah isn't one of them.

'I met an old man today,' she says. He feels her breath against his neck. Her voice is low, yet loud because it is so close to his ear.

'Mmmm?'

'A nice old man. He bought me a cup of tea.'

'What did he want?'

'He said I reminded him of someone. Dunno who; he didn't say.'

Jude makes a moue with his mouth, his eyes widening for a moment, his mouth stretching down at the corners, and then returning to normal, grinning, knowing she has seen.

'Jude! He was nice. Polite. I liked him. He was Polish. He invited me to an exhibition.'

They are quiet. For almost a minute neither of them moves or says anything. They are still. Jude has nothing else to say about the man. He doesn't ask about the cup of tea – where it was drunk, why it was bought, nor about the exhibition, and whether she will go – and suddenly she doesn't seem to want to say any more. His hand reaches out, fishing for the book. The moment has passed. She wriggles out of his encircling arm and sits up. He watches her rise and leave the room before he picks up the book again and finds his place.

Since that night in the restaurant Jude has been distracted at odd moments by the thought of Hari. Or more specifically by the thought of Hari and Sarah. Has been thinking, frivolously, whether it might not just be possible that there is something between them. After all, she always seems so different, so much happier, when he is around, as if he sparks something which he himself is unable to reach. He sometimes has the feeling that he is extraneous, that he can only ever be at the periphery of her life. Whereas Hari . . . He just seems more *there* than he feels himself to be.

Although he has tried not to, he has started to notice how she is when she is with Hari. Has started to check whether her pallor rises at all at the casual mention of his name. He can't say he's found anything to alarm him, to set his suspicions jangling, yet he doesn't feel easy.

ᕲᗃ

The old man's name is Jozef. The folded invitation he pressed into her hand as they parted outside the café a week ago doesn't give any more away; his first name only is handwritten on the glossy, printed card, so that it reads 'Jozef and guest(s) are invited to . . .' She wonders if there will be others, or if she is to be his only guest.

The gallery is a pristine white cube of a room. Large, colourful canvases are dotted around three walls; the fourth is made almost entirely of glass. Outside she can see there is a balcony, and a view across the river. The twenty or so other people in the room are dressed smartly, and there is a low murmur of conversation as they mingle, clutching the stems of wine glasses, the occasional flurry of laughter or greeting escaping like fizzy bubbles. She spots Jozef quickly, his arm linked with that of a tall woman in a dark red suit. They are deep in conversation, the woman's face bending towards him, and Sarah feels she would be intruding if she approached now. He hasn't seen her, so she takes a glass of red wine from a passing tray and sips it as she looks at the paintings.

'What do you think?'

She turns round. Jozef is standing behind her, still arm in arm with the woman.

'I like them,' she says, feeling this, on its own, is a bit of a lame comment, but not knowing what else to say.

'Good,' he says. 'So do I. I'll introduce you to the artist if she

49

ever stops talking to those people.' He indicates a tight, animated group on the other side of the room, all of whom seem to be talking at the same time. Sarah had wondered briefly if the woman by his side might be the artist.

'So you're Sarah,' she says now, holding out her hand. Sarah is surprised to be known. One of her fears about coming was that Jozef might have completely forgotten their meeting, the hour they spent together. She takes the woman's hand.

'Yes,' she whispers. The woman smiles kindly. Sarah notices her perfectly painted lips, the colour an identical shade of red to her suit.

'Jozef's just been telling me about you,' she says. 'I'll leave you to it.' She disengages her arm from Jozef's and leaves them.

'Hello again,' he says.

They walk in silence around the paintings, Jozef standing quietly at her shoulder as she looks at them, and then they take advantage of a vacant bench on the balcony, where small groups of guests are smoking, talking, laughing, or leaning on the rail, looking out over the river at the lights of the darkening city.

'One disadvantage of being old,' he says wanly, 'is that one is always half watching for a seat!' She feels horrified, suddenly, that she hadn't thought, and that he had remained steadfastly beside her while she looked at the paintings.

'Oh,' she says, 'you should have—'

'No, no,' he interrupts her. 'I have a seat now. Yes?' And when she still looks concerned, 'Don't worry. Really. I like to . . . to join in. It is no good for me always to be sitting and watching.'

She wonders whether she should have offered him her arm. She isn't sure what she had assumed about his relationship with the woman in the dark red suit but their linked arms had suggested that there was perhaps an intimacy between them.

Although the woman was much younger. But no, perhaps he was just leaning on her arm.

'I'm very glad you came,' he says.

She smiles. 'So am I.'

'I feared you might not.' She doesn't say that she almost hadn't, but she has a feeling that he already knows this. That, somehow, he has also been struck by the fragility of this as yet unknown friendship, and is as delighted as she is to be sitting here, now, in the slight chill, as the night gathers over the river.

ତ୭

When everyone has left and the restaurant is ready for the cleaner in the morning, all the tablecloths spinning in the washing machine and the chairs piled heavily onto the stripped tables, Balu calls a minicab and, casting a last glance around the darkened restaurant before locking up, rides home in a car which smells of dog, cheap perfume and stale cigarettes. The interior is nicotine-yellow and the ashtrays moulded into the door panels are brimming over with twisted cigarette ends. He winds down the window and feels the rush of night air on his face. It has been raining, and the large round drops on the rear windscreen speckle dark, moving shadows on the back of the driver's seat, riding endlessly upwards, pushed on in a silent shepherd's scale as each passed street light takes up the relay as they enter the deadness of the suburbs.

The fare is always the same. At the end of the journey he will pass a note to the driver through the gap between the seats and climb out. He rarely needs to say to keep the change, his gestures make it clear. It isn't that he is deliberately unsociable, but he has been feeling tired recently. After a busy night in the restaurant he needs to unwind before he lies down to sleep. And besides, if he felt like chatting, what was there to say?

He settles back into the seat with a sigh and closes his eyes. In India he remembers how, during the day, bicycles mingled with the motor cars, weaving amongst them, stopping and starting, the sound of their bells shrill amidst the throaty hootings of car horns.

It stirs a deep sadness, this night journey out from the restaurant to his cold suburban home. Not cold in the literal sense; indeed with the new central heating system and the hermetically sealed rooms he often finds his face beaded with sweat as he perches, self-consciously huge, on the new sofa beside his tiny, neat sister-in-law. The coldness is in the place itself, the feel of it. Built from identical smooth red bricks with no imperfections, no gradations of colour, it is a manufactured home. The walls are smooth, the ceilings low, the internal doors flat and hollow, made from fire-resistant fibreboard. He thinks lovingly of the cracked plaster and the panelled wooden doors in the flat above his restaurant. The creaking stairs and the chugging noises in the water pipes. Even now, with every wall painted gleaming white, it still has contours. In his new home there is nowhere for the house spider to conceal itself, neither cracks in the skirting board nor gaps beneath doors. Sofas are pulled out from the wall weekly and Hoovered behind. Balu finds himself longing to run his finger over a surface and bring it away with a coating of dust. On the immaculate, pale-coloured carpet the spider has nowhere to run. Of course it's just as well with a baby in the house, Sharmila would argue. If he sees a spider he will gently scoop it onto a piece of card and carry it into the garden. But if Sharmila spots it first it will be dispatched smartly with the aid of a rolled up *TV Times*.

Balu feels wrong there.

He isn't made to feel unwelcome. He is hardly ever there in any case, and when he is, he is very often in his room. He sits at the desk at the end of his bed, reading, for hours on end. Sharmila is years younger than he is, but still she thinks of him as she might of an obedient foster child doing his homework. She speaks softly to him, fears he feels left out. She says come down and sit in the lounge if you'd rather, sit at the big table. Sit wherever you like, it's your home too. But it is an open-plan house, and the TV or the child or just the lack of privacy would disturb him, so he declines politely and softly closes his bedroom door.

He is meticulously tidy in the house. Unlike his brother, he will carefully rinse the basin after shaving and open the window a notch to let the steam out after his shower. He will erase all traces of his ablutions. If he were to be asked he would say without very much hesitation that he is happy, that his new situation suits him perfectly. A warm and welcoming family home with a chuckling baby to bounce on his knee. An unmarried man could not ask for anything more ideal, could he? He would still be alone in that old flat above the restaurant, he would explain in patient, persuasive tones, if it were not for his brother's kindness.

And yet, alone in his single bed, beneath the sweet-smelling poly-cotton duvet cover Sharmila has chosen for him, he listens to the silent cul-de-sac. Occasionally, a taxi swings round in the wide road end and halts at a driveway, its tyres crunching against the loose gravel on the new road surface. Shoes scuffle on the ground and lowered, whispery voices rasp out clearly in the hollow air.

He cannot ever remember silence like this. At the restaurant

in the evening there is a constant hubbub of voices, the intermittent percussion of cutlery scraping on plates and the clink
of glasses. In the kitchen, a sizzling, hissing fury of heat and
steam and smell. The shouted orders as the waiters rush in and
out. Colin, regaling him with anecdotes above the din, everything about him loud. Laughing until tears are rolling down his
cheeks. And the background to all of this, the white paper
beneath the strokes of colour in the kitchen, is the radio,
churning out a constant stream of the current clubby pop
music Colin and the waiters like to listen to.

At home, too, there was always noise and colour, the bustle
of activity. The windows of the bedroom he remembers from
his childhood overlooked the market, and from five o'clock
every morning there would be the arrival and unpacking of
produce, the sleepy talk of stallholders and the scrape and thud
of heavy crates being moved and cleared. And in bed each night
he would listen to the sounds of the town winding down after
a dusty day: the chatter of a group of young men sauntering
down the middle of the street, the whirr of insects' wings
against the blinds, mewling tomcats. And the electric fan on the
ceiling rattling round and round and round through the night.

His meandering thoughts are interrupted tonight by the
driver. As the engine throbs impatiently while they wait at
traffic lights, like a tensed cat waiting for its moment to pounce,
the driver turns round to him.

'Mind if I smoke, mate?'

'Not at all,' Balu replies flatly, feeling, as usual, tired, used up.
The driver shakes a single cigarette loose from a packet on the
dashboard and inserts it between his lips straight from the
pack.

'So,' he says, flaring a cheap plastic lighter and holding the flame just in front of his chin. His voice comes out tight, as if it, too, is gripping the cigarette. 'Mountain of Light. Where'd you think up that name, then?'

Balu was born in Mangalore in 1952, on the day of the coronation of Queen Elizabeth II in London. The Koh-i-noor diamond, his mother told him, set into the crown of state which the Queen wore for the first time that day, was the most famous diamond in the world. Diamonds, like spices, she said, held both help and harm in balance. A diamond worn next to the skin could ward off evil spirits, and a house touched in every corner with the precious stone was protected from lightning strikes and all manner of other disasters. Yet, ground to powder and ingested, a diamond was a powerful poison. Koh-i-noor meant Mountain of Light, and Noor, or *Nur*, was a girl's name in Arabic, just as *Clair* was in French.

Another time, as she cradled him on her knee, her belly already swollen with his brother, she told him about the Peacock Throne. Her voice took on the rocking, soothing tone she used when she sat down from her work to rest her feet and make the most of the remaining time she had alone with her boy. The Peacock Throne, she said, was the most magnificent throne in the world. It was made of gold, and was so high there were three little steps made of solid silver leading up to it. It was built for Shah Jahah, the Emperor of Persia, and its back was shaped like an open peacock's tail. Balu had reached forward then, and touched the magnificent picture-book bird his mother held in front of him, fascinated by the fan of dark eyes and the gold the artist had painted on the very tips of the feathers.

She told him how they said the Koh-i-noor diamond had

once been set into the biggest of the peacock's tail eyes, right in the middle, so that it hovered just above the Shah's head, and the human spirit living inside protected him. The Peacock Throne had disappeared over two hundred years ago. What stories that diamond could tell!

Balu had grown so fond of the picture-book peacock that the page became dirtied and smudged with his fingerprints. In the end his mother carefully cut it out from the book and put it on the wall by his bed. When his brother was born and his mother was too exhausted for a while to tell stories, he would look at his picture before going to sleep, and imagine all the eyes gazing back at him.

Of course he doesn't say all of this to the driver, but he explains about the diamond in the coronation crown.

'Me dad seen that on the telly,' the cab driver says. 'The coronation. First time he saw a TV set. Weird that, innit? Can't imagine it now, can you? Life without the telly. The kids'd go ballistic!'

In Jayesh's much sought-after Enfield cul-de-sac, the stillness is like a muffler. Balu lies flat on his back with the duvet pulled up neatly to his armpits. His pyjama-clad arms lie flat, uncovered, at his sides, pulling the duvet taut across the hill of his belly. The thin flounced curtains let in the sodium glow of the street lamp and he blinks at the pale blue ceiling, the delicate paper lampshade and the decorative border running round the wall at waist height.

Sharmila chose the decor for his room – her little present to him, she said. It coordinates with the rest of the house. An icily feminine look. Impersonal. Every night he feels as if he is a temporary guest, carefully folding himself into a stranger's spare bed, staring up at an unfamiliar ceiling.

He has placed his books on a shelf and below that he has hung the tiny, framed photographs that used to be on the wall in the flat, in an attempt to inject something of himself into the room, but the effect is of an unfortunate, unworkable collision. The wrong pictures on the wrong walls. Himself and Jayesh before they left for England, looking green and fresh-eyed. With Jayesh standing outside the new restaurant, looking slightly older, himself slightly fatter. In this photograph he holds a kittenish black cat in his pudgy hands. She is peering at the lens, stretching her thin neck, eyes wide, in response to a sudden sound or movement, so that she, too, appears to be posing for the picture.

ଚ୬

They meet a week later at the National Gallery, at the top of the steps in the central hall, where there is a row of plump leather upholstered seats on either side and another down the middle.

Jozef is already there when she arrives, leaning forward on one of the seats, his elbows on his knees as he studies a gallery plan hanging in a sagging concertina between his hands. She rushes up the steps and sits beside him, a little breathless.

'Sorry.'

'You aren't late,' he says bluntly, straightening up. She feels a momentary irritation but then she sees the smile he is trying to hide and notices the leaflet trembling slightly in his hands, and she says nothing.

The Sainsbury Wing, where the early Renaissance collection is housed, is, he says, a favourite haunt of his. In the early mornings, before the tourists make it impossible to find seclusion, he often comes here and sits in his coat, looking at the paintings he knows so intimately.

He knows this building inside out, she thinks, he doesn't need a plan. He just needs an occupation for his hands, and she thinks again of the phantom cigarettes he must still feel at times between his fingers.

'Shall we walk?' he says, a little abruptly, clumsily refolding the leaflet so that it doesn't lie flat and poking it roughly into his pocket.

They walk slowly through the deep red rooms of the West Wing, the succession of grey marble doorways, heavy and square, making her feel as if she is travelling down some kind of living spine. They cross through room after room without stopping. Sarah sees a succession of old paintings as they pass, which she cannot fix in any time or place.

'They are High Renaissance,' Jozef says airily when she asks. He does not grace them with even a glance. 'They come after our paintings.'

Ahead, the deep, warm red gives way to a cool, classical grey, and the doorways are suddenly high and arched.

The gallery is quite empty, and suffused with a quiet calm. In each room, bored-looking attendants with walkie-talkies attached to their belts droop on chairs and stare past her, through her, as she walks slowly beside the old man, stopping when he stops, looking at the paintings he looks at and passing over the ones he does not.

They sit down in front of an ornate and rather eerie Madonna and Child.

'Have you noticed,' Jozef says, as if she is as familiar with the rooms as he is, 'the preponderance of birds in all of these paintings? Of animals in general, actually, but birds particularly.'

Sarah gazes at the canvas in front of her. She has never seen it before, has never heard of the painter whose name she reads on the label on the wall. She looks again at the painting. It is almost nauseatingly opulent. Every inch of the canvas is filled with minute, photographic detail, and draped everywhere with fat, heavy fruit. The figures look sallow and evil, as if the fruit has somehow sucked them dry. She searches for a bird.

'"*La Madonna della Rondine*,"' he says musingly. 'See, the swallow is there, above the Virgin's head. A symbol of rebirth, of resurrection. Swallows were thought to hibernate in mud through the winter and then re-emerge in spring.' He looks at her. 'Before they knew, I think, about migration.'

She steps up close to the painting and has another look. He's right. The swallow is there, a tiny dart of deep, Prussian blue, invisible as a shadow. Without him beside her she would have missed it entirely. She examines the whole thing again more carefully, and notices more. The bottom plinth of the painting, part of the frame really, is divided into five tiny panels which she feels she could almost disappear into, they are so detailed, with such long perspective. In one a figure is strung up in a tree like a marionette, as archers aim arrows at him and a morose-looking lurcher dog stands impotently at one side. In another a vulture towers over an old, kneeling man.

'That is Saint Jerome,' he says, seeing her examining the tiny, penitent figure. 'And the other is Saint Sebastian. They are the two figures in the main painting.' She wonders how Jozef can know so much. She feels ashamed to be so ignorant. She turns and sits down again beside Jozef, eager for him to tell her more, her interest captured in a way she would not have expected before today. The way he talks about the paintings makes them come alive, gives them a meaning and a story which she would never have found on her own. She is suddenly fascinated.

'Birds are everywhere in these paintings,' he says. 'In Mantegna's "Garden of Gethsemane" behind us there are vultures; their symbolism is well-known. Elsewhere, in Netherlandish paintings, and others by this master of the ornate, Crivelli, in front of us, there are partridges for truth, peacocks for immortality. Did you know that a peacock's flesh was supposed never to rot?'

၆၃

He designed the skylight deliberately to be faceted and angled like the surface of a diamond. 'Don't you see?' he said to Jayesh when his brother questioned why it had to have quite so many tiny bits of glass in it. 'It's representative. It's a symbol. It's not meant to be just practical.' Jayesh had shaken his head and Balu had seen the smile he tried to hide and knew he thought him ridiculous. It had made him angry that Jayesh was treating his idea with such levity and making him feel the way he always made him feel – like a child who needed to be humoured. A lovable buffoon.

He couldn't expect his brother to understand something that went beyond function, it just wasn't in his character. And it would be difficult to explain to Jayesh just how much the restaurant meant to him.

For a while after coming halfway across the world to the harsh, unforgiving city of London in January, at the tail end of the 1970s, Balu had been desperately and silently unhappy. It was really only finding the job here as a waiter that had got him through. In those dark days, the bustle and community, and above all the smells of the restaurant, had provided a link with home, with his mother's kitchen and her steady, soothing food preparation. If he was honest, he wasn't very good at change, he was slow and dogged. He needed time to percolate and process things, and working in the restaurant had given him that.

His restaurant, now, was the centre of his life and his skylight was so much more than a way of getting more light into the front of the restaurant. It was a way of putting something back, he supposed. A way of showing how important the restaurant was to him. Even the idea had come about in a significant way; it had sprung initially from a throwaway comment by one of his more regular diners, a woman he had grown rather fond of, who always came with a man she seemed not to like very much. She had been touchingly flattered when Balu took up her suggestion and treated it seriously. She seemed unused to being listened to and Balu worried that she might be unhappy with the man. He found himself thinking about her sometimes, at odd moments, wondering when she might next visit. But it was typical of Jayesh that all of this human side of things should have passed him by completely.

ನಿ

'Euclid thought that vision was produced by rays, emitted from the seer, which travelled towards the perceived object and gave it visible form.'

Sarah's meetings with Jozef are filled with such nuggets of information. She enjoys being swept along on the crest of his accumulated knowledge. In Poland before the war he had lectured on Canaletto and his lesser known nephew Bernardo Bellotto, who had lived in Warsaw and painted it in such minute and accurate detail during the 1770s that his work was used as a guide when the capital had to be rebuilt after the Germans destroyed it during the war. There were people who had spirited the paintings away when the future of the city became uncertain, unaware of the value they would have later, worried only that they might be destroyed.

'He called himself Canaletto,' he says. 'He hoped the more famous name would help his pictures sell. The paintings here, you know, many of them, were stored in a slate quarry in the centre of a mountain in Wales, during the war. The whole centre of a mountain, hollowed out then abandoned. Filled with priceless works of art stacked against the walls. And then, when danger was past, back they all came. I came here for the first time not long afterwards.'

She sits beside him and listens as he talks, punctuating himself with asides and parenthetical comments, almost as though she were not there at all. Sometimes she tries to imagine him as a young man in Poland in front of a class or a lecture hall full of students at Warsaw University. Through his tangential commentaries she is building up a rather idiosyncratic and patchwork knowledge of Renaissance iconography and philosophy and who knows what else. She has noticed, though, how Jozef has avoided, so far, talking about himself. He has met what few polite questions she has asked him with a guarded obliqueness and she has started to become curious. And yet he has shown an interest in her, has asked her to tell him about herself. And because he is, in a way, someone outside her life, she has confided things in him which she would not normally voice. There has, for instance, been a growing remoteness in Jude lately and, although she has scarcely realised it has been bothering her, she has found herself telling Jozef about it. She tells him she feels, sometimes, that he is behaving almost as if he were jealous, but there is nothing for him to be jealous of.

'Do you think it might be me?' Jozef asks, joking really, and she thinks, well, it's possible, and then in the next moment, no, of course not. But there's nothing else for him to be jealous of.

They sit for a long while and look in silence at da Vinci's 'Madonna of the Rocks'. The deep blue of her robe. Her serene and eerie face. Jozef seems to have nothing to say about this painting. There is something about the dark brown of the rocks and the ground and the air which seems to Sarah to be brooding and unwholesome. The four faces, and the chubby, naked limbs of the infants seem to glow in the deepening gloom. She is reminded of those strange, luminous fish which silently populate the black depths of oceans. She would like to move, to leave, and she straightens up and fiddles with her hair, looking around the room, feeling, unexpectedly, a little awkward.

'It's my birthday next week,' he announces suddenly. It is the first really personal detail he has given. He has seemed a little strange today and she notices that he looks tired and drawn.

'Do you know,' he says next, just as abruptly, as if he has not mentioned his birthday, 'Leonardo said that only mathematicians should be allowed to read his work. He thought it should be a prerequisite.' He turns to face her then and, after a lengthy pause, asks, 'Would you like to come to tea?'

ॐ

She has made him a birthday card. She gives it a final inspection, checks the message she has written inside, then slides it carefully into an envelope, seals it, and writes his name on the front. Jude is still in bed when she leaves. On her way to Jozef's flat she wonders briefly what they will talk about without the paintings.

Jude stretches out luxuriously, reaching his toes across to the opposite corner of the bed, where her warmth still lingers. As she comes in and out of the room he is dimly aware of drawers being opened, and the wardrobe door squeaking on its hinges. He has his back to her; sleepily, he watches the reflected ghost of morning light swing across the wall and back as she closes the wardrobe door to check her hair in the mirror.

She's going to see the old guy again. He thinks it's weird, this friendship she seems to have struck up. And a bit creepy too, the way she can just go off to his house, knowing practically nothing about him, or nothing she's told him anyway. The old man probably fancies her, gets a hard-on having a young woman paying attention to him. She probably doesn't realise that. He flumps over onto his other side. She's wearing a dress and she's pinning her hair up, her mouth prickling with hair-grips as she grimaces and tries to tame the wayward coils of hair that won't quite stay put. He loves her hair. Loves it all free, hanging round her face and falling over her shoulders – it was one of the first things he noticed when they met – or veiling his face as she sits astride him, leaning over him to make a dark cave of hair. It's a red dress, simple and sexy, curving round her hips and shadowing the narrow concave hollow of her lower back. He's not sure he's seen her wear it before; maybe it's new. He remembers the first few weeks they were together, when everything she had was new to him and each time they met her clothes were different. She glimpses him watching her in the mirror and her eyebrow twitches upwards minutely.

'What?'

'Nothing,' he murmurs, reaching out his hand, wanting her to come to him, wanting suddenly to touch that part of her where the dress is slightly loose, at the back of her waist. She smiles quickly, and pulls a face at herself in the mirror, fiddling still with one of the grips, trying to iron out some invisible kink in her hair.

'You're going to a lot of effort.' He doesn't exactly mean to say this. He hears it, querulous, slightly vulnerable, and wishes it immediately unsaid. She turns round and looks straight at him.

'It's his birthday.'

She sounds sharp, defensive even. He tries a dismissive, half-apologetic smile, but feels she is more angry with him than she would admit to if he asked. He does wonder, though. Since she met this old man she has been skipping off to meet him as she might a lover. Yet that cannot be the pull. Obviously it's not: he's over eighty or something. But even so, there's something about this other life, away from him, that seems to be taking over from the absorption she had in him at the beginning, that makes him feel second-best. He wants to get that intensity back again, wants to spend entire days with her in bed, sharing wine and talking, as they did when they first knew each other, needing nothing more to make them feel fulfilled and happy. He's not sure how to get back to this, or what it is that this Jozef character is giving her that takes her away from him so often.

On her way out she kisses him lightly on the mouth and he catches her hand, encircles her waist and pulls her closer. They kiss briefly, but he can feel the spring of resistance in her body.

* * *

65

She kisses him on the forehead and stands up. He smells of stale sheets and sleep; his breath is sour, making her more aware of the toothpaste taste in her own mouth. She needs to go, but she feels uneasy. There's something a little febrile in Jude's behaviour at the moment, in his need for constant touching and sex. He's become different, somehow, more sombre, more dogged. He used to be fun, they could laugh at themselves, laugh as they made love; now it's always so serious, as if it's all the more meaningful for having a bit of solemnity. But she can't stop and think about it now or she will be late.

The bus comes almost immediately; she sits on the top deck and watches out of the window as the Mountain of Light disappears into the distance. Glad to be free of the worry that she might be late, she thinks about where she is going. She is quite excited about Jozef's birthday. If she's honest, she feels a bit chosen, a bit special. She is just some girl who knows nothing, really, about anything very much, and yet he thinks enough of her to want to make her his friend. Knowing that makes her happy.

His flat is small and dark, and is in one of those buildings which feels as if it has igloo-thick walls. He lives on the fourth floor and the muffled sounds from outside, traffic and street noises drifting up from below, remind her of childhood stays in Wales with her mother's boyfriend, Uncle Stefan, during the Christmas holidays, when thick snow seemed to wall everything in and absorb all the colours and sounds. She has never experienced such deep, all-enveloping snow since and hasn't even thought about the house in Wales for years, till this moment, stepping into Jozef's flat.

There are two old easy chairs, the type with wooden arms and cushions slung over sagging elastic straps for the seat, pulled up to a small gas fire. Although it is quite a warm day, she sees that it is lit on the lowest, blue-flickering setting. He has gone to so much trouble she feels terribly sad all of a sudden. He has opened out a tiny tray table beside one of the chairs, and has already set out a plate, knife, cup and saucer and paper serviette. Beside the other chair, on a larger table also seemingly brought out for the purpose, stand a teapot, milk jug, and the same arrangement of cup, saucer, knife and plate. He gestures her to the seat with the tray and she sits down, asking if there is anything she can do.

'It's all done,' he says, pleased, and disappears into a tiny, crammed-looking kitchen. He brings out a plate of neat little sandwiches, carefully covered with cling film, and another one of Cadbury's Mini Rolls. The sadness rolls over her again as he hesitates, a plate in each hand, and she realises he's left himself nowhere to put them. She makes room on his little table and his nervousness subsides a little after he has sat down and shakily poured them both a cup of tea. He has a knitted brown tea cosy in the shape of a tabby cat; it has curled-up knitted ears and a knitted pink tongue licking round an impossibly wide smile. She wonders how long it has been since he has had a visitor.

'Happy birthday,' she says at last, fishing in her bag for the card she has brought. When he opens it he looks so fondly at it and spends so long reading the short message she has written inside, she feels she won't be able to contain the sadness if it keeps welling up at every single thing. He eventually closes the card, looks again at the pressed flowers on the front, and places it on top of the gas fire, angling it carefully so that it faces him. There is only one other and she wishes she had thought to buy him a present. He sees her eyeing the top of the fire.

'The other one is from Teresa, an ex-student of mine. I also knew her father. You have met her, I think. At the private view?' Sarah remembers the woman in red who had been arm in arm with Jozef and nods. He smiles. 'She is always telling me I should reminisce, as if it would be good for me, like doing exercises or taking bran. There are groups for the old, you know. They sit around in institution chairs boring to death some young community worker until afternoon tea and a doze.' He catches her eye. 'You think I am ungrateful?'

Sarah shakes her head quickly, catching the sharpness in his voice.

'Not at all,' she says.

In the silence that follows he picks the cling film off the plate of sandwiches and holds it out to her. His arm is unsteady and wavers slightly as it hovers in the air between them. She fears all the careful triangles will slide onto the floor so she quickly takes two and places them self-consciously on the plate at her side.

Without the paintings there isn't the obvious stimulus for easy conversation and as they chew their sandwiches they talk in a faltering, uneasy way. But then, as she listens to the slightly irritating, edgy ticking of a clock on the wall, he does away with the need for her to say anything very much at all for the rest of the time she knows him. He leans forward slightly in his chair and clears his throat.

'On that day I met you,' he says, and stops, his eyes locking with hers. 'I was reminded . . . you . . . reminded me of someone.' He has already told her that, but she nods slowly, waiting for him to say more.

Two People and a Snowflake

As he begins to talk it is as if something starts to awaken in him that has been asleep for so long he has almost forgotten it is there. His eyes seem alight, but also tentative, as if he is fearful of what he might find as he shakes away the dust. The paintings in the gallery, although he has talked about them eagerly enough, have never animated him as dramatically as this. Sarah is transfixed, her sadness about the sandwiches and his lack of birthday presents forgotten as she watches him come alive.

'Ewa was nineteen years old when I first knew her. I engineered it, I'm afraid. I lay in wait for her. It wasn't sinister, wasn't meant to be. Not an ambush or anything like that. But I had seen her and I wanted to speak to her.' He pauses. 'I had fallen in love with her,' he says, enunciating carefully the words 'fallen in love' as if they were something brittle, the long, ungainly legs of a glass foal, perhaps, Sarah thinks. 'She had a way of walking up the street while still buttoning up her coat and pulling on her gloves. A disarranged person, I thought. An imprecise person. I had always been someone who would hold up my scarf, find the middle and place this part at the nape of my neck and then cross the two ends on my chest. I would check my coat, my collar, in the hall mirror and put on my hat. All before I even considered opening the front door. And here was this girl streaming up the road with her scarf waving in the wind, or else trailing down her back. Totally unconcerned.

'I knew nothing about her. All I had was that picture of her as she was leaving the Warsaw Grand Theatre, jumping the few worn steps that led down from the stage door in one go and dashing round the corner to the front of the building and the main road. I didn't know she was a dancer then, I just assumed she was. The way she held herself was so . . .' He stops, his eyes fixed on a point on the ceiling as he searches for the words. 'She had *composure*,' he says at last, stressing the word slightly as if to affirm what he is saying, 'and I was utterly captivated. She took me completely by surprise. She brought me out of myself; I was disarmed, I was so unprepared for her. For falling in love. Suddenly *being* in love.

'I took a short cut always when I was in that part of town and it took me behind the theatre building. Often the huge doors to the stage would be open and I would see people working inside, all ladders and ropes, a hive of concentration, the curving banks of empty seats climbing up into the darkness of the roof. I've always loved the technicalities behind things, the secret labour behind what's shown.

'That first time,' he says, 'that chance passing near the stage door at the back of the theatre, when she nearly ran into me – she would have if I hadn't stepped aside – I had my wits about me then.' He turns to Sarah suddenly, as if expecting her to dispute this.

'She was always running, always on the verge of being late. All I had, that first time, was a glimpse of her face. Mostly it was her back I saw. Her scarf, and her hand grabbing for it, feeling blindly for it, trying to tame it and wrap it round herself. It was enough. That glimpse brought me back to the same spot the next day, and the next. I gave myself unnecessary errands which involved passing the theatre. I left the university at a slightly different time each evening, hoping to catch her, if she was a dancer, arriving for the evening performance.

'The Balets Polski had arrived in Warsaw about a year earlier. Perhaps less. I had been, at the time, involved with a young lady who rather liked ballet, and so I remembered some facts I would not otherwise have known. Without realising, I started to dredge my months-past memory for things I had learnt from this girlfriend – Anna, she was called. She had told me, for instance, that the company's director had some impressive credentials. He had once worked with Diaghilev and Pavlova. Even I had heard these luminous names. And on one occasion in that short time we spent together she persuaded me to take her to a performance in Lazienki Park, and we walked along the east bank of the Wisła, arrived early and strolled along the oak-lined promenades before taking our seats in the Orangery where the performance took place. I don't remember the ballet.

'And so, a year later, I hung around the stage door every evening and prayed that my bewitching young woman, almost certainly a dancer, would reappear. On the third day my perseverance was rewarded. I saw her again and felt myself stumbling stupidly into love with her. She looked straight at me, or through me.

'When I lost sight of her I tried to remember her face and couldn't. It had gone. People I have met only once – an academic, a librarian, a woman swaying opposite me on the packed tram from Praga, breathing her onion breath in my face – I remember their faces for ever. I can see them there in my head, behind my eyes if I close them. But Ewa. No, she flowed in and flowed out again. I couldn't fix her. I lay in bed trying for hours and had to give it up. I got up again, drank two measures of vodka and fell asleep in a chair.'

ა

Sarah hugs her knees under her chin and peers down through the skylight into the restaurant. She is thinking about what Jozef has been saying about falling in love. She wonders whether it is possible to fall in love at all, let alone to know for certain when it has happened. But Jozef's conviction, his utter transformation, even that afternoon, in front of her, sixty years later, was absolutely genuine. Maybe, she thinks, she's thinking about it the wrong way. Maybe it's just different for everyone and it's pointless trying to make comparisons. Perhaps she will never experience Jozef's kind of certainty because she just isn't like that.

She sees Balu, down below in the golden glow of the restaurant, glide slowly by, like some large, hospitable fish, and bend silently over one of the tables, talking to a diner. It looks busy tonight. She often imagines the restaurant as an aquarium: in its silent depths, distorted by the sharpness of the angle from which she is looking, strangely shaped creatures pulse and move, always seeming to be in slow motion, flashing colours and then disappearing. Occasionally a human face will turn upwards, pale and round as a moon, and it will surprise her, peering curiously, vulnerably, out into the dark void of the sky. If they see her hovering above them in the darkness it never registers in their expressions.

Of course, she thinks, even if love is different in every person, that doesn't explain why some people are so sure of it, know it for what it is the instant its flickering light is squinted at, while others, herself, walk round and round it, trying to work out what it is, and whether it's worth stopping at and stoking up on.

୧୬

'The next time I saw her, the day we first spoke, the city had been clamped under a thick layer of ice for a week. It was January 1938. Nevertheless, I set off from my flat and made my tentative way towards the tram stop, my anxiety at knowing that this time I intended to try to speak to her made all the worse by my faltering progress. My heart was pounding as I climbed down from the tram once I was over the bridge and in the old town, and I slithered my way down the ungritted side streets towards the back of the theatre. I didn't yet know what I was going to say to her, but I was beginning to feel rather conspicuous, hanging around behind the theatre day after silent day, and I knew that this time I really would have to try.

'And then, as I laboured up the street, each breath standing whole in the air in front of me like some sort of fog balloon, I saw her coming towards me.

'What must I do? Must I walk past and ignore her? Can I? I begin to panic. I will give myself away, I am sure. A smile or a nod then, or must I stop and introduce myself? All the time she is getting closer, and I really do not know what to do. I am in a dreadful panic. But Sarah, it is she who speaks to me!' He looks across at her, incredulous.

'"I have seen you here before," she says. "Yesterday." Her words are perfectly enunciated. Her lips envelop them, shape them.

73

'"*Tak*." My mouth is dry, the saliva has thickened into a gum which clicks as I say the word, gluing my tongue to the roof of my mouth. *Czuję się głupio*. I feel stupid. Stupid.

'"Aren't you going to offer me your arm?" she asks, her voice glibly confident.

'I do as she asks and escort her stiffly down the road, feeling more awkward by the minute.

'"Where are we going, by the way?" she asks eventually, once we have laboured a little way in silence. I feel her face turned towards me, open and expectant. She is amused by me and I wonder if she is not having a little game with herself at my expense.

'"Where *were* you going?"

'"Why? Am I still going there?" Well, I don't know how to respond to this. I feel as if I have been winded. I cannot speak and find myself mouthing shapes like some sort of gross, beached fish or an imbecile, even. I who have such self-control!

'"I . . . we . . ." I try to say something, but I fail miserably and instead shrug my shoulders helplessly.

'She stops and turns her whole body towards me, her arm in mine pulling me to a standstill beside her. We face each other in the middle of the pavement. Snow has started to fall, meaning it must not be as cold as it was, but I am sweating inside my coat while my feet have no feeling. My own micro-climate. The only reason I know it is snowing is that a flake has landed on the brim of her grey felt hat. The world is reduced to two people in a street, and one snowflake.

'"I saw you yesterday, standing in the street in the cold." She speaks more gently now. "And I saw you the day before that from the dressing-room window, only by the time I'd collected my things and had my coat on you were gone. You were waiting for me?" This last is tentatively questioning. She is not entirely sure; she knows it is possible she could be quite wrong, although I fear I must have given myself away absolutely.

'I lower my head. "Yes," I whisper, my scrap of voice almost soundless.'

৶

Balu brought with him to London the kitchen secrets of a dozen Mangalore matriarchs and the studied traditions of the whole of India. His mother passed on to him all she knew, and what she hadn't been able to tell him he learnt from others. As he grew older he branched out beyond Mangalore mothers and discovered how ingredients were used differently in Jaipur, for example, and the Keralan region in the south. Before long, he could provide a tour of the entire subcontinent, criss-crossing from east to west to south between each dish. The mothers who had nurtured his interest as a child now tasted the fruit of their teachings when his mother invited them to the house to sample his cooking.

Now, he is the undisputed master in the kitchen at the Mountain of Light. But despite his love for it he knows that it was there for the taking. This authority was not something he had to fight for. It was not hard-won, as Jayesh's success in business had been. He just grew into it; it was as natural as mothering. While he chose to stay with his mother in the kitchen when he was a child, Jayesh played outside, kicking balls with his friends, running in the fields, shinning over walls and coming home with grazed knees, his clothes filthy with red dust and bike chain oil. Nobody had ever suggested that Balu leave the kitchen, and so he had not. As always, he was doing what was expected of him. The difference was that in the kitchen he was happy. There, he concurred rather than submitted.

He never felt lonely when he was cooking. Ingredients responded to him, took their cues from him, as if the whole act of preparation and cooking were a kind of dialogue. He was like the conductor of an orchestra, maestro of a limited but, for a short while, all-encompassing realm. Balu was careful to take happiness where he found it and not question it too much, and if he missed out on some of the things that Jayesh or the young couples who came to eat at the restaurant seemed to take for granted, then that was just the way it was.

Pools of Silence

'Paintings? And that's all you talk about?'

Sarah drops her eyes sideways. She hasn't told them yet about Jozef's latest topic of conversation. 'No, not all.'

'What then?' Hari persists. 'Come on, don't be so mysterious. Tell!'

Hari's eyes are on her, unwilling to let her go so easily, wanting to tease more from her. She looks up at him, briefly angry. She wishes he wouldn't be so . . . so what? She's not sure what it is. But he's so puppyish around her sometimes, as if he thinks they could still fool around with each other if they wanted. Sometimes she wonders whether Jude can tell. Whether each connection with another person, however brief, leaves something indelible behind.

'It's difficult,' she snaps. 'He just wanders around. He forgets I'm there. I don't think I should even talk about it.'

'You're not.'

Balu straightens up in his chair to reach across the table and places his chubby hand over hers.

'Take no notice of Hari,' he says. 'He is being most indelicate tonight. I don't know what's the matter with him.' He pronounces the word indelicate with the utmost delicacy.

Hari looks guardedly at the round face turned to his, the raised black eyebrows crumpling the shiny forehead with four horizontal furrows. Balu's dark eyes look steadily at him, as if trying to transmit some tentative warning. After an awkward silence Hari laughs a laugh which sounds like a shrug, brushing the comment off in a way which somehow makes it resonate and linger.

Sarah and Jude sit at opposite ends of the table. She looks across at him. He is a little apart from them – they have pulled their chairs up towards her end of the table. He has slid down in his chair so that his head rests on the velvet upholstered back which he now uses as a pivot as he looks from Hari to Balu and back, absorbed, she thinks, by this sudden tension between them. She cannot see his legs beneath the table, but she can tell from the depth of his slouch that they are outstretched, possibly crossed, reaching almost to the centre of the table. Mid-pivot he catches her looking at him and as a slow smile creeps across his lips a little of the sense of something not being right ebbs from her.

She draws herself up in her chair and pours more wine into her glass, and this movement, its necessary precision, together with Jude's smile, is sufficient to break the momentary spell.

'He talks about himself, his life, when he was younger,' she says at last. She feels evasive. She does not want to tell them.

While their eyes are fixed on her, Jude looks again at Balu and Hari. Watches them watching her.

'It's nothing really,' she says. 'Just his life. Lovers, that sort of thing. I think he just wants to remember. He's old.' She doesn't know what's wrong. Jude is quite obviously sulking, and it's a part of him she has never seen before. He is refusing to show any curiosity about her friendship with Jozef, and he is slouching in his chair as if he would just like to go upstairs to bed. Well, go then, she thinks. She knows it's ridiculous of her to be so short-tempered with Hari, who is itching for her to tell them about her new friend. But it's Jude she wants to be curious. She looks across at their reflections in the tiny mirror squares on the wall behind and notices how the back of Jude's head – the top of it, the rest is hidden by the chair back – cuts off Balu's face. And how the unnevenness of the tiles fragments their reflections so that their little group seems like a jumbled huddle of backs and fronts, faces and shoulders, and all the different colours of their clothes are mixed up together so she can't separate them out into four distinct people.

∞

'When I first met Ewa I was already seeing someone. A girl called Magda. I say a girl; she was a young woman, of course. She was older than Ewa, a little nearer my own age. She was in love with me, although she had never actually said as much. But I think I'd worked it out.' He sighs deeply.

Sarah notices the tremor in his voice and looks at him. As if in answer, he meets her gaze, and his faded blue eyes are filmed with tears. He must be feeling a stab of pity for this Magda, she thinks. She already has a picture of Ewa in her mind, the dark straight hair and strong features. This new character in the story, Magda, she can't yet imagine.

'Of course Magda knew something was wrong. I think, without realising it, certain things, guilt especially probably, make you act differently. She was very hurt. She tried not to show it; she was very closed about her feelings, very protective. I hadn't been fair with her. I hadn't acknowledged her feelings for me. But it was very difficult, you know, when she herself could not express them either.' He looks quizzically at Sarah. 'I'm not saying you should excuse me,' he says quickly. 'I behaved wrongly, I know. But . . .' he pauses, weighs his words, looks across at her again. 'With Magda . . . with Magda it was very difficult to know where you were. Whereas with Ewa. Well. At the beginning everything was so simple.'

❦

Always two conversations, she thinks. The one they are having – a few sentences draped across an afternoon, dropped into pools of silence and swallowed – and the one they are not having, in which they both stop what they are doing and talk to each other properly. They never seem to any more, the way they did at the beginning. Sarah looks at Jude. Looks at him in the garden, standing on the other side of the skylight, looking down onto the road. He has his back to her and, she supposes, is unaware she is watching him. Perhaps we have talked ourselves out, she thinks. He certainly never talks, anyway. She watches as he leans further over the wall and his head disappears as if it is a sun sinking behind the horizon of his shoulders. He closes himself off from things. When she sat at the table in the restaurant opposite him last night she could feel it, his barrier, as he sank lower into his chair and stretched his feet out underneath the table.

She remembers the first time she and Jude were in the restaurant together. It had felt a little as if she was bringing her boyfriend home to meet the parents. They had gone in the back way, through the kitchen, and halfway down the fire escape Jude had caught hold of her hand and stopped her, wanting to keep her to himself a moment longer before they went inside.

She can feel his barrier, his unwillingness. But there's something else. There is a petulance now. She doesn't know why.

He calls down to someone in the street and she hears Hari's voice shout something back. Jude's arms are spaced wide apart on the wall as if he is embracing the late afternoon, his shoulders pushed up so that she can sense the valley between them beneath his T-shirt, the warmth she would feel if she were to place her hand there. She imagines the contact of his hands, flat-palmed, with the bricks. Their smoothness against the rough surface. He stretches, flexing his fingers and arching his back, yawning loudly, and then once again peers over the wall to the pavement below. Greyness. The pavement, the road. It is that time of day just before twilight when, on an already dull day, everything visible becomes almost entirely monochrome.

He can feel her behind him. Knows she is there, and imagines her watching him through the open door. Imagines that, cross-legged on the sofa, she lifted her eyes from whatever it is she is reading and followed his back as he picked his way past the flowerpots surrounding that glass monstrosity and reached the wall. That cat on the chair. As he spreads his hands out against the bricks and feels the surface hardness individualise each finger, he thinks of the cat's feet and the tip of her tail neatly arranged in a bundle. Five legs. Mentally he grasps them and ties them all together with a piece of ribbon. A bunch of feet. That cat. When it blinks, the thin, smiling crescents of its yellow-green irises simply disappear and reappear in its blackness, that is all. Lamps switched off and on in the dark.

He takes a deep breath, filling his lungs and then releasing the air slowly. Sarah seems so right in this place, so self-contained. He has moved all of his things in now; she has pushed her clothes up in the wardrobe to give him space, and

81

crammed more of her clothes into fewer drawers so that he can put his clothes away. His books fill the available shelves and overflow onto the mantelpiece and floor. Yet somehow he still feels as if he is a guest, someone just passing through on his way somewhere else.

He wishes he could stop thinking of that thing Balu said in the restaurant. The evening they were talking about Othello and he said, well, imagine Sarah was sleeping with Hari. Of course she isn't, he knows that, but still. Why did Balu use them? Why did he use such a specific example? Jude knows it must be affecting his behaviour, that it must seem as if he's sulking or something. He smiles to himself. Of course there's nothing. There's nothing at all.

She notices it most when she talks about Jozef, this new sulkiness in Jude. At first she thought he just wasn't interested. But it isn't lack of interest, it is a deliberate closing off. A shutting out. As if he is anticipating some kind of sadness which he doesn't wish to be drawn closer to. And she thinks he is jealous too. He feels threatened, somehow, by this new relationship which excludes him. And how it comes out, how it translates to her, is as rigid boredom. An almost arrogant dismissal.

She blinks and realises she is staring at the same page, has actually got two-thirds of the way down it and has no idea what she has read. She turns back to the previous page, trying to find the point where she drifted away. Ah, here: '. . . *No, it's a useless journey you're making,*' she mentally addressed a party *of people in a coach and four who were evidently going on an excursion into the country. 'And the dog you are taking with you won't help either. You can't get away from yourselves.' Glancing in the direction in which Peter was looking, she saw a workman,*

almost dead-drunk, his head swaying, being led off by a
policeman. 'He's found a quicker way,' she thought. 'Count
Vronsky and I did not find our happiness either, though we
expected so much . . .'

They have said so little in the passing of an afternoon that
began dully and is now being steered into dusk. The street
lamp outside the restaurant has come on and its round orange
glow increases in confidence, in brilliance, as darkness slowly
surrounds it, lapping at its furry extremes. Outside in the
garden, peering down into the road, Jude sees Hari leap from
the footplate of a bus he has hardly noticed. He shouts down
to him and sees the surprise turn to recognition in his face,
remembering, oh yes, that is what it's like. You are switched
off, allowing your body's blind familiarity with its routine to
steer your course, when a shouted greeting, or a question from
a stranger, drags you back. And all in a moment you have to
reassemble everything, remember who you are, where you are
going, before you can recognise the question or greeting, or
whatever it was. That is what he sees in the usually composed
figure standing on the pavement below. The beautiful face
lifted up to him, for a fleeting moment completely disarmed.

And then Hari goes inside the restaurant and Jude is alone
again. He turns his head and looks over his shoulder, down
through the hole in the roof, sees Hari walk through the
restaurant, remove his coat in one swift movement, and disappear out of sight. When he turns back, the street light nearest
to him comes on. One thing different, he thinks. Just one thing
different, a second here, a second there, and I would have
missed that. And he leans out over the wall and looks down
the road as all the lights blink on in silent sequence.

If he is honest, it's the fact that Hari is so fucking gorgeous, and that he knows it, that grates so particularly. He is impossible not to like, yet it's this very amiability that has begun to set Jude's teeth on edge. He knows it's unfair; Hari has done nothing to provoke such antipathy except be himself, but if he were less perfect, less comfortable with himself, he would be so much easier to get on with.

He stays outside until the pale violet glow warms to orange and the darkness grows around him until the road seems punctuated by regular spots of orange and the phrases of illuminated shop and restaurant signs. Then he goes back indoors, to where Sarah is sitting, cross-legged still, with her head bowed over the book she is reading. Sita lies curled on a chair, wakened only when he comes back into the room and bangs into the chair, too near the door.

'Shit.' He grabs at his ankle and stumbles into the room as the chair empties itself of the roused cat which stalks into the centre of the room, instantly awake, and begins abrasively to wash. Finally, reluctantly, Sarah looks up from her book.

They have said so little. He could have asked her what she was reading so intently, but might she not have resented his intrusion? She looked so absorbed, her posture so inwardly bent, so protective. And yet the afternoon has not passed unpleasantly. So little needed to be said. When he came up the stairs and found her there, cross-legged on the sofa opposite the opened shutters where the feeble afternoon sun was lighting one end of the long room, she looked up at him and smiled a smile which felt like physical contact.

'Hello.' That was all. It was true, he thought; so little needed to be said sometimes. And what he had thought of as hostility in her could have been nothing. She was reading, that was all.

When he comes clumsily back into the room, catching the chair with his leg, he blinks the street lights away and sees her momentarily bowed in a pool of light at the other end of the room before she looks up.

She closes the book and puts it on the cushion beside her, then pats her lap. Jude sits beside her and lies down gratefully, suddenly tired. He feels her fingers pulling gently at his hair, twirling strands of it round her fingers, then bunching clumps of it together and smoothing it with her palm. He closes his eyes. Maybe he just wishes sometimes that she'd talk to him as much as she talks to the old man, he thinks. Since he's been living in the flat with her it's as if they have outworn the things they used to talk about so easily. It's envy, he supposes, or sadness that she has taken her absorption elsewhere.

As she strokes his hair Sarah is thinking about Jozef, and the distress he was obviously feeling as he told her about Magda. He hurt Magda, betrayed an unspoken love. What happened to her, she wonders. What happens to people whose love is not returned?

ം

Hari has the evening off. All afternoon he thought idly that he might phone a friend, go for a beer a bit later, but as the evening crept closer and the phone call remained unmade, he realised that he wasn't going to phone anyone. The room has gradually darkened around him, so slowly that he has remained oblivious, and the curtains are still wide open, the lamp in the corner unlit, shadows dancing on the wall in the blue light from the television. He lifts the remote control from the arm of his chair and zaps the TV off. There's nothing he wants to watch. He glances at his watch in the gloom; it's just after 9.30. Without meaning to he remembers wine drunk in Sarah's garden from a single glass, the Verve's *Urban Hymns* drifting through the open doors. He cannot hear any of those songs now without being crowded by memories, must switch off the radio if he hears the too-familiar, prefatory threads of songs they played over and over last summer. He glances at his watch again. He isn't going to phone anyone. But now he's had this memory pang he has to do something; he can't sit here, letting its destructive floodwaters course through him. In a series of movements so swift they appear as one single, fluid action, he rises from the chair, picks up his keys, leaves the flat and is walking at a clip down the street.

The pub isn't busy. He buys a pint of lager and carries it over to an empty table in the corner. He rarely smokes, would never call himself a smoker, but now he digs in his pocket and sorts through his change to see if he has enough for a pack from the fag machine.

He can't even remember the last time he smoked, hasn't done it for months. As the unaccustomed sensation fills him, making him feel a sudden rush of nausea and a dizzy loosening of the tension in his body, he glances around the room. Aside from a couple of men sitting singly on high stools at the bar, staring stolidly into space, everyone else is with others. Either as part of a group of three or four, or as one half of a couple. There is a low buzz of conversation, woven through with individual voices which he can pick out and identify. The animated, musical voice of a compact, sharp-featured girl at the next table, with brown, smooth shoulders and neatly crossed legs, leaning in to whisper something to her companion. The confident, open voices, swinging easily back and forth between a group of three men, two of them still in work shirts with loosened ties. Hari drinks his beer quickly, in agitated, angry gulps, and buys another. His head is singing slightly: the mingled effect of the rush of alcohol and nicotine. He pulls out another cigarette and gets a light from the smooth-skinned girl, who holds the tiny flame steady in front of his trembling hands.

He has never been here with Sarah, he thinks. She has never seen this room. She has never seen most of the places he has known all his life; she was content to know him again and again in that one place which was always there, over his head as he worked. Which is there still.

☙

It is a bright day and when she arrives Jozef suggests they walk in the park. He takes her arm and they walk slowly, stopping at the frequent benches to rest. It's a relief to be outside instead of cooped up in the tiny, dark flat, but he seems so frail out of doors, as if the space and air somehow make him smaller. She has got so used to seeing him in his armchair now, in the airless sitting room, that he just looks wrong anywhere else. She notices, too, how difficult his breathing seems to be as he walks.

He soon picks up the thread of his rememberings, left hanging since the last time they met.

'Ewa was a graceful, beautiful woman, but you have no idea how deformed her feet were by the age of twenty. Really, sometimes she would be almost weeping in my arms from the pain of them and I would take them in my hands, both of them, and rub them, soothe them. I pitied her so much that sometimes I would bathe them. Her toes were calloused and ugly, horribly misshapen and red, and the nails which she still had were all stunted and split. I couldn't believe, at first, how something as beautiful as dancing could cause such disfigurement and pain. After a performance they would be rubbed raw, blistered and bleeding. But you could see none of this, none of the pain, when she was actually dancing. She once said that when she was on stage she could cut herself off from it, the same way she closed her mind to everything else – the audience, the world outside. Everything immediate was reduced to sound and movement; nothing beyond this existed, she said. She was at her most beautiful when she was dancing. The pain only reattached itself when she left the stage and the world came spiralling back into view.'

Back in his flat he seems quite exhausted. A greyness has crept into his cheeks, and when she offers to put the kettle on for their cup of tea he doesn't protest. When she comes back into the room he is bent double in his chair, still in his coat, fumbling with his shoelaces. In the silence of the room his breathing is heavy and laboured.

'Here,' she says, and she kneels beside him and tackles the knotted laces herself. He sits up gratefully and smiles a feeble smile as her fingers untangle the laces which have become tight and sodden in the dewy grass. His breathing slows and he leans back, closing his eyes.

'Why are you telling me all this, Jozef?'

'What?'

She hadn't meant to ask the question. It just comes out suddenly in the silence as the electric kettle hisses in the kitchen. She is angry with herself for needing to do this. Angry for this sudden, selfish need for him to see her. For him to step out of his story for a moment and see her there beside him.

He looks at her, and he wonders how it would have been if he had not approached her that day they met. If he had not touched her elbow and asked if she was all right. It was her expression, the fleeting habitation of her face by another's, which had been the start, reminding him so arbitrarily but so painfully of his first encounter with Ewa outside the theatre.

He knows he is neglecting her. That in a way he is using her as a conduit to his memories rather than treating her as a friend. But he thinks of her as a friend now. A dear friend. The truth is that he has not thought about any of this for a long time. He has blotted out his loneliness, his loss of Ewa and even of Magda, and all the guilt and jealousy and suspicion he had fallen victim to. But for a long time he has known it must be revisited. That he must somehow make peace with the rest-less ghosts from his past, and with his own voiceless yearning. When he was a younger man it had been much easier to bury all those things that felt unfinished, and simply to keep busy – he has found no shortage of occupation. But a deep unease has been rising in him in the past months, disturbing the compacted, flattened years and threatening collapse. It is perhaps partly due to his sense that the current work he is doing is of little academic relevance. He has, in a way, left the highway of his own expertise and is exposed and alone. He knows that his usefulness is behind him. That the focus has already shifted elsewhere, and it won't matter greatly if this current project never sees completion. More than this, he is beginning to realise that he doesn't much care any more. And with the waning of his carefully constructed professional self has come a waxing of the self he has suppressed, still bristling with its insecurities and rages, as if it has been taken out of the deep freeze and thawed out to trouble him afresh.

It occurs to him that, once again, he has unwittingly fallen into dependence; he needs Sarah now, possibly more than he has ever needed anyone. He cannot bear to be lonely any longer. Since meeting her his life has started to shrink away – gradually at first, but then more and more quickly, like disturbed scree gathering speed and slipping away irrevocably – until it consists of little else but her arrival and departure, and the story he is unravelling, finally, for her. But yes, he is neglecting her. And knowing this he reaches out his hand to her. She takes it and, for a moment, they are two people – a young woman and an old man – together. Nothing else.

 familia

Sarah wonders how it must feel to be at the end of life, looking back at what it has been. She has her own memories – is brimful of them – and they feel as much a physical part of her as her hair or the skin on her knees. Yet to Jozef she must seem so untried and fresh. So empty still. But of course a person's capacity must grow with their years, so that at any stage in their life they are as full of the past as they are able to be.

He is standing at the window, his silhouetted head angled sharply downwards, as if he is looking intently at something particular in the street. He hasn't heard her come back into the room, she thinks, and closes the door as noisily as she can without it seeming deliberate. He turns sharply. She smiles, suddenly a little embarrassed – he forgot, she thinks. Just for a moment, he forgot that I was here. She squeezes past the tray table with the teapot and milk jug on it and joins him at the window.

'What were you looking at?'

'Oh nothing. Just looking out,' he says, and he offers her a watery, pathetic smile and goes back to his easy chair. It's a small window and there isn't room for two people to stand and look out together. She follows what she imagines to have been the line of his gaze. On the other side of the road is a sandwich shop. It is one of those sandwich shops which employs three or four attractive young Italians or Spaniards to deal with the lunchtime rush and then closes early. A slim, olive-skinned youth in a short apron is vigorously wiping tables near the window. A woman, further inside the shop, half hidden by the reflected street in the plate glass, stands with her back turned, doing something at the till. The outside paintwork is a bright, sky-blue and the broad step up to the shop door is tiled with mosaic squares of the same colour, chequered with white.

'It makes me think of the seaside,' she says absently, not yet remembering why, although the memory of a holiday in a ramshackle B&B starts to trickle back. She has the habit of remembering the smallest details of a place she has been, an encounter she has had, and recalling them later on, out of nowhere, and having them bring back the rest of the memory with them, flapping behind like a streamer. But it is the tiny, unconnected fragments – the colour of the paintwork – which are the triggers that set her off.

It is nearly four o'clock. The sandwich shop is about to close. A third aproned figure is sitting at one of the tables and, as she watches, the woman at the till joins him and lights a cigarette.

They look tired. They look as if they couldn't care less whether they are being watched or not. But she feels suddenly intrusive.

Jozef is looking at her intently.

'The seaside?'

Her mention of the seaside has sparked another memory.

'I remember Ewa on the beach in Poland. I remember a crowd of swans. What do you call it? Gaggle? Murder? Anyway, a whatever-it's-called of swans. They looked so odd against the sand. As if they were in the wrong place. They may well have been, I don't know. Do you get swans on beaches?' Sarah doesn't know.

'They were milling around, waiting for one of them to make a decision to move, or so it seemed to me. Well, we thought, let's go and have a look at them. They were only specks when we first saw them. And so we walked over the sand, across the dry untidy part and onto the darker compacted bit. I always liked that, how the sea could tidy up after people. The stretches of sand it never reached so bleached and kicked up. All those scraps of so many people's day on the beach swept up and left in a neat line. I've always respected the way the sea does that.

'The swans had collected underneath the pier. Around its barnacled piles.' Sarah pictures the huge iron supports, the tide lines on them, wrapped round with the glistening bright greens of seaweed and the ancient studding of barnacles. 'As we approached them they turned their heads and eyed us suspiciously. Ewa started clucking at them, the way she always did with animals that weren't sure of her. A soft sound in her throat. I once heard her use it to coax a nursing cat from my cellar. Where I had failed she persuaded it to drink milk, crouching down beside it in her stockinged feet for over an hour.

'I noticed how the sun disappeared as we went beneath the pier, and how it was suddenly cooler. She was entranced by the swans. Slowly, they started to come towards her and surround her and I began to feel terribly alone. It was her experience, I was the observer, and in that role I quietly pulled out my camera and took a photograph. She didn't notice. Afterwards I told her and she was surprised. Not so much at the photograph, I don't think, as the fact that I was there at all. It was the same as when she was dancing and I knew that she had shut everything out. I am sure that at the moment I opened the shutter nothing else existed for her but the swans and the density of wet sand beneath her feet; I felt a fleeting need for reassurance which I swallowed immediately. The click of the shutter made the picture seem like a mockery. I don't know, I can't explain. Like a cheapening. As if I was trying to force entry into an experience which was not mine to have, and trying to capture an image of something when the image was the most insignificant thing about it. That's the trouble with photographs, I think, isn't it? You expect too much of them.' Sarah isn't sure, but she thinks she understands what he means.

'They closed around her so that I couldn't have stepped any closer without frightening them. I have always been a little afraid of swans. Something my mother said when I was a child about their being able to break your arm with one beat of their terrible wings if they were so inclined. And so naturally I assumed they were always intent upon harming small boys. She showed me how you could tell if one was angry – the way it held its wings away from its body and arched them over its back. And how it lurched through the water, ploughing into it and leaving a long, widening V in its wake.

'These swans weren't angry though. They stood around her like sentinels. I thought, "Nothing can harm her. Nothing can change her, change this."' He lets his hands drop limply into his lap.

'There's a fairy tale, you might have heard it; it's by Hans Christian Andersen. A doomed queen is to be burned at the stake, but her swan brothers come and she changes them back into men with the shirts she has sewed in silence and she is saved. Do you know it?' He looks up at her and she realises that the room is almost in darkness. His pupils are large, thinly rimmed with blue, searching her face. Looking for something she can offer him, something he has not yet thought of. Her stomach plunges; something awful happened, she thinks. For him to say that, something terrible must have happened to Ewa, mustn't it? But the queen was saved . . .

'In the evening, walking beside the sand, a small circle of light danced along the pavement in front of us, sometimes catching under our toes as we caught up with it, and then darting off again to wait for us. "Look," she said, laughing, and she pointed up at a window in one of the pale hotels along the front. She had traced the light back to there. Stroking her eyes along the sweep of its beam until she found the two grinning children at a window, shining a powerful torch down onto the opposite side of the road, where promenaders stopped and turned to look, once again, at the sea. She played along for a while, skipping down the promenade and jumping this way and that, trying to catch the light, oblivious of the unimpressed glances of strangers out for their evening strolls, while I walked soberly behind. What was it about me, do you think, that made

94

the children not include me in their game? I thought I might take another photograph, but then I remembered how alone I had felt out on the beach with the swans, and something uncharitable in me stopped me from enjoying their innocent fun.

'But she found it delightful that these two boys who should have been in bed were sitting at the window in their pyjamas, playing their wordless game with strangers. How many brief friendships had been made that night, she asked me, how many smiles and waves of recognition had there been, up at the two white faces, silent behind glass?'

ରେ

She drags the Hoover savagely up the three flights of stairs to the top of the house, hauls out the flex and plugs it in. When she starts it up, the noise is almost comforting. She drags it by the hose into the larger of the two top-floor rooms and noses it carefully around the floor as it roars. Tiny bits of dirt and dust rattle up the tube and disappear. She loves the sense of absolute stillness in the empty homes she inhabits briefly, like a visiting ghost.

The buzz of the vacuum fills her head as she humps it, stair by stair, down to the next landing, Hoovering each step as she goes, as if erasing her own footprints. When she arrived she removed her shoes and left them just inside the front door. She feels less like an intruder barefoot. More invisible.

In the baby's room she switches the Hoover off while she tidies up a little. She likes this room the best. She empties the bin, puts some little clothes away, and straightens the cot. Hanging over it is a musical mobile dangling little blue birds.

She winds it up and watches it. The birds turn gently as the tune tinkles out. The blue is the same blue as the one the day before, at Jozef's, which reminded her of the seaside. She closes her eyes as the music slows and slows and stops. It's the blue in the sky over the sea, she thinks. The bite in the air. Sunlight without yellow warmth. The blue in the pebbles which at first you think are grey. And the peeling paint on abandoned beach huts strung along a promenade.

The silence is broken by the sound of a key in the lock. Sarah quickly rouses herself and goes out onto the landing to peer down the stairs. The people who live here never come home; she has only met them once.

'Hello?' she calls, suddenly feeling self-conscious with her bare feet. There's no reply. She can hear the child crying and the mother trying to calm him. They have brought a tension into the house with them and Sarah wishes she could just disappear.

They are in the kitchen. When she gets to the bottom of the stairs she sees that the door is closed. She senses suddenly that the woman hasn't realised she is there, even though her shoes are in the hall. She can hear her voice more clearly now; she is on the telephone. 'Hello? . . . Hello? . . . Well, would you find him, please . . . Yes please.' Her voice is curt and strained. The child's whine has risen to a lusty wailing. Sarah takes a deep breath and opens the door.

The moment she walks in she wishes she hadn't, but it is already too late. The woman grabs the child and pulls it to her. Although it's an instinctive movement to protect him, Sarah can't help noticing how she also seems to be shielding herself behind him, as if she is somehow more able to face a stranger with a baby in her arms.

'What the hell do you think you are doing in my house?' she shouts above her son's screaming.

'I . . . I'm cleaning,' Sarah says weakly. The woman glares at her and then, realising her mistake, turns to the baby and starts bouncing him roughly on her hip.

'Shhh shhh shhh,' she says briskly. 'Silly Mummy. Silly Mummy. It's only the cleaner.' She turns back to Sarah. 'I'm sorry,' she says, her voice still hostile. 'I thought . . . I forgot . . .' Sarah takes a step forward, as if to re-introduce herself. 'Look,' the woman says, her body stiffening again, 'could you just leave, please? How much do I owe you?'

At home, exhausted, Sarah peers out of her bedroom window. There is an afternoon lull in the traffic and she can hear her own breathing as she looks out, her face up close to the glass. From here she can see her garden fully only if she unscrews the catch and pushes up the lower sash, hearing the squeak and protest of the wheels inside the hollow rope chambers on either side. If she leans through the open window, high up in the wall of the house, she can imagine her garden as a plan, a diagram, the irregular sprawl of small shrubs hiding the circumferences of the pots beneath them. In the centre the miniature panes of glass in the skylight reflect the sun in shapes against the bricks. Jude says it is like a replica of a glasshouse at Kew Gardens, or the Crystal Palace; he laughs at Balu's design, thinks he is ridiculous. She squints her eyes. It *is* like Kew Gardens, she thinks. Only the plants are on the outside. She gazes down admiringly at the encircling ring of small pots she has placed round it, containing lemon thyme, purple sage, applemint, savory, French lavender. She looks at the top of the wall, remembering Jude, a few days ago, walking out of the room beneath, into the garden. Going to the far side and resting his weight on the low wall, his splayed arms straight as he leaned over and peered down into the street.

Up here the noise from the street is slightly dampened. She closes the window and backs into the room, sitting on the edge of the bed when she feels its shape pushing at the backs of her legs. She remembers the money in her jeans pocket and pulls it out, unfolding the two crumpled notes. Two twenties. She wonders whether the woman even knows how much she has given her. She was so anxious to get her out of the house she scarcely looked as she fumbled in her wallet. And she kept the child in her arms, like a barrier between them, as she followed Sarah through the hall towards the front door.

I wonder what happened to her this morning, Sarah thinks as she lies down from her sitting position, leaving her feet on the floor at the foot of the bed. The door squeaks open slightly and she feels the silent landing of cat's feet on the bed beside her. Sita seeks out her hand and runs the two sides of her mouth against it. Sarah feels the cold nose; the black rubber lips catch on her fingers and pull away loosely from the pink gums. The furry head rotates inside her hand and she feels the warm, folded triangle of ear. She closes her eyes.

The cat that gave birth in the cellar of the house where Josef lived was a mixture of tortoiseshell and tabby. He didn't describe her like that. He said she was all sorts of colours: white, black, ginger and stripy, flecked brown. He didn't know about cats, he said. And she was neither long-haired nor short-haired but somewhere in between.

As she drifts towards sleep, Jozef's voice replays in her head.

'Ewa was the only person who had the patience to sit at the top of the cellar steps with a shawl round her shoulders and some scraps of meat in a saucer, trying to coax her out. We didn't know she was pregnant – we saw her so fleetingly at first. She must have been making her nest. I don't think I would even have noticed her if Ewa hadn't pointed her out.

'And then she disappeared. Finally, after politely knocking and asking at the flats above and below me, Ewa opened the cellar door and crept down the first few steps in the dark. She was sure the cat was in there. Sometimes she was like that, so firm in a belief that it would not cross your mind to question her. If she had a conviction, it stayed.

'She stood there in the darkness, listening, then switched on the torch she had taken with her and disappeared down the steps, dancing the circle of light in front of her onto piles of bricks and damp rubble. She saw the kittens, pink and squirming in a heap in a box of old newspapers. She turned the torch off, stopping the switch with her thumb so that it wouldn't click and startle the cat if she were near, and retreated. She closed the door behind her. 'Kittens,' she said, and she marched straight into the kitchen to see what she could leave on the steps for the hungry mother.'

Something moves in the room, on the bed, pulling her a little away from the brink of sleep. Sita is circling beside her, making a dent in the eiderdown and kneading the outsplayed edge of her skirt, catching at it with her claws, before she settles warmly down. Being careful not to disturb her, Sarah draws her feet up onto the bed, turning slowly from her back onto her side, pulling her knees in to her chest, curling round the cat, encircling her.

The World of Tomorrow

Jude wakes with a start and flings his arm out to reach Sarah, to catch her and pull her away from the thing he has been dreaming about. It thwacks down on the mattress. He sits up, his heart pounding so hard he can feel it in his throat and wrists. His mouth is dry. The curtains furthest from the bed, on Sarah's side, are half open and, seeing this, he remembers her drawing them back earlier to let in some light for herself. He falls back onto the pillow, relieved, but with a strange residual irritation which he can't account for. She had got up early for work again; that's where she is now.

With effort, he swings his legs over the edge of the bed and sits up slowly. His head is spinning a little, and the air in the room is close and stale. He drinks some of the water from the pint glass beside the bed, but it has been there for days and tastes dusty and old. The drunk water leaves a tidemark behind.

There was a time when, if he woke with a hangover after a night of drinking with Sarah, she would wake with a worse one and they would both lie in bed, prisoners of a shared sickness, until one or other of them felt better and went to make tea. He remembers the breakfasts she swore by as a hangover cure. And the Bloody Marys she would make on gloomy Sunday afternoons, which they would drink in front of the television, praying for the phone not to ring and intrude on the tenderness of feeling ill together. He can't remember the last time they did this.

101

A solitary hangover is a far more miserable affair. He sits on the edge of the bed, wishing he could bathe his eyes, the inside of his head, in cool water, in a soothing milk which would smooth away the desiccated state he has woken to.

He feels a sudden prickle of warning and a wave of nausea engulfs him as he struggles to the bathroom, his mouth filling with the familiar precursory swell of saliva. He kneels in front of the toilet, hating Sarah for not being there, hating the silent, empty flat and this lowly homage he must pay, swaying helplessly over the toilet bowl as the first rush of vomit heaves upwards from his belly.

Back in the bedroom he pulls last night's clothes back on and then treads carefully down the stairs and out onto the roof, falling weakly into the deckchair. He'll phone work later, throw a sickie, no one will give a shit – the job's only for another week anyway. He can't stand being alone inside the flat any more. Out on the roof it is a little better, a little less suffocating. He pulls a half packet of tobacco from his pocket and sits, eyes closed, with it in his lap. He hasn't even the strength to roll a cigarette.

He can remember what he was dreaming, now. Sarah had been astride him, kissing him, but he could tell from how she was kissing, and from her taste, that she had already been kissing Hari and that she was still thinking about him. Her expression betrayed her. Everything betrayed her, as if her secret passion were being shown in a film reel on the ceiling as he lay on his back between her straddling legs, unable to turn away from it.

He leans forward and presses his face into his palms. Fucking stupid dream, and now that would plague him too and make his miserable solitude, his confinement in this flat, even more unbearable. He is starting to loathe the restaurant too, having to sit in here, hovering above it night after night, knowing that Hari and Balu are scurrying about below him with things to do, with purpose. They don't have the time he has to dwell on stuff so minutely. He wonders what they think of him – with a fucking first-class degree and not even a glimmer of proper work, just crap casual stuff. A week here, a week there. And he is constantly aware of Hari, so near, glimpsable sometimes, if he glances down through the skylight at the right moment.

Hari is wary of him; that is clear enough. Oh, there's the friendliness on the surface. The four of them will sit together until late in the restaurant, and talk into the night. But there's a guardedness, a reticence between himself and Hari, which he notices more alongside the comfortable ease which Hari shares with Balu and Sarah. But it's an unacknowledged strain, and maybe it's only the two of them who are aware of it.

ॐ

'In May 1939 Ewa travelled, with the Balets Polski, to New York City to perform at the New York World Fair. I sensed adventure and followed her there. I had never seen her as alive as she was then and I couldn't bear to be away from her. In April there had been a tour to France and Luxembourg, and a seven-night stay in Kowno in Poland, during which time I had painfully borne the enforced separation. Then they had returned and performed nightly in Warsaw, and in those intense weeks she seemed to retreat from things not directly connected with the constant round of dance class, rehearsal, performance, and yet at the same time be minutely attuned to her surroundings. She was suddenly questing for life, hungry for experience. I felt so old beside her; she was like a puppy that cannot get its owner to play soon enough or long enough. She became edgy and slightly impatient. But when she was not dancing she seemed glad of me. She wanted me with her constantly. Needed me. As if she was too tiny and fragile to survive alone. She made me think of one of those humming-birds which have to keep on feeding, constantly on the wing, in order to keep themselves going. And then, with the coming trip to New York, there was something about her excitement which was almost fearful. She had to have me within sight, within touch, as if she was terrified of losing me. A touch, that was all it needed to be. The merest brushing of her fingertip against my neck just above the collar, fluttering, scarcely resting before taking flight once again.

'As I watched her with other people, I drew into myself the essence of that touch and held it for as long as I could, as if holding on to it meant I was holding on to something of her.

'I began to drink. To need to be drunk. Needing that sensation beyond myself, as she seemed to need the momentary connection of fingertip with neck, chin with shoulder, like a diver coming up for air. Except that each time she submerged she was able to remain underwater for longer. Until finally, I feared, she would no longer need me.'

He shakes his head, smiling wanly, abrasively. 'There was this growing sense of something. Not wrong; it wasn't so much something wrong as something changed which was causing me this sense of uneasiness. I translated those butterfly touches of hers, those traces of tenderness she left across my skin, into apologies, compensations, for this new strangeness between us.'

∽

At ten o'clock Sarah is still not home. Jude has spent the afternoon and evening in an agonised stew of self-loathing and self-pity, moving from room to room, switching the television on and flicking angrily through the channels before switching it off again, then attempting to read, to sleep, to strum his guitar. Nothing can rid him of the edgy, anxious feeling that everything is wrong, irretrievably wrong and fucked up and he doesn't know how to make it right.

At some point he goes out for more tobacco, just for something to do, striding energetically down the road, his face like a caged animal's, so that the trip, which he had hoped would fill up more time, takes barely fifteen minutes. Too soon, he is back in the flat, more restless than ever. The phone rings but he is too unsure of the sound of his voice to answer it and it rings out hollowly.

Outside, the day has inched, agonisingly slowly, into the semi-reassurance of darkness. He has been sitting for over an hour in the deckchair, smoking and listening to the buses lumbering along the road, the occasional siren and constant zipping of mopeds, and has worked his way steadily through the bottle of wine he bought when he went out for tobacco. The monstrosity, that expensive and useless confection of glass which Balu is so naively proud of, is lit up like a Dickensian window at Christmas, all yellow and glowing. He stands up and stretches, yawning loudly, and steps nearer to it, feeling a sudden, peevish urge to spy on the unsuspecting people below. He crouches in front of it and peers in, his knee jostling a pot of lavender. He freezes as it knocks audibly against the glass, but nobody down below hears anything and the two rows of heads directly beneath him, flanking both sides of the long table – clearly another birthday party – remain bent over their plates. Secretly, he is nursing the seed of an idea: Hari is meant to be working tonight. He remembers this because, lately, he has been remembering lots of things Sarah says about Hari. Has been noticing, in general, how often she talks about him. So if he's there, if he watches for long enough, he ought to see him, oughtn't he? He leans forward a little more, steadying himself with his hands against the glass. It vaguely occurs to him that he doesn't know whether he wants Hari to be there or not. If he's there then he's not with Sarah, but that doesn't bring her back, does it? Doesn't fix anything. And if he's not there, well, that doesn't really mean anything either. It just stretches things out more and intensifies what he is already feeling.

A familiarly clad figure flickers briefly into view and his stomach lurches, but he doesn't think it is Hari. He waits a little and the figure returns with a round tray of drinks and sets about distributing them, leaning across the table to plant opened bottles amidst the mess of plates and glasses and candle-powered warming trays. It isn't Hari, it's another of the waiters, with the same slicked-back, black hair, although he can see now that he wears his hair longer than Hari and it is pulled back in a stubby ponytail.

He is beginning to feel ridiculous, and is just about to leave the bustling restaurant to its business when Hari does appear. He streaks across his field of vision and disappears into the front of the restaurant, hidden from view. Jude waits, his tensed arms beginning to ache. It isn't long before Hari re-emerges, his arms piled with plates and stainless steel dishes smeared with sauce and dotted with stray grains of rice. It is unfortunate that he is so laden because, when he suddenly glances upwards into the glassy darkness above his head without warning, Jude cannot move away quickly enough and the shock of seeing him hovering there in the darkness throws Hari's balance right off and he lurches forward with a small cry of surprise, the pile of dirty dishes sliding with a crash to the floor.

෴

'My arrival in New York was intended as a surprise. I had the address of the residence near Corona Park where the company were staying – Ewa had written it down for me before she left, along with the telephone number, and I still had the scrap of paper, a piece torn from the bottom of a page of my own discarded notes, folded into a pocket of my wallet, and so I made my tentative way to Fifty-ninth Street and across the bridge to Queens in search of a room. A lukewarm bath and a shave later, I asked the proprietress of the small hotel I had found for directions to Corona Park and made my way to where Ewa was staying, half anxious at what her reaction might be. I drank alone that evening.'

'Did you not find her?'

'Oh yes. No, it wasn't that. I found her at some reception.' He pauses, breathing in carefully, slowly, as if he suspects the air might be laced with tiny shards of glass. As if he must filter it carefully if he is to avoid the harm it may do him. 'Ewa was very particular,' he explains, frowning slightly. 'I think her family had something to do with it. And having someone, a lover, turn up, well, I think she would have liked a little warning. And then there was this *something* in her, this change that I had not so much noticed but subconsciously felt in the weeks before her departure for France, and during her absence, coupled now with my rogue presence in New York. Arriving there without me, ahead of me, it was as if she had the measure of it and I had not. She had spent so much time away from me by then. I don't know; whatever it was, it had risen to the surface. It was as if my arrival had solidified something that was distancing us from each other. When I presented myself to her, for a moment she looked horrified, and suddenly I felt as though I had followed her there unfairly, like some sort of snoop, as if I suspected her of infidelity and had hoped to catch her at it.' He swallows loudly. 'I felt as a stranger might; I was like an intruder.'

He looks up at her. Sarah drops her eyes from his face and looks at his hands – one cupping the other – in his lap. There is a change in Jozef now. Today she has noticed that he is not waving his hands around in explanation of this or that thing he thought or she said. His face is not flickering with relived emotions, recovered moments. There was a time, months ago, when he would hit upon some memory, some story fragment linked tenuously, if at all, with his main thread and his face would be awash with the fleeting, momentary life of something awoken. She would see his inward smile, the rush of warmth of remembered love, remembered laughter. A sudden, demented grin, and the desire in his eyes to be again dancing or running through rain or hanging on to her legs as she reached bodily from an upstairs window for the largest icicle she had ever seen.

He has changed. Remembering how he was just a few months ago, Sarah sees the pale absence of the joy she once felt she had revived.

'I felt I couldn't stay,' he says. 'And so, after a decent interval, I made my excuses. Claimed fatigue. And I left Ewa, surrounded by strangers, so occupied and happy she scarcely noticed my departure.'

Hari freezes. His arms feel useless as spaghetti and the dirty plates and cutlery and dishes he had carefully piled up are littering the floor in front of him. He shoots another glance up into the skylight above his head, but the ghostly face, framed between two white, starfish hands, has disappeared.

The crash of breaking crockery and rattling cutlery has brought Amil, the other waiter, scurrying to his side and he is down on his knees, smirking, picking fragments of plate from between chair legs before it occurs to Hari to help him. The chatter in the restaurant has come to a dead stop and every face is turned towards him.

'Sorry,' he mutters, trying to smile. 'Sorry, sorry.' Turning round almost a full circle so that he encompasses everyone in his apology. 'Sorry. Tripped over my own feet.' He tries to laugh it off. 'Hah! No tips for me tonight!' He urges everyone to carry on with their meals, and shuns offers of help from one or two people who have risen from their seats. He kneels and starts gathering the explosion back onto the tray. Balu pokes a worried face round the door into the kitchen, lifts his eyes heavenwards and disappears. A moment later he reappears with a dustpan and brush.

Gradually the chatter begins again and increases in volume, and the mess is cleared and forgotten.

'Take a break,' Balu says, a look of concern deepening the creases in his forehead as Hari tips the contents of the dustpan into the kitchen waste bin. He goes outside and sits on the bottom step of the fire escape, fumbling a Marlboro from its packet. His hands are shaking.

'For fuck's sake!' he spits into the darkness. What the fuck was Jude doing, staring down at him like that? He lights the cigarette and pulls deeply on it, holding the smoke in his lungs for as long as he can before releasing it in a long, steady breath. In the past he could have dashed up the fire escape in his break and stolen ten minutes with Sarah. He often had. They would have laughed at something like this. Back in the days before Jude existed. That tortured, malevolent-looking face staring down at him like a bad fairy. And those two hands, the rest of him in darkness, so that he had seemed, for one hideous moment, like some pale, suckering sea creature stuck against the glass wall of its tank, staring inscrutably out.

Hari wonders whether Sarah is up there with Jude. Whether she, too, was out on the roof peering down at him, out of sight. But there was something about the urgency of the face, and the way the hands were pressed against the glass – Jude must have been crouching down and leaning forwards purposely to have got close enough to be visible – that told him he was in the flat alone. That look he had caught in his face, for the fleeting moment they had locked eyes, was not a look he would have worn if she had been there. It was a hunted, secret expression. Some kind of lonely desperation had seemed to fuel it, and Hari had caught its full force.

He takes another drag from the cigarette and leans forward, resting his elbows on his knees, his head bowed. It has been a busy night and he is tired suddenly. He can't face the thought of going back inside, of clearing more dishes and scraping them endlessly into the bin in the fluorescent-bright kitchen before rinsing them in the vast sink. He can't face the people out in the restaurant who had all turned to look at him when he dropped the plates, or the requests for bills, or more drinks, or dessert menus. Or the whole palaver of clearing all the candles and flower vases from each table and stripping the tablecloths once the diners have gone, wiping the tables and piling up the chairs for the cleaner in the morning, and, finally, sweeping the kitchen and setting the dishwasher for its last wash of the night. All of this before he can go home, and then the same tomorrow and tomorrow and for ever.

Why had Jude looked at him like that? He can't shake off the malice he had felt in that look. But there's no reason for it. And there's never been anything before. Even if Jude knows about him and Sarah, so what? There's nothing between them now, he surely knows that. How could there be?

Slowly Hari lifts his head and tips it to one side, rolling it gently round, first in one direction and then the other, trying to ease away some of the tension he is feeling. He only looked up at the skylight because he did sometimes, especially in the summer, knowing that Sarah might be there, just above his head, going about her invisible life. Before Jude, of course, he had often glanced up at it excitedly, knowing that in an hour, half an hour, he would be up there with her, perhaps lying on that pile of blankets and cushions on the roof if the weather was warm, peering down into his own, temporarily abandoned, life below. And then kissing her, touching her pale, delicate face and her thin, white body, knowing, always knowing, that she was only on loan to him.

'The following evening was the opening night. I couldn't afford a seat of course, but Ewa let me in through the stage door and I watched the performance from the wings, sitting on a three-legged stool.

'I was beginning to see her differently. I was noticing, for the first time, that she had a life beyond just the two of us. Well, I knew that, of course. She told me such stories all the time – gossip, that kind of thing. Performers cannot resist a bit of cattiness and Ewa seemed always to be in the thick of chatter, piecing together scraps of hearsay, desperate to brew up a scandal. And so I knew from her stories who was sleeping with whom, who was in favour and who was out, who was pregnant, who was drinking and so on. But it was all at a distance from me; I was not involved with the everyday parts of her life and she was not involved with mine. In Warsaw her life with me was quite distinct from anything else. It took place almost entirely in my rooms. And I had no desire to become involved in this other part of her life; I suppose, selfishly, I wanted her all to myself. Yet suddenly, in New York, I was seeing for the first time this other Ewa, the Ewa she was for other people.

'They danced *Harnasie* on that first night.'

Sarah frowns.

'The *Brigands*.' Jozef reads the question in her face. 'It was one of the repertoire they took to New York. It is about a young girl who is carried off, in the middle of her own wedding, by the man she is really in love with. Fokine used the same story in *Chopiniana*, which later became *Les Sylphides*. You have heard of that?' Sarah nods, although she hasn't. 'One of the famous Romantic ballets staged by Diaghilev. But *Harnasie* is a Polish ballet, set in the Tatra Mountains. The bride's lover just carries her away and her husband-to-be is left standing, alone, on the stage, gazing up at the mountains. He never sees her again.' Jozef stops speaking and gives a rueful laugh before continuing.

'I had seen her in this ballet I don't know how many times. In Warsaw, shortly before the company left for New York, seeing her dancing and twirling her skirt as a wedding guest, the whole corps de ballet dressed in the same, brightly coloured peasant costumes, and spinning like dervishes so that their skirts became a sea of whirling, coloured discs, I loved how untouchable she seemed, loved the fact that nobody was watching her specifically. She was part of the overall movement and picture but only I could know her. And yet I loved to play a game with myself, where I, too, would watch as if I had eyes only for the abducted mountain girl and her roguish brigand. And I would ignore Ewa, adopt the view of her I suspected the man sitting beside me or in front of me must have. And then I would seek out her familiar lines, her familiar movements, and feel again the pleasure of knowing her. And each night as she recoiled in horror, hands clasped high at her throat, the exaggerated expression of pain on her face at the sight of the young bride being carried away in the arms of her lover, I saw her standing frozen in the hallway of my house, at the top of the cellar steps, a tiny dead kitten held to her chest.

'But this time I pinned my eyes on her for the whole performance. When she was not on the stage I shifted impatiently on my low seat, my fingers twitching for a cigarette as I waited for her to return.

'After the performance I mingled uncomfortably with the ticket-holding members of the audience, all patrons of the arts and journalists. Americans with money and status. It's funny how such things can show in a face, isn't it? Amongst them I felt sallow and undeserving. It was while trying to avoid making eye contact with any of them, and at the same time keep my antennae pointed in Ewa's direction in the hope

113

that she might come and rescue me, that I met George Hopper.

'George Hopper was an all-American male. He was handsome in that engaging and satisfying way that such young men are. Lush dark hair flopped over his face and his eyes were ripe and sparkling, with an instant magnetism. There was a sort of completeness, a rightness in his appearance, if that makes any sense. And he had a nervous, intermittent habit of chewing at the sides of his fingernails, during heated exchanges especially, I noticed, and this appealed to me. He kept drawing back from speaking, as if he sensed that he was somehow unqualified, inexperienced, and must defer to others' more intimate knowledge of a subject, and his eyes darted backwards and forwards as his teeth gnawed at each upraised finger in turn.

'I must have looked a little ashen, because he came over specifically to speak to me, handing me a tumbler of whisky at the same time as he introduced himself. He asked me politely, a little awkwardly, how I had enjoyed the performance. I liked him instantly.

'We talked, in that halting way people who have just met at a party talk, and he told me he worked for his father. His route through life seemed to have been mapped out at an early stage and, so far, he had not deviated from the plan. I thought, utterly without malice, how easy a time he must have had of it; how, clearly younger than I was, he was already firmly established, "on the map" so to speak, while in Warsaw I hammered out hopeful articles bound for obscure journals on my rackety typewriter which dotted my page with filled-in Os and Qs, smoking my cigarettes until the lighted end burnt my fingers.

'I would have had to admit to feeling envious, shortchanged in life, had I not taken this instant liking to him, and he to me. Despite the seeming security of his occupation, his whole life, I sensed that he felt awkwardly slotted in, as if he were simply the wrong-shaped peg for the hole into which he was being pressed. I, on the other hand, was someone who could become so deeply involved in whatever my current piece of work was that I could lose my sense of place and time easily and entirely forget that at the end of the week I would be hard pressed to pay the bills I owed.

'I suspected he rather admired me – my unconventional occupation, my passion for my work. Even my relationship with Ewa.

'During the rest of the evening, he mingled amongst the guests and I drew back into a safe niche, from the cover of which I could observe Ewa and my new acquaintance without drawing too much attention to myself. I noticed how slightly ill at ease Hopper was with other men, how he sipped a little too often from his wine glass, passed it rather too many times from one hand to the other, and how his body, like a repelling magnet, seemed to pull away from each man in turn, as if he were struggling hard to stand his ground. They didn't seem to notice; they bore down on him just the same, wanting to talk to him about his father's this and his father's that. I think I must have been the only man that Hopper actually approached himself that night. The only one he didn't have foisted upon him because of some connection with his father or something to do with someone his father knew.

'With women he was entirely different. I watched as he spoke to two nervy-looking wives and within minutes their heads were bowed towards each other, they were sharing jokes, their voices and laughter mingling. More women seemed to join them from nowhere, and he sat easily astride the arm of a sofa in their midst, his discomfiture seeming to leave him entirely.

'I was distracted for a time – someone who had seen me talking to Hopper came over, and for a while I turned my back to the party to speak to him. He soon left when he realised I was nobody important, on the pretext of getting another drink, and I turned round to find Hopper and Ewa laughing together. As I watched, she passed him her drink, hitched up her skirt a little, and demonstrated a rather formal curtsy in front of him. I noticed the colour rise in her cheeks as she took her glass back and their fingers accidentally brushed together on the stem.'

Sarah fumbles for her keys and unlocks the street door to her flat. The bulb in the narrow passageway has gone, so she runs her fingers lightly along the wall beside her to steady herself in the darkness as she climbs the stairs, and finds the key to the flat door by touch. George Hopper, she thinks as she lets herself in. I wonder how important he will be.

The flat is in darkness; Jude must already be in bed. She looks at her watch – it's after one o'clock. She had no idea it was so late. That bus she got must have been a night bus and she hadn't even noticed. She has spent all day cleaning and her hands feel swollen, the skin smooth and tight, burning slightly. She is hungry too – she hasn't eaten since morning.

The shutters are still open in the living room, the street light outside throwing leafy, wavering shadows from the garden across the carpet. There's also a slight breeze, and she can hear the road too clearly; she looks again and sees that one of the doors is ajar. She feels a momentary throb of panic, but Jude is in, his manky trainers are lying in a jumble in the middle of the floor, his tobacco and Rizlas still arranged on the hardcover atlas which he has left balanced on the arm of the sofa. There's no burglar, he's just forgotten to close the doors. She crosses the room in the orange half-light. He's obviously been outside; there's an empty wine bottle standing next to the deckchair, and a half-full glass of wine. She leaves them where they are, too exhausted by tidying other people's homes to bother with her own, locks the doors and folds the shutters across them. As she's leaving the room to go up to bed, she notices the light winking on the answering machine. There are two messages. Funny. Jude usually checks them when he gets in. She's too tired to listen to them now. She yawns. Whatever it is can wait till tomorrow.

In bed she thinks again about this new character, George Hopper. He has to be important – Jozef spent so long talking about him. She fears for him in New York now; he is alone and alienated there. She is scared of what will happen next.

'I rather arrogantly believed that Ewa used me as her touchstone,' he said earlier, 'as a way of judging the measure of other men, of ranking their worth. But that was my way; it was what I did with her. In fact it was far more like Ewa to take each new person as he appeared to her and judge him according to himself rather than slot him into some mental scheme as I might do. But seeing her at that moment with Hopper, I suddenly felt frightened. I remembered how easily she had captured me, how quickly I had forgotten Magda, how that momentary encounter had changed my life so utterly.'

When he first wakes up, for a moment Jude thinks everything is all right. It is as if the night has cleansed him of the disturbing thoughts he had been having before he fell asleep. But as the seconds pass, and he slides more firmly into wakefulness, he feels a sinking sensation and everything that was worrying him last night again swirls into sight.

He hears a sigh, and turns over. She is still asleep beside him. She must have come back late; he doesn't remember. He sits up carefully, pulls his T-shirt on and creeps quietly from the room. He doesn't want to wake her; he needs to think. His head feels fuddled and slightly woozy; he can't remember the last morning he got up without a hangover.

He pads barefoot into the kitchen and fills the kettle. Sita comes dashing in after him with a long, low purr and stalks round his legs, her tail vertical, gazing imploringly up at him. He lowers himself into a kitchen chair, trying to ignore her, while he waits for the kettle. He knows Sarah wasn't with Hari last night. So where was she? She can't have been with the old man till so late, surely.

Armed with a cup of tea, he wanders into the living room, Sita following hungrily at his heels. He notices the answering machine flashing and remembers the unanswered phone yesterday. He stops himself leaping to suspicious conclusions as to who might have phoned – Hari has never, as far as he knows, phoned the flat. Why would he when he's just down-stairs? And if they were having a secret liaison he surely wouldn't phone here. Jude hates himself for even contem-plating such stupid thoughts. Jealousy, he is beginning to realise, can destroy a sense of reasonable perspective more quickly than anything.

He checks the messages anyway. They are both for him, from his boss at work, wanting to know where he is. He sounds slightly tight-lipped and annoyed in the first one, and down-right angry in the second. Jude wonders whether he can be bothered concocting an excuse for his absences, or whether it mightn't just be easier to pack the job in. He presses rewind quickly and listens to the mechanical voice telling him the time and that there are no messages.

'The next day I got up early, determined to stop the uncomfortable thoughts that had been crowding my mind since my arrival in New York. I had spent much of the night tossing and turning, allowing that image of Ewa and Hopper at the party to return and linger each time I awoke, too hot, and tangled up in my bedclothes. Once up and breakfasted I was able to see things more sensibly. The city of New York was in the grip of World Fair fever; since my arrival I had been bombarded with images of it on subways and billboards. Every newsstand sold postcards of little else and it seemed to have galvanised a frenetic energy in the city, or so I thought at the time. Perhaps I was wrong. New York may always have had such a charge, I suspect it probably had. But I don't know, I have never been back.

'I decided, anyway, in the clear light of day, to stop feeling edgy and to persuade Ewa to come to see the World Fair with me and so I telephoned her hotel.

'Downstairs in the lobby, the landlady grudgingly pushed the telephone halfway across the counter to me and looked pointedly at the dirty flex it trailed behind it before resuming her nail-filing, one leg swinging backwards and forwards, a high-heeled, patent leather shoe dangling precariously from her toes. She was humming faintly, just enough for me to hear and find distracting. A humming which blatantly failed to disguise the fact that she was listening.

'I dragged the phone closer and wrenched the receiver from the hook, trying to close my ears to her humming as I was put through. I cleared my throat.

'"Good morning. May I speak to Miss Ewa Kamzowa?"

'The answer came back immediately. "I'm afraid the young ladies have gone out, sir. Mr Hopper arrived early this . . ." I felt a plunge in my stomach, but swallowed it down. This was nothing, after all.

'"Do you have any idea where they might have gone?" I asked as pleasantly as I could, determined not to let this minor irritation spoil my day.

'"Mr Hopper mentioned that one of the young ladies had expressed a wish to see Macy's department store, sir, if that is any help."

'"Thank you." I punched down the receiver button, cutting off the receptionist abruptly. Try as I might to conceal my annoyance at this disappointment I could just imagine his smug, courteous face at the other end of the line. I took the receiver away from my ear and replaced it silently, clenching my teeth. Then I piled some coins beside the telephone, deliberately leaving more money than was necessary.

'I did find them in Macy's. For some reason I decided not to approach them and watched from behind a display stand of hats as the dancers draped silk scarves around each other's shoulders and held differently coloured swatches up against themselves in the tiny mirror they were crowding around. I briefly caught sight of one of the dancers' faces in the mirror as Hopper lifted a deep, shimmering green colour to her hair. She was called Alicja; she and Ewa were quite friendly and Ewa had mentioned her often in those afternoons in my rooms in Warsaw. Alicja's expression was heart-stopping. She was gazing at him with her dark, thoughtful eyes, and had clearly already fallen in love with him.

'They took so long over it. Hopper, unfailingly charming,

seemed to have enlisted the help of an employee who was now holding out even more scarves to the delighted foreign women, and speaking in loud, slow sentences at their eager but uncomprehending faces. Hopper shared a joke with Ewa but I was too far away to hear it and suddenly I couldn't bear to watch the silly, slow-motion procession of diaphanous nonsense any longer. I backed away from the sheltering hat tree, my feet soundless on the deep carpet, pushed my way through a set of heavy double doors and found an elevator. Alone inside, I pressed my forehead hard against the panelling and breathed deeply, feeling a sudden rush of fear, of complete powerlessness. I think it was Alicja's face more than anything. It reminded me of how I had been when Ewa and I had first met. There were some people, it seemed, who had this attraction, this lure. I had been magnetised by Ewa, and if Alicja had been similarly drawn by Hopper then . . . The fear that I might lose Ewa slowly settled into a kind of certainty that, with someone like Hopper in the equation, I would never be able to keep her.'

๑

Hari hasn't seen Sarah or Jude for days. Not since the night when he caught Jude watching him through the skylight. There's something wrong, there must be. He has never gone so long without a glimpse of Sarah, a quick hello. She hardly ever comes down to the restaurant any more. He stands up and weaves his way between the seats and down the stairs as the bus swings round the corner. Maybe he should go and speak to her, ask if everything's OK.

He likes this final bit of his journey to work. He always rides the footplate, hanging on to the bar and leaning outwards as the bus speeds along the straight stretch of road, whizzing past the familiar façade of the Mountain of Light then slowing as it reaches the bus stop. He always jumps free before it stops, for a moment feeling as if he is still travelling forwards, flying alongside the bus, before his feet hit the pavement and he is jerked to a dead halt. He hitches his bag up on his shoulder and walks back towards the restaurant, glancing at his watch. He is early. There was a time when this would have meant a few stolen minutes with Sarah. A time when he would have arrived purposely early. He reaches the door and pushes through it, walking into the rich scent of layers and layers of mingled flavour which always seems so overpowering the moment he walks through the door but which then seems to withdraw and disguise itself within the turmeric walls, the wine-red ceiling, and the deep, plum-coloured carpet.

Balu is standing at the till, extracting the night's float from an assortment of little transparent coin bags, tipping each one carefully into its allotted compartment in the till drawer before tucking the emptied bag underneath. He greets Hari without looking up; he has his lips pressed tightly together, the upper slightly overlapping the lower, and a frown of concentration straddles his brow as he lifts the cover and carefully checks the till roll.

Hari goes through to the kitchen and hangs up his bag. Everything stands ready: trays of neatly parcelled samosas and pakoras ready for deep-frying; a vast array of Tupperware boxes filled with the bright, traffic-light colours of sliced peppers; green, loofah-shaped okra; tiny, tight-skinned aubergines; diced onion; chopped herbs and tomatoes. Colin is already working, singing along to the radio as he lifts the lids on all the different vats on the enormous hob in turn, stirring each one with the long-handled ladles which poke out through the lids.

Hari pulls a packet of cigarettes from his bag and goes outside, glancing up at Sarah's kitchen door at the top of the fire escape. He could go up, just quickly, and see if she's OK. He hasn't been up there for a while, but she wouldn't mind, surely, if he just said hello. He takes a drag from the cigarette. He'll finish it, he thinks, before he decides.

Up at the top he knocks tentatively at the door. The blind is still there and he can't see in. She doesn't come to the door. Suddenly he feels wrong there. Fears that she isn't there at all, and that Jude might open it instead. He realises he doesn't want to see Jude, would not be able to be normal with him now. He would feel awkward speaking to him, explaining what he was doing. That awful, desperate, accusing face which he keeps on remembering could mean only one thing, and if he is caught knocking at the back door it will only make things worse. He hurries back down, his steps ringing lightly through the metal so that he can feel the vibrations in the soles of his feet.

In the restaurant, Balu has done everything he needs to do for the evening but he has a residual unease, as if there is something he has forgotten. He feels on the shelf underneath the till for a duster and can of Pledge and starts to polish the mirror-tiled border running round the restaurant walls. Sometimes, when he feels like this, he needs to get on with some kind of mindless, repetitive chore to wind himself out of the tension he is feeling.

He wishes he hadn't been so absorbed when Hari arrived. He hasn't really spoken to him since the night he dropped the dishes, and he is worried something is wrong. He hasn't seemed his usual, jokey self recently; there has been less banter with the customers, less of that particular brand of mild flirtation that works so well in creating a good atmosphere, and which Hari is so particularly skilled at. Balu smiles to himself at how something which has always eluded him can come so easily to someone else.

He wishes Hari would get more involved with the restaurant. He has tried to encourage him, to discuss his new dessert ideas with him. But, despite his fondness for him, he has to admit defeat. Hari just isn't interested; he has no ambition, no goal beyond passing each day in as pleasant and easy a manner as possible. Which isn't for one moment to say that he is lazy. Quite the contrary; he works consistently long, hard hours, and is always on call to do extra. Has never let him down in that sense. But it would be so satisfying to Balu if they could, perhaps, share a little more. He wishes he could make him understand how happy it would make him.

He glances back at what he has just been polishing. There are a few smears where he hasn't rubbed quite hard enough. He goes back and rubs at them vigorously. Jude's been behaving strangely too. Whenever he sees him he seems so strained and distracted. And Sarah, spending her time with a lonely old man who has no one else. What sad preoccupations his young friends seem to have all of a sudden.

He steps back again to appraise his work. The smears have vanished. He pulls out a chair and sits down gratefully, puffing a little. When Hari comes in from the kitchen, he decides, he'll ask him to run up the fire escape and ask Jude and Sarah if they'd like to come down this evening. He can try out his latest idea on them all, see if he can't make things a bit more cheerful.

ও

'I finally managed to speak to her alone that evening. As innocently as I could I asked her where she had been all day and she gave me a puzzling, slightly wary look.

'"*Wiesz*. You know," she said simply, and looked back at the magazine open on her lap. She was sitting in a chair in her tiny room and I realised it was the first time we had been alone together since my arrival in New York. Her legs were crossed and I noticed she was wearing fine stockings. They looked like silk, although I had never actually seen silk stockings before, but they were certainly different from the stockings she wore at home.

'She noticed me looking at them. "I went shopping," she said in a blunt, flat voice. "You telephoned this morning and Michael told you." Typical of Ewa, I thought, to know the name of every bellboy and chambermaid. They would probably give her flowers when she left, and photographs of their families. I remembered my sour encounter with the manageress of my own lodging house that morning and winced.

'She must have seen me flinch. She carefully closed the magazine and laid it on the round table beside the chair and fixed me with a patient, stony look.

'"What have *you* been doing all day?" she asked. The exaggerated tone in her voice was not lost on me. She was angry with me. Panicking, I wondered whether she had seen me in Macy's. I didn't know whether I should confess that I had felt abandoned and lonely and had tried to find her, but I didn't dare. I had never seen her like this before. There was a coldness in her expression, a self-containment, which made me feel as if she was too far away from me for us to communicate. I smiled at her, wanting to dispel the feeling, and asked what she was thinking and she stood up abruptly and walked across the room to fiddle with the things on her dressing table, keeping her back to me. With a sinking heart I realised that she didn't want to be in the room with me. She must have seen me in Macy's, and was feeling too angry even to speak to me.

'"Ewa?" I took a step closer to her. I wanted to break this sense of separation between us, but I could tell she was starting to feel hemmed in by my presence and she avoided me, fiddling some more, hanging up some clothes, rearranging their order in her wardrobe as I looked on. Eventually she turned to face me and, after a beat, asked me why I had come. How had I been able to afford to come? she asked. How had I arranged time away from the university? What was I going to do here alone while she rehearsed and worked night after night? What did I expect her to do?

'"But aren't you glad I'm here?" I asked, sinking impotently into the chair.

'"I just don't know why you *needed* to be here," she said, and picked up her handbag and left the room.

'After she had gone, I sat, half waiting for her to reappear, until the realisation dawned that she wasn't going to return any time soon. I tried to work out what was happening between us but I felt dulled and stupid and horribly ashamed of myself. I couldn't yet admit to feeling jealous, but the sensation was there. My dreams of the previous night had been saturated with images of her dancing, spinning, twirling round the dance floor with Hopper, and it was this that had sent me creeping around Macy's in search of her. And that glancing, accidental touch on the cool stem of her wine glass.

'I suppose, sitting alone in the silent hotel room, I caught a glimpse of the possessive, pathetic drinker I was becoming, and of the real Ewa, a woman I had never really fully seen until now, whose life did not revolve exclusively around me, as mine now did around her.

'The following morning I sat hunched, uninvited, at the back of the stalls in the empty theatre, lulled by the thud-thudding of the dancers' feet on the silent stage as they warmed up for an afternoon performance. There was something very comforting about the sound, and about the stopping and starting, the short, murmuring bursts of speech in my own language, interspersed with the heavily accented French commands from the dance master.

'But I couldn't feel comforted. As I sat there I watched Ewa closely. I had always known how dancing was her escape, her way of shutting out the world, but now it seemed that this shutting out was a way of withdrawing from me.

'I'm making it sound as though it wasn't deliberate, aren't I? As though it was something that took her over which she was powerless to resist. And perhaps it was, I have no idea. But it felt deliberate. I had noticed a few cautious glances thrown in my direction when I walked into the auditorium and I thought, they know something I don't. She will talk to them while she shuts me out.

'Of course New York was the catalyst, that was all. As much as I blamed it all on that brash, hateful city at the time, the potential for this rift must have been there in our relationship always, from the very beginning. But it wasn't so easy to see this then. I could only keep reminding myself that in Warsaw, where we would, after all, shortly be returning, everything had been fine. I sought reassurance from the fact that normality would resume once we were home, that the difficulties we were having were as transient as our presence in this city which was so very different from our own.

'But it was clear she couldn't bear to be alone with me. A kind of restless disgust overtook her in my presence and she could settle nowhere. She was energised and alive to the city, thriving within its heat and din, while I had become suddenly old, my body slow and heavy with alcohol, constantly missing the beat, unable to adjust my pace. I suppose I must have grated unbearably.

'I was so unprepared. I'd been so sure of her. And suddenly here she was building a wall round herself to keep me out, when all I wanted was to crawl into that space she was making and be walled in with her, reason with her, prove to her that the fault was not between us at all.'

He lifts his head and looks at the window; sees sky, clouds. His creased, grey face, open and vulnerable in the cold, pallid light from outside, seems to admit defeat. Sarah feels the silence, feels the slipping edge of his story, like a breakaway piece of ice on a frozen river. He looks down almost bashfully, she thinks, watching as his finger traces the wood-grain patterns on the arm of his chair. When he begins to speak again she feels as if she has been holding her breath.

ॐ

Balu is feeling pleased with himself. His vermicelli pudding has been a resounding triumph and Jude, Hari and Sarah are together for the first time in ages. Even Jude, usually so withdrawn these days, is leaning forward, both elbows on the table, seemingly filled with some new-found enthusiasm. He has been talking about the eclipse coming in August with uncharacteristic fervency. Once or twice during the evening Balu has noticed Sarah shooting him the briefest sideways glance, a telltale sign of some discomfort she is feeling, but apart from this the evening is going well.

Hari gets up to fetch a fresh beer for Jude and himself, uncaps the bottles and carries them to the table at the back of the restaurant.

'He says Romania,' Sarah is saying as he sits down, the faintest dusting of ridicule coating the surface of her words, her enunciation minutely exaggerated. Hari notices, and his left eyebrow twitches up and down again in an almost invisible movement. Sarah smiles. 'So how exactly would we be able to afford to get there?' she asks, her tone brittle, turning her attention back to Jude.

'We'd manage. It's weeks away yet.'

'How?'

Jude flings himself back in his chair, suddenly exasperated. 'We just could,' he says. 'It's not that difficult to get a bit of money together, you know.' He throws Hari a savage look. 'Well, would *you* be up for it?'

Balu gathers up their empty bowls and piles them on another table, where he has coffee waiting. Hari jumps up automatically from his chair to take over but Balu tuts at him, shakes his head; he wants the three to talk together like they used to.

'Yeah,' says Hari, straightening up in his chair a little, sounding, to Balu, riled by the distinctly combative tone in Jude's voice. 'OK, yeah. I'd be up for it if you two are.' He looks apologetically at Sarah but she won't meet his eyes.

Balu carries the jug of coffee over to their table and lowers himself carefully back into his chair.

'Up for what?' he asks innocently, as if he hasn't quite heard the conversation.

'Oh, it's nothing,' Sarah says quickly. 'Jude and Hari are just being ridiculous.'

Balu's eyes widen.

'But it's a *great* idea,' says Jude, his voice mocking, slightly wheedling. 'Don't you think, Balu? Us three, going to Romania to see the eclipse?'

'Just drop it, Jude,' she says quietly. 'Who's having coffee?'

Balu studies Hari's face surreptitiously. He looks perfectly composed, but there's a waver in the smile he gives him when he notices he is being watched.

Jude refuses coffee, instead getting up and helping himself to another bottle of beer from behind the counter. Balu watches him nervously as he stands for a while with his back to them and swigs two or three times from the bottle before sitting back down beside Sarah again, the beer already half gone.

ॐ

'You have made it beautiful, Sarah. I never would have dreamt it could be made so beautiful.' Balu hasn't been up to see Sarah's garden for ages. She has kept his deckchair diligently folded and propped against the wall; now she sets it up for him and he sinks gratefully into the striped sling seat. He leans forward, studying his skylight intently, a thought suddenly occurring to him. 'You can see into the restaurant,' he says. 'You could spy on us!'

'If I wanted. Yes, I suppose I could.' Sarah sits down, cross-legged, on the cushion. She has always been far more concerned about whether people in the restaurant can see her. He leans back in the deckchair, his scrutiny of the skylight at an end.

'So,' he says, feeling a little self-conscious suddenly. 'How is your old gentleman?'

'I'm not sure,' she says. 'He just seems to get sadder and sadder. I wish I could do something. You know. Really do something to help.' She bends down to scratch Sita under the chin. She is stretched out in a long, thin patch of sun and at Sarah's touch she gives a chirrup of surprise and lifts her head.

You're probably helping already, Balu thinks, watching her bent over the cat. He wants to ask her whether everything is all right with Jude. He worries about her sometimes, worries that she is the sort of person who could so easily step off the narrow track of her life and wander so far from it that she wouldn't be able to find her way back

'I think the main thing is that he's lonely,' she says, straightening up. 'He lives in that flat all alone and I don't think he really sees anyone other than me.'

௸

'I went to the World Fair alone. I'm afraid I wasn't in the right frame of mind for it. I drifted from exhibit to exhibit, everything that was happening with Ewa swimming around in my head so that I scarcely knew where I was going. I fetched up at one point at this thing called the Westinghouse Capsule.' He closes his eyes briefly. She sees the muscle in his jaw tighten then relax. 'Have you heard of it?' She shakes her head. 'It was a time capsule,' he says, when he has opened his eyes again. 'Westinghouse was a big manufacturer. Fridges, domestic appliances. Still is. They buried this cap . . . capsule . . .' He winces suddenly, raising his upper body slightly, as if to try to lift himself above some internal pain he is feeling, and she wonders whether he is all right. But whatever it is seems to subside and he continues speaking. 'And it wasn't supposed to be dug up for five thousand years. Five thousand years! I tried to tell Ewa about it that evening at a party I had followed her to, but she wouldn't stay put for long enough. She said it was too depressing to think about – the fact that everything that was "now" would be like some kind of ancient civilisation – and floated away, back to the dance floor. But to me the timescale made it more bearable. I couldn't feel troubled by something so distant, so removed, while the immediate future, in every direction, seemed so unsure.

'This time capsule, ah, it was like an exercise in thoroughness. I think that was what really impressed me. Absolutely everything was thought of. They put in something from every area of human endeavour they could think of. There were examples of different manufactured materials, different metals, swatches of fabric, plastics. All sorts of everyday items – they were my favourites – shaving brushes and wristwatches, pens and tobacco pouches. Each one meticulously labelled with the name of the manufacturer. Seeds, microfilms of literature, radio shows, newspapers, photographs of contemporary life. It fascinated me. I bought a guide which listed absolutely everything that had gone into it and couldn't stop myself from reading it. Just a list of things!' He smiles broadly, chuckles and then takes a sharp breath, as if the chuckle has joggled his insides too much.

'I bought a present for Ewa, too, although I never gave it to her.' He pauses momentarily. 'It was a paperweight. You know, one of those things, when you shake them . . .' He looks at her and Sarah thinks that his face seems to have shrunk a little.

Sarah nods. 'A snowstorm.'

'Is that what they're called? Inside was a tiny Trylon and Perisphere – they were the main exhibition buildings. You shook it and snow swirled around inside. I thought she would like that.' He stops speaking for a moment and smiles wanly before continuing, staying close to his subject, not allowing himself to drift.

'In 6939 this capsule will be unearthed. A book was printed in permanent ink and a copy was placed in monasteries, and every major library around the world. Inside, it gave detailed instructions on how to make some kind of electro-magnetic equipment to find the exact burial place. They even thought of a way to get round the fact that people might not speak the same languages any more. They put in a key which showed how to decipher English. And a request for the written contents to be translated into new languages. There was no eventuality which had not been considered. The whole thing was made of some sort of alloy of silver and copper, and it was lined with glass. It was, literally, an encapsulation of a moment in history. The tragedy of it is that it must ever be found and torn apart.'

❧

Balu has been thinking about Sarah's lonely old man and it has struck him that, in some small way, they might have something in common. He feels a little ridiculous thinking this. After all, this Jozef is an academic, has taught in universities in who knows how many different places, while he has spent most of his life in kitchens. Nonetheless, he has been wondering about him and feeling rather sorry for him sitting alone day after day waiting for Sarah. When he next sees Sarah, he decides, he will ask her to invite him to the Mountain of Light and he will cook a special dish for him. Nothing too overpowering, he is an old man, after all, but something tasty and a little uplifting. He would like to do that for him.

When Sarah buzzes Jozef's entryphone there is a long wait. She wonders whether he has fallen asleep and hasn't heard. Of course she could go home and come back tomorrow, but she said she would be here today, and he will worry if she doesn't arrive. And anyway, she wants to hear more of his story. She is terribly afraid of what is going to happen and has started to jump ahead, to try to guess. The few clues she has don't hold out much promise; there are, for example, no framed wedding photographs, or any photographs at all, come to think of it, decorating Jozef's walls and mantelpiece. And all of this happened just before the war. Wasn't Warsaw occupied? Weren't thousands of Poles killed? She is beginning to fear something of this sort and, worse, of Ewa being taken from him before they have a chance to resolve this problem in communication, or whatever it was, that had grown between them.

She waits another thirty seconds and then, impatient, gives the button three longish, firm presses, just to make sure he will hear it. Of course it could be broken, she thinks. I could be here for hours on the doorstep. How funny that they have never thought to exchange phone numbers. She assumes he has a phone, but now she thinks about it she realises she's never seen one; Jozef's is a peculiarly empty flat. She is just deciding how long she will wait when a woman opens the street door from the inside.

'Sarah?' she asks.

'Yes, I . . .' How does the woman know her name? She ushers

Sarah into the vestibule and looks at her urgently, as if she has something to say. Sarah is still trying to explain that she thinks Jozef's buzzer might be broken and she's sorry if she disturbed her.

'Jozef has been taken in the hospital,' she says, slowly and clearly, as if she is explaining something to a child. Sarah stares at her stupidly.

'Hospital,' she says again, in a louder voice. Her accent is stronger than Jozef's and she is old and frail-looking. Sarah wonders if she, too, is from Poland, or if she is from somewhere else entirely, with a lifetime of her own stories tightly coiled within her.

'He go to the hospital since two days. St Bartholomew's. They ask me to tell you.' Sarah wonders who 'they' are. Maybe the ambulance people.

'Was he taken in an ambulance?' she asks. 'What happened?' But the woman knows no more and simply repeats what she has said, and hands her a piece of paper with the hospital address on it.

'They give this for you,' she says.

Sarah thanks her and, after she has said goodbye and is outside again, she sinks down onto the top step and wonders what to do. She is stunned. Jozef is old, she knows that, and he is thin and is certainly looking thinner and greyer than when they first met. And his storytelling has become more urgent lately; she has felt he wants her to stay with him for longer each time she visits. Sarah feels terrible. Last time she saw him she stayed so late. Perhaps she exhausted him. But he talked on and on as if he would never stop. She left as soon as she could.

* * *

He refuses to be in bed for the visit, says there is no need, and sits in his chair like a stubborn wooden doll. When the blanket across his lap slips a little and threatens to fall off completely, he looks at her desperately, hating not being able to do such a simple thing as catch it himself. She pulls it round him, carefully tucking it in where she can, to stop it slipping again. It is four days since she saw him last, but how different he looks. She doesn't know if it is merely because he is in pyjamas and in the bright hospital light, but he now looks ill and drawn, and his breathing, she notices, is more laboured and heavy than usual. She feels a pang of something she can't identify – worry, panic, guilt, sadness, she isn't sure. It feels most like a deep and stirring sadness, as if she has lost something.

She sits down opposite him, in the uncomfortable-looking visitor's chair and sheds the top she pulled on before she left the flat. The ward is hot, although most of the windows are open. It is the evening visiting hour and groups of people in outdoor clothes are clustered around each bed, leaning in close to pyjama-clad relatives to regale them with tales from the world that is still turning outside their shrinking compass. She looks at a couple of the drawn faces, trying desperately to appear interested but exhausted by the effort, their connection to this noisy otherworld increasingly irrelevant. Here and there, single figures sit alone in dressing gowns with their reading lamps pulled down low over books and magazines.

She has been thinking about Jozef in the four days since she last saw him, worrying about what seems to be happening to him and Ewa in New York. She wonders whether a place can have such a catastrophic effect on people, bringing things so rapidly to a head. But now that he is here, now that his health has put him in hospital, he probably won't want to go on with his story. She feels selfish for thinking this. A middle-aged couple in matching corduroy outfits walk down the ward to a bed at the far end, their shoes squeaking on the lino. She pulls her chair closer to Jozef's, determined not to let her eagerness for him to continue with his story show.

'So,' she says, 'are you OK? I mean . . .' She feels horribly intrusive, unsure how to ask him about his health. They have never really talked about such things before. 'I mean, what happened?' She is aware of having coloured slightly, and hates herself for it. Why does illness have to be such an uncomfortable thing to talk about?

'I am dying, Sarah.' Her stomach flips over so dramatically that she fears she might be sick, and she can hear the blood suddenly surging in her ears. He smiles apologetically. 'All those cigarettes. I left it too long before giving up, I'm afraid. The damage is done. But let's not talk about it. I have so much else to tell you. Please?'

'Oh, Jozef,' she gasps, her stomach flips now subsiding, leaving her with a tipped-out, trembly feeling. Several fat tears well up and spill down her cheeks, splashing onto her arm, but she nods. She won't ask him about it if he doesn't want her to, she is determined; if the rules of their relationship are going to change, it will be his decision.

'The evening of that day at the fair I went to another party. Ewa didn't invite me; she was still angry with me for following her to New York. But I went anyway and was allowed grudging entry by the doorman.

'Again, I watched Hopper. I noticed his gentle manners with Alicja, whom he spoke to alone now, and his love of fun and frivolity as he flirted and chatted in the midst of the dancers, like the dark centre of a flower, a single black bead within their sparkle and colour. Ewa and Maria were shrieking with laughter at each other's American accents. *"Oh sure,"* they drawled at each other, in between giggles. *"Couldya tell me the wayda the subway?"*

'I was jealous. He was charming. He was younger than I was. He was American.' Jozef laughs ruefully. 'He was attractive to women and I knew I was not; I was madly jealous. In my pocket I clenched my hand round the gift I had bought for Ewa at the fair. Before coming to New York she would have loved it. But this city, the new people she had met . . . She had gained a knowingness, was losing the slightly innocent sense of fun I knew so well and I felt my present was ridiculous. She would accept it politely and then laugh at it with them behind my back. And the bulge it made in my jacket pocket seemed to single me out as some kind of simpleton, coming to a party with my pockets stuffed to bursting. I would gladly have left right there and then, but I decided I had to talk to Ewa first.'

He stops, exhausted, and breathes laboriously, heavily, leaning forward, away from his pillows. Sarah half rises from her seat.

'Shall I . . . ?' Shall I call a nurse, she wants to say. Shall I help? Shall I go, and let you rest? She feels uncomfortable doing nothing, just sitting there waiting for him to catch his breath and go on. Suddenly she feels afraid and on the verge of panicky tears. Talking is clearly exhausting him. He looks up, his breathing calmer, softer, and puts his hand on her sleeve, as if he fears she might run away from him.

She cannot bear the thought of his spending visiting time alone like many of the old men she has noticed in the ward who busy themselves with books and feigned sleep or requests for the curtains to be drawn round their beds so that their solitary state might gain some feeble authority. It's funny, she thinks; it is women who live longer than men, and yet this ward is full of old men with no visitors. And here she is, visiting one of these old men who has nobody. Who has nothing but the past.

'I watched her dance with Hopper, my morose mood aggravated by the sight of his contact with her and hers with him. Alicja, dancing with another dinner-suited fellow, turned her head this way and that, so that her gaze remained fixed, for the entire dance, on Hopper, his face, his profile, the back of his head. I felt a pang of fellow feeling with her partner.

And then suddenly there Ewa was, standing beside me with her butterfly fingers at my neck. Perching, exhausted. Something wild and guarded. Unreachable. I put up my hand to touch her but she took flight and was lost again. A little later she pulled me aside, took my face in her hands and looked at me, seeming, at last, to be still. But I couldn't reach her. I felt as if I was behind glass or underwater when I tried to speak. Just for once, she saw my distress. She pitied me for long enough to take me by the hand and lead me from the room and out into a high-ceilinged corridor.

'"What do you want, Jozef?" she asked. "Why are you following me like this?"

'"I . . . I love you," was all I could say. I heard my voice, all chewed up and ugly, as if my tongue were too big for my mouth. "I love you."

'"Why don't you leave?" she asked, as gently as she could, but the irritation of the past few days was stitching itself back into her voice. I thought she meant leave New York, go home to Poland. I still don't know if she did or whether she just wanted me to leave the party.

"'Leave?' I was incredulous. I heard my voice, loud and unsteady, unthreading. It started shouting at her. "Leave? Leave? Is that what you want me to do? Go away so that you can screw your American boy all you like and have him buy you all the gifts I can't afford? Is that it? Is that what you want?" I was astonishing myself with what I was saying, I had never spoken like this to anyone, but I couldn't stop. Although what was happening was terrible, I was thrilled by the suddenness of it, the exhilaration. She backed away from me, her hand raised halfway to her mouth. I ought to have stopped right there – I had already said too much – and left, like she said, but I couldn't. I had unleashed a passion which I couldn't rein in quickly enough. I tried to but it was all spooling out of my mouth; it seemed to be beyond my control. "I've seen you," I growled. "I've seen you together." By this point several people had come out of the dance hall to see what the noise was about and were standing a little way behind Ewa. Hopper was among them. They only served to make me raise my voice even more; I was now performing for an audience. "You think I don't know what's going on?" I felt I had the upper hand now. "I've been following you. And I've seen the way you are together, all touching fingers and secret smiles. Well," I flung out my arm dramatically in Hopper's direction and pointed an accusing finger, "it's true, isn't it?" Hopper stared at me dumbly. He looked even younger then than his twenty-five years and it struck me for one awful moment that I was probably completely wrong. That this might all be some hideous folly of my overworked imagination. But it was too late now. And I was too proud to change direction. The previous night I had

had another dream, that Ewa was being driven away from me in a huge American car. She turned in her seat to watch me through the back window and I saw her face grow smaller and smaller until I could no longer make it out.

'A general murmuring had arisen and, as I stood there facing them, feeling a little light-headed but still surging with euphoria, the doorman who had let me in, along with one of the burlier of the dinner-suited guests, approached and set about removing me, taking one arm each and frogmarching me to the exit. I turned wildly, calling out to Ewa, shouting that they were making a mistake, that I was wrong. Ewa stood and watched, her expression frozen, her hand still at her mouth, and I lost sight of her as I was escorted round the corner.

'They threw me out into the night. I vomited copiously on the steps, spitefully hoping that every guest would have to tread through it, wove my way to the subway and rode ingloriously back to my room in Queens.'

He turns down the corners of his mouth slowly, pressing his dry, paper-grey lips firmly together. His face has lost all its colour. He is beginning to look like an old faded photograph of someone long dead. He has not had a shave for several days and whiskers are growing defiantly on his hollowed-out cheeks.

'Excuse me. Are you Ewa?' the nurse asks as she is leaving. It is nine o'clock and the lights have been dimmed. Sarah looks back at the ward, at Jozef, tiny in his chair at the far end, and it seems almost cosy. It is so calm and quiet. Jozef has been speaking in a low murmur, warm and yellow in the glow of his reading lamp. Once or twice he fell asleep and she simply sat, looking at the changing expressions which passed across his face like slow clouds, silently, distantly covering and uncovering the sun, and at the pink and blue early summer sky through the window as the evening lengthened.

'I'm Sarah,' she says, and shrugs her shoulders with a smile before walking out through the heavy swing doors.

'The nurse says he's been saying her name in his sleep,' she says to Jude later. 'And when he's dopey with the morphine.'

'Does he fancy her?'

'Ewa's name.'

'Sorry.' He looks at her. 'Joke,' he says, his voice laced with something a little barbed.

She goes out into the garden and watches him angrily through the half-open doors. He has not reacted at all to the news of Jozef's illness. He was sitting forward on the edge of the sofa with the atlas on his lap, rolling a spliff, half watching the muted TV when she came home, in need of some kind of recognition, of comfort. She perched on the sofa and told him, her voice unsteady and small, but he only half-listened, did no more than glance up at her, so engrossed was he in his delicate task. And he said nothing, really, just murmured some half-thing and only spoke properly to make that stupid joke. He is rolling another spliff now. She sees him deliberate, his hand hovering over the tiny block of resin, deciding whether a bit more is needed. He holds it delicately to the lighter flame for a moment and slowly crumbles a little more along the length of the Rizla. Then, carefully, he picks up the loaded paper in both hands and rolls it with the tips of his fingers, poking out his tongue to moisten the edge, his eyes now fixed on the silent screen.

She thinks how inexpressible it is, the feeling she gets when she watches Jude, anyone, just doing something ordinary like that. Just doing something, anything, unaware of how vulnerable, how lovable he is in his actions. He rasps the lighter and purses his lips round the end of the thin cigarette, drawing on it. The end glows orange and she imagines the crackle it makes, the taste of the smoke. Perhaps he is regretting that joke, she thinks. Or perhaps not.

There's something very wrong, she knows that, if he can't even bring himself to put his arm round her to say, 'I'm sorry your friend is dying,' but she feels too battered to think about it. She has no idea what's happening but he is shutting himself away from her, bricking himself up into his own little fortification, and she doesn't know how to get through. She thinks of what Jozef said about how Ewa suddenly started distancing herself from him, and she shivers as she goes back into the room.

'I'm going downstairs for a bit,' she says. He lifts his head and looks at her, gives a vague, dismissive nod. It's as if they've had an argument, she thinks. It's like that sulky aftermath. But there has been no argument. And she doesn't want to have to think about it; she wants someone other than herself to care that Jozef is dying.

'Ah,' Balu says when he sees her. 'Good. I've got something to ask you.' He draws her through the kitchen and ushers her eagerly into the restaurant. It is busy; even their table at the back, which is usually free, is in use. Everyone is in summer clothes and the air is heavy with trapped heat and the mingled smell of food and perfume and sweat and smoke. For a moment she wants to go straight back up to the dark flat again, but Balu notices her swollen, red eyes, and pulls her back into the kitchen.

'What's wrong?' he asks. 'What has happened?'

'It's Jozef,' she says, tears welling up in her eyes again. 'My old man. He's in hospital. He's going to die.' Balu puts his hand on her shoulder. She knows he must be feeling awkward, but she cannot help it, she starts to sob. Balu puts his arms round her and she leans her head gratefully against his blue and white striped apron.

'What were you going to ask me?' she says. The restaurant has quietened down a little and they are sitting at the table at the back, drinking masala tea. Hari is working; he has been flat out all evening, flitting from table to table, never looking hurried or overwrought, his face so expertly fixed. He catches Sarah watching him, puffy-eyed, and winks at her from across the room, making her smile.

'Oh,' says Balu, 'it was nothing. Just another idea. I think I need to cook it more in my head before I let it out from the bag.' He reaches over and squeezes her hand. In adulthood, he realises, apart from dandling his baby niece on his lap occasionally, the hug he gave Sarah is the first physical contact he has ever had with another person. He excludes shaking hands and things of that sort. He isn't used to comforting people, to holding people. But when he put his arms round her, it had seemed the easiest, most natural thing in the world.

He has comforted her a little, but the warmth, the living, fluttering fragility of another person which he felt when he held her has filled him with a sudden yawning emptiness and aloneness which he hasn't felt since coming to London all those years ago. For a moment he wonders what his life would be now if the dark-haired beauty his parents had chosen for him had agreed to their marriage after all. Or if he had met someone else at the restaurant. He remembers the sad woman with her husband. Maybe if there had been someone like her, but without the husband. But he shrugs the thought away.

ھ

Sarah dips the squeegee mop into the bucket and gives it a few vigorous plunges up and down before pulling it out and ramming down the lever, folding the yellow sponge in on itself and squeezing out the excess water. She has found a new cleaning job to take the place of the house with the mad woman and the crying baby and this is the first time she has been here. She starts in one corner of the freshly swept kitchen and puts her back into it, taking a grim pleasure in seeing the quarry tiles darken and glisten under their coating of soapy water. She works her way to the adjacent corner then returns to the bucket. As the mop skims the surface of the tiles, tiny wisps of steam rise and disappear.

She feels better here, calmer, in the silent, empty home of someone who knows nothing at all about her life, and the repetitive, mindless yet quite exacting physical work she is doing lulls her far more than sitting at home waiting would.

Jozef has taken a turn for the worse and has been moved to a hospice. She finds it almost unbearable to see him, knowing that they are now both waiting for an end, that his telling of his story is to be so prominent a summing up, and that, very soon, his voice in her head, with its precise intonation, its carefully chosen words and irregular, lilting rhythms will be all that remains of him.

She is dividing her life into two functions: working all the hours she can, polishing, sweeping, scrubbing kitchen tiles until they gleam, Hoovering whole houses twice over, and, when she is not doing this, sitting interminable, motionless, agonising hours with Jozef. This simple contrast is all she can manage, as if one can somehow cancel out the other and leave her emptied, feeling nothing. At night she comes home to the Mountain of Light and climbs the stairs wearily in the dark, falling asleep as soon as she climbs into bed, dreaming nothing. Dimly, she is aware of Jude on the periphery, breathing quietly beside her, miles away.

The hospice is called the Camellias. It smells of air freshener and disinfectant in the corridors, and the decor is predominantly frilly and feminine. Framed prints of old Pears' soap adverts grace every available wall and artificial flowers cascade over the sides of wicker jardinieres in every corner. It is very quiet. Quieter than the hospital. All the staff wear pink tabards over their uniforms, like doll's house dinner ladies.

'Too much fuss and lace,' he says, in a voice which is gruffer, thicker than usual. 'Don't sit down. Take that curtain away. I want to see outside.'

She goes to the window and takes down the net curtain and stuffs it in a drawer which smells of chipboard and emptiness. She stays at the window, looking out into the garden. It is a ground-floor room and there is a garden door. Outside, a railed ramp leads gently down to the lawn. For the first time in their acquaintance Sarah feels uncomfortable. The present has caught them; its urgency is drawing a veil across everything familiar, and she doesn't know what to do, how to be. Their friendship had settled into a routine. Now he is helpless, too weak, she realises, to take the lead. He needs her now more than ever. But she doesn't know if this is true, or if she is the very last thing he needs. She feels a sudden coating of tears, and she opens her eyes wide to stop them pooling and spilling down her cheeks. She concentrates on watching a blackbird scuttle about beneath a glossy rhododendron. The shrub has bright pink, blowsy flowers that match one of the colours in the curtains. On the dark soil and at the edges of the grass lie fallen pink blooms, crumpled and collapsed, and the blackbird hops about amongst them, grubbing for worms.

She swallows hard and turns back into the room. You could sit outside, she is going to say. I could get someone to help us. But he looks terrible, is probably glad just to lie still. 'It's a pretty garden,' is all she says.

She goes back to the bed and sits in the chair beside him. 'Jozef?' she says.

He opens his eyes and the hunted look is still there, is not going to go away simply because he is too weak to bear it any longer. She wants to touch him, to hold on to his bony hand, to dispel the sudden awful feeling of aloneness that is coursing through her body like cold rainwater. His eyes close and slowly open again.

'You're tired, Jozef. I'll go. I'll come back later.'

He nods. 'Promise?' he says. 'Later.'

She promises, and leaves.

Jude has clearly not been around all day; the flat is full of stale, dusty heat. When she returns from the hospice she sits in the garden, but no sooner has she fetched a book and cushion and sat down than she decides she doesn't want to be outside at all. She goes upstairs, closes the bedroom door, removes her socks, and gets into bed.

On her way back to the hospice she buys Jozef some flowers

and thinks again how little she really knows about him. She doesn't know what to choose, even whether he likes flowers at all. In the end, remembering something she once said to him about a certain shade of blue reminding her of the seaside, she buys cornflowers.

'I'm back,' she says.

After a long silence he speaks.

'I never saw Ewa again,' he says. His face is half in shadow. The curtains are still open and she can hear the unbearably melancholic trickle of blackbird song which makes her shudder and feel, suddenly, that everything has stopped and she doesn't want it to start again. His voice is husky and has become threaded through with a dark, even tone. A deadness.

'I went back home to Warsaw and began the long wait for her return. I busied myself with all sorts of things. I found I had endless time on my hands. I hadn't realised how much I had let the rest of my life slip away. I contacted a couple of friends I had neglected. I did some work. I attempted to smoke more and drink less.' He stops suddenly and takes a long, deep breath. 'I waited and waited. For weeks. Then months. The war started and Warsaw was soon occupied. Still, she didn't come back.'

He is staring straight ahead, at the pink wall. His eyes seem pinned there. Neither of them speaks. The blackbird song continues and Sarah feels as if she has been tipped out of herself. She feels a raw, gnawing anger and an awful iron rigidity. She wants to run to her mother and bury her face against her softness, even though this is something she has rarely done. She wants her mother's arms round her. She wants to be in bed, wants the comfort of her covers and her pillow.

She wants Jude. She wants her mother. She cannot blink or swallow or move.

ॐ

Balu has been telling Hari about Sarah's friend, about how ill he is and how unhappy she is. Balu is puzzled; where was Jude when she was so upset? Why did she have to come down to the restaurant? Hari shrugs. He feels impotent. He would like to run upstairs to the flat right now and put his arms round Sarah, tell her everything will be OK, but he can't. He doesn't dare, not now, with the feeling he gets every time he sees Jude that his is the face he would most like never to see again.

But the restaurant isn't busy, and he can't keep his mind away from her. When a couple come in he pounces on them and ushers them to a table, handing them menus before they are out of their coats. Balu, watching from the back of the restaurant, beckons him into the kitchen.

'Go upstairs,' he says. 'These are for the old man.' He hands him a small confectioner's cake box, tied up like a parcel with a length of gift-wrap ribbon. 'It's some biscuits,' he says, answering Hari's question before it is out of his mouth. 'Take them up.'

Hari takes the box without protest and goes out of the kitchen into the area at the back of the restaurant where the bins are. He wonders whether Balu really wants him to check on Sarah, make sure nothing is wrong, or whether he is simply rescuing him from the restaurant for a few minutes. He sits at the bottom of the fire escape with the box on his lap. So like Balu, he thinks, twisting a curled end of ribbon round his finger. Trying to look after them all, wanting everything to be all right.

If Sarah isn't there, he decides, he'll hand the box over to Jude with a quick explanation. If there's no one in he can come down again and ask Balu what he should do with it. Somehow he knows Sarah isn't going to be there. He wishes he had thought to bring his cigarettes outside with him.

At the top of the fire escape he pauses, his knuckles an inch from the glass. He could just go back downstairs and say nobody is in. That he knocked but neither Sarah nor Jude came to the door. But he's being stupid. Nothing's going to happen, he just gets this edgy sense whenever he's around Jude now. And the two of them are never alone together; he imagines how awkward they would feel without the buffeting presence of Sarah and Balu.

When he knocks, there are a few silent moments when he thinks there is nobody at home. But then a light goes on in the kitchen and the blurred shape of a person appears in the frosted glass. It's Jude.

'Hi.' Jude looks at him blearily, as if he has just woken up. 'Sarah's not here,' he says with surprising baldness, already turning to walk back into the flat. Hari follows him inside.

'No? Well, it doesn't matter.' He holds the box out in explanation but Jude's back is turned so he places it silently on the kitchen table and follows Jude into the other room. The shutters are only half open and the air in the room is heavy and blue with cigarette smoke. Hari isn't sure what to say next. He doesn't know why he has followed Jude inside, but here he is. Jude has sat down on the sofa and pulled a large book covered with threads of tobacco and torn Rizla packets onto his lap. Hari, standing in the centre of the room, casts around desperately for something to say. He catches sight of the stripe of sky and vivid green leaves between the shutters. 'Garden's looking good,' he says. 'Can I . . . ?'

'Sure, take a look.'

Outside, Hari feels just as awkward. He wishes he hadn't come in. It might have seemed rude to hand over the biscuits and flee, but anything has to be better than this. What the fuck is Jude's problem? He's acting like there's nothing wrong, but with such a deliberately flimsy veneer – it seems deliberate anyway – it's as bad as if he were towering over him hurling accusations. Of what, he can only guess, but he assumes it would be over Sarah. Maybe she's told him about them. Well, what if she has? He peers down through the skylight into the restaurant below. There's nobody in sight. He crouches down and leans nearer, trying to get the view Jude must have had on that night when he dropped the plates. As he's pressing his hands against the glass and wondering whether he dare lean any more heavily against it he hears Jude come through the French windows behind him and out onto the rooftop.

'What're you doing?'

Hari pulls guiltily away from the window. Jude must remember, he thinks. He must know what I was doing. 'I'm just taking in the bird's eye view,' he says, his tone over-bright. 'The place looks so much nicer from up here.' He stands up and steps away from the glass. 'Don't you think?'

Jude doesn't answer. He shrugs his shoulders with a tight, almost invisible movement and stands there, as if rooted. Hari wishes Balu hadn't sent him up. He wishes he was anywhere but here, stuck in Sarah's garden without Sarah, with her sullen, aggrieved-looking boyfriend blocking his escape.

'Why're you here, anyway?' Jude asks eventually.

'Balu made some biscuits,' he says. 'For Sarah's old man.'

Jude gives a dismissive huff.

'What's your problem, Jude?' Almost as soon as the words are out of his mouth Hari wishes them back in. He knows that he has inflamed whatever thing there is between Jude and himself tenfold. Jude's eyebrows are arched, his forehead scrunched into a tight concertina and his mouth has turned up mockingly at the corners.

'*My* problem?' he says. 'What's *my* problem?' He raises his eyes skywards. 'You're the one who's sleeping with Sarah. *You* tell *me* what the problem is.'

'This is crazy.' Hari has had enough. He makes to leave, but Jude is still blocking the doorway. They stand for a couple of seconds, chest to chest, neither one prepared to stand down.

'*You* tell *me*,' Jude repeats.

'I'm leaving.' As he tries to push past Jude, Hari feels himself being shoved backwards. He stumbles, scrabbles to stay on his feet but cannot, and lands with a dull thud on the grey roofing felt. His arm, flung out to try to steady himself, breaks his fall and knocks over a couple of the plant pots surrounding the skylight. They crash against the glass, falling away in pieces from the pot-shaped mouldings of soil and roots, like broken chocolate eggs. Hari hears the glass crack, then a moment of silence before the broken panes smash onto the wine-red carpet in the restaurant below.

Balu feels sad that Sarah's friend won't now be able to visit the restaurant. He had rather hoped he might meet him. He hopes he will like the biscuits; his mother used to make them for him when he was ill. She would cut out the dough in diamond shapes, pressing the biscuit cutter carefully into its freshly rolled smoothness, and spread half of them with jam. Then she would cut a smaller diamond shape in the centre of each remaining half and carefully sandwich them all together and fill the holes with jam before baking them. He remembers lying on the rug in pyjamas with a sore throat or an eye infection, sniffing the warm, sweet smell as it drifted into each room of the house.

He wanders into the restaurant. It's still quite dead; just three tables are filled. He thinks it's something to do with the summer heat. In this country Indian food is not so welcome when the weather is warm. Or maybe it's just the heat and bustle of restaurants generally, he doesn't really know. But tonight the air is close and he can understand how people might prefer to sit at outdoor picnic tables in pubs and bars rather than come and eat indoors. He pads across to the plate-glass window at the front and looks out onto the street. There are three or four young lads coming out of the off-licence opposite with bulging, blue and white striped plastic bags – the cheap kind. Further down there's a pizza place, but he can't see whether anyone is in there. The pub on the corner has benches outside and they are mostly occupied. Again, it is young people; they seem to populate the summer, to flower and come into their own, somehow. He always feels older, more at odds with the world during London summers.

He turns back into the restaurant to check on the meagre sprinkling of diners. As he turns he glances up into the blue-glowing skylight space hovering over them and catches a shadow, a movement, then nothing. Hari hasn't come down yet. He wonders whether the three of them are sitting in the garden together. He hopes so; they are young and they deserve nights like this. He is about to clear the empty dishes from one of the tables when there is another, closer, more sudden movement, and a sound which rises above the gentle music he is playing tonight. A muffled thump and a crashing sound which causes all the heads in the restaurant to look up in alarm. And then a shattering right above their heads and for a moment it rains glass as the broken panes fall into a crazed, jagged pattern on the carpet.

Balu is distraught.

'What is wrong with you all? What is happening?' he cries in confusion when Hari walks back into the restaurant. His face is pale and puckered with worry. He gestures at Hari, at the customers – all of them looking very uncomfortable caught in the midst of this sudden drama – and at the debris on the carpet.

Hari grabs the dustpan and brush, storms over to the little pile of broken glass and sweeps it up angrily.

'I don't know,' he says. 'Jude's going crazy up there, I know that much. Fucking crazy.'

Balu winces at Hari's bad language but he tries to draw him out further. Has he said something to annoy Jude? Did they disagree about something? Hari feels such welling tenderness at the sight of Balu's confused, concerned face and wishes he could explain more. But how can he explain that their lives are not the way Balu sees them? That there is no such thing as carefree, love-filled youth. It is just as shitty to be any one of them, himself, Sarah or Jude, as it probably was for Balu twenty years ago.

He tries to reassure Balu, says Jude is probably just stressed out or something and that he's probably had a bit to drink and will be down first thing in the morning full of apologies.

'Well, I hope so,' Balu says, unconvinced.

Later, they survey the damage together; there are only a few broken panes and Hari says no problem, he'll get it fixed in the morning. Balu, still worried, calls his nightly cab home to the suburbs and leaves Hari to lock up.

She is in the dark garden with a blanket wrapped round her shoulders. Too much has happened today. Too much. She doesn't know whether she can bear it any longer. She pulls the blanket more tightly round her shoulders and rests her forehead on her knees.

Hari sits in the restaurant alone after Balu has gone (he refused to let him go with him in the taxi and see him home; Hari was worried about him, he had been so shaken by the night's events). He sees Jude leave, a huge, bulging kitbag slung over his shoulder. He hasn't seen Sarah come home, but now at last he can leave the restaurant and check if she is there.

Upstairs in the dark kitchen he can just make out Balu's ribboned box of biscuits, still sitting in the middle of the table.

When he walks out onto the rooftop he doesn't see her immediately; the wounded skylight, still radiant, seems to have consumed all the surrounding light, leaving a black emptiness he cannot peer into. It flits through his mind that the place has been abandoned – doors have been left unlocked, curtains undrawn. He imagines seeing Balu in the morning and saying she has gone, she has left us. Then he senses movement in the darkness and steps towards it, his hands feeling for someone he can recognise.

She hasn't spoken since leaving the hospice, doesn't know how long she has been sitting here. When she got home Jude was gone. The flat was frighteningly tidy and out in the garden there were broken plant pots and a few panes of glass gone from the skylight, so that she could have reached inside the dark restaurant if she'd wanted to. But she has been sitting here for so long that when Hari's arms find her she cannot move; he has to shake her into life, shake the tears from her.

She clings to him. 'He's dead,' she whispers into his shirt, breathing through the fabric the mingled smells of sweat, washing powder and zingy sports deodorant. 'Jozef's dead. And Jude's disappeared. I don't know where he is.'

Ryszard

A sound far away, from somewhere behind, drags her up through fathoms to the surface. She opens her eyes. She is sitting at the table with her head facing the bed, resting on her folded arms. The room is in darkness. She tries to lift her head but it is too heavy.

Someone places a tray silently on the table beside her and she realises she hadn't heard him come in; it was the shudder, the coldness in the air which she felt as the opening door rippled it across to her. She wonders if she can no longer hear but then he picks up a bottle from the tray and she hears the rasp of the lid unscrewing, and the transparent slosh of vodka in two glasses.

'Sarah?' It is half question, half just the sound of her name. A word said. He sits on the side of the bed and gulps a measure down in one mouthful, exhaling the shock of it slowly, looking at her.

She blinks in the light he has brought in with him – for a brief moment forgetting where she is and who he is – and sees that the window has become a deep blue square in the pale wall.

'*Jestés chora?* Are you sick?'

Sarah drags her head up at last and reaches out for a glass of vodka.

She is in Poland, in a town a few miles from Lublin, in the house where Jozef grew up, and the person fixing her now with his intent, concerned gaze is Ryszard, Jozef's great-nephew.

She feels the vodka fill her hollowed-out body and gasps a little at the sudden bite of the alcohol in her mouth and throat. On her cheek is the inverted impression of the knitted texture of her sleeve. She shakes her head.

'No. I'm not sick.'

'You don't sleep at night?'

'No.'

So much has happened recently that Sarah has been in an almost constant state of agitation for weeks. She is starting to feel as if she is living in some tortuous parallel universe which looks the same as the world she ought to be living in but where she is made to function with the briefest snatches of restless sleep, well spaced between heavily draped hour upon hour of wakeful anxiety.

Everything has gone wrong at once. Jozef died much sooner than she had expected and she wasn't really prepared for it. And, the same day, Jude just disappeared. Even now, she doesn't know where he is or whether he intends to come back – he has left her no clue, has simply gone, leaving hardly a trace of himself behind. On that day, when she returned from the hospice to find the minutes-old message on the answering machine saying that Jozef had just died, she went into each room in turn in search of some kind of comfort, but the flat was uncharacteristically tidy. The brimful ashtrays which usually graced at least one surface in each room were gone, and when she pulled the swing top off the kitchen bin and looked inside for the orange, screwed-out stubs that would show, at least, that she hadn't simply been imagining Jude all along, the sack was empty. He had collected up and emptied all the various saucers and little bowls which had gradually been employed as ashtrays during his short tenancy and had meticulously washed them up and put them away, as if it were part of the process of severance from her. She found them in the kitchen cupboard. One, a dainty porcelain gift from a friend years ago who had gone on a trip somewhere or other, she found shining and empty on the mantelpiece. Another, which had started life as a soap dish, she found perched smugly on the side of the bath. She picked it up and sent it hurtling into the corner where it broke in two. Even his smell was gone; she wondered whether he had deliberately opened all the doors and windows while she was not there, erasing all evidence of his presence in her home, determinedly blowing himself out of her life.

'I was just looking at the letters,' she says feebly, putting her empty vodka glass down silently on the tray beside Ryszard's. 'I wish I could read them.'

He pauses noticeably before replying.

'I can read them,' he says levelly, spacing the words out, a little guarded. She looks up at him, a lurching, desperate feeling welling up. She can't be sure he was actually offering.

'Please,' she says. 'Would you?'

He holds out his hand and she passes over the sheet of paper on which she has been unwittingly sleeping. He takes it and she watches him pour himself another half-inch of the vodka before he looks at it.

It is a letter from Ewa, dated 14 April 1939. The handwriting is large and looped, the plentiful Polish 'z's dangling long, seahorse tails into the lines below. The pen she used must have had a wide nib, because the strokes are broad and confident, the uprights thick and sensuous. It's a reckless, rather exuberant hand, difficult to read, she imagines, even in a familiar language. She had been thinking this before she fell asleep, as she was glancing through the six pages which must have been pulled from a notebook – the upper edge of each one is ragged where it has been torn out.

Ryszard clears his throat and carefully scratches his arm, then the back of his neck. She looks at him, suddenly conscious of how curious it must seem to him to have her, a complete stranger, come bursting into his life with the missing pieces of a puzzle which has absorbed him periodically throughout his life – during his childhood, when he first became aware of it, and for a spell during adolescence, when it took on a rather private magic – but which he was certain would never be found. She feels suddenly a little awkward and guilty. She had been so absorbed with finding Jozef's 'own little Westinghouse Capsule' as he had called the box into which he had crammed all Ewa's letters and photographs, his lips stretching in a wide, death's head smile too large for his sunken face.

'Yes,' she says. 'Please.'

Ryszard clears his throat again, studying the letter which is trembling slightly in his long fingers. Then, halting at phrase ends, the words round and fat in his heavily accented English, he begins to translate for her:

My darling,
    I wished for you so much today . . . I really think . . . thought . . . that you may appear to me . . . I want you so . . .

'No!' It is too much. Sarah stops him urgently, leaning forward and grasping his arm, suddenly pained and uncomfortable hearing Ewa's private words to Jozef in a language she understands. 'No.'

160

Ryszard is finding this embarrassing too, perched on the edge of a bare mattress in the empty attic room of his home, reading out a fifty-year-old love letter to a virtual stranger. Especially in a language in which, although competent, he feels unsure and self-conscious.

Right now, Sarah just wants to hear the words as they were written, unstilted and sure. 'Read it as it is. Do you mind?'

'But . . .' She won't understand it; that's what he's about to say.

'It doesn't matter. I just want to hear it.'

He begins again, and the words, freed from meaning, sound almost comforting as they wash over her with their whispery, angular syllables. Ryszard still feels a little awkward. He stands up and turns slightly to one side, not facing her, as if in this way he can distance himself from the words.

Near the end, when Jozef had told her about the wooden box he had sent to his parents' home and wondered aloud whether it still existed, she had known that she would try to find it.

When, after leaving New York, he had returned to his rooms in Warsaw, on the east side of the Wistula River (she has searched for this on Ryszard's map of the city, has found the area, Praga, Jozef told her about) he had found a Chinese enamelled bangle beneath his pillow. The ashtray was still where he had left it on the table and the cigarette ends in it were his and Ewa's combined. 'When I knew she wasn't coming back,' he said, 'I crammed everything to do with her into that box. Letters, photographs, newspaper cuttings, scraps of memorabilia. She had left a scarf draped over the back of a chair. I found hairpins on the table beside the bed; a darning needle threaded with shoe-mending silk which had dropped onto the rug and disappeared into its pattern.

'Everything belonging to her, connected with her, I threw into the box, and when this was done I pushed it under the bed. It stayed there, never quite forgotten, for the duration of the war.'

Towards sunrise they are still together in the close, suffocating air of the little attic room. They have plundered the wooden box, pulling out its viscera, examining yellowing photographs, faded letters and unfolding brittle pages torn from newspapers. Sarah had been tentative, as if fearing that, at her touch, the contents of this time capsule might prove as insubstantial as the air and dust enfolded within them, between them, in the gap beneath the glass of a photograph frame, the space between one word pressed, face down, against another.

She has touched everything. Each envelope, each page, each picture. The glut of textures: the powdery surface of aged paper; the curled yellow newsprint. And the smell of it, and the ink dried on it. The imagined brush of Ewa's hand across the surface as she wrote. Within the fibres Sarah has searched all night for Ewa's scent. The smell of her hair, the perfume transferred from her wrist as her hand hovered over the paper, waiting for the right words. She has fed greedily, a little guiltily, vulnerable in her need to do this.

'Sarah.' Ryszard lifts out two pairs of ballet shoes. One pair tiny, a child's, the other full-sized, made of pink satin, thickly darned and re-darned at the toes in a web of strong silk thread, dirtied and fraying. When Sarah takes them from him they hang heavily from her fingers, trailing long crumpled ribbons. He didn't tell me he had these, she thinks, and feels a ridiculous flush of annoyance at Jozef, and at the arbitrary significance of

162

the things he did tell her. It's all so impossible to hold, to fix, to remember. There is so much she doesn't know. So much that is lost.

She looks again at everything they have emptied out of the box and sorted into little piles on the red carpet and sees for a moment through cold, detached eyes – perhaps Jude's eyes, she thinks – the worthlessness of it all. Ryszard self-consciously places the tiny, flattened shoes side by side on the edge of the rug and it strikes her as the saddest thing she has ever seen, such quiet reverence, and all of it suddenly seems pointless.

'What are we doing?' she asks.

Ryszard freezes in the middle of sorting through a handful of photographs. All of these things are familiar to him; when he was younger he, too, looked through them with the breath-held fascination he has been watching in Sarah for the past hours. He has been too embarrassed to tell her but the beautiful, dark-eyed woman in the photographs fuelled, in the absence of any more robust stimulus, his nascent romantic imagination as a boy. The mysterious dancer who, along with his great-uncle, had disappeared from the face of the earth. His mother hadn't actually ever said so out loud but he had thought privately, later on, that this sloe-eyed beauty must surely have perished in one of the death camps during the war. And this thought had added a tragic lustre to his innocent first love. He remembers his mother being, for a time, quite taken with trying to find her uncle and discover what had happened to the woman. The letters in the box stopped suddenly in April 1939, and the most recent clue was a newspaper report on the return of the Balets Polski to Warsaw in August 1939 after a successful visit to New York. That was where it stopped. So, his great-uncle's dancer had returned to Poland and – what?

Sarah is staring at him, the pair of ballet shoes now clasped on her lap. He puts the photographs down and, aware that he is blushing as she watches him, straightens them into a neat little bundle on the rug.

'What are we doing?' she asks again.

He looks at her. For the briefest moment, he thinks he sees this young woman through the eyes of his great-uncle. Of course! There is, in the shape of her face, the slight almond slant of her eyes, a flicker of something recognisable. When she told him about her first meeting with Jozef he had hardly taken it in, but now he recognises it for himself, fleetingly. And then it is gone, and she is just Sarah again, an English girl whom he has known of for just over two weeks and met less than forty-eight hours ago.

She stands up now, all resemblance to Ewa gone for the moment, and sits on the edge of the mattress. He stays where he is, kneeling on the rug, surrounded by the spoils of their plunder. He has an idea of how Sarah is feeling: sickened and guilty with over-indulgence. They have looked at everything, just as his mother did years ago, and she is feeling guilty, intrusive, blundering into the buried past and stirring it all up again. Maybe that was why his mother had given up on it in the end. Maybe it was just too sad; too old and sad and lost. But going through the box with Sarah, watching the care with which she touched, unfolded and seemed to caress each letter and each photograph with her eyes, has rekindled his interest in it all, as if she has somehow transformed it into something new and exciting.

'Have you got a girlfriend?' she blurts out in the middle of this thought.

Ryszard feels the tingle of a blush again, and fights to keep it down. There's something about the way she looks at him that unnerves him.

'No,' he says. 'No. Not at the moment. There was . . .' He smiles, absolutely sure she doesn't want to hear about that right now. 'No,' he says again, decisively.

'Me neither,' she says, with mock brightness. 'A boyfriend, I mean. At least I don't think so.' She is twisting and untwisting the ribbon of one of the ballet shoes around her finger. He can feel his heartbeat twitching in his neck. He's not sure what to say.

'How do you tell that it's over?' she asks, and as she speaks the tears spring into her eyes and she seems not to be able to hold them back. He jumps up and sits beside her, pulling her to him. She rests her head against him briefly then pulls away, the tears stopping almost as soon as they started. She is still fiddling with the ribbon, wrapping it round her finger like a bandage, then unwrapping it and pulling it straight.

'The more I know Jude the less I know him,' she says. 'It's like we've worked backwards to the first time we met and now there's nothing. I don't know him. I don't feel as if I've ever known him, and now I'm here and I don't know what I'm doing here when I can't even know him. How near to someone can you get?'

Ryszard says nothing.

'We never spoke about Jozef once, you know, not anything about how it was, how it came about, how I felt – even how *he* felt. It just wasn't said. I don't know what it was. What is it that makes people shut themselves off like that?'

She seems suddenly tiny and dishevelled; too much alcohol, he thinks, and too little sleep. She is probably exhausted. She looks apologetically at him.

165

'Why don't I just shut up?'

Warsaw was utterly destroyed during the war. She hadn't known that. When she arrived on the coach and made her way across the city to catch a train to Jozef's town, she peered closely at the solid, old-looking buildings in amazement, remembering what he had said about it.

'When the city was finally liberated, there was nothing left; it was like Hiroshima, only that hadn't happened yet. If you go there now it looks exactly as it did, but it's all new. The whole city was rebuilt afterwards, brick for brick, the same as it had been. It took ten years.'

Just before the liberation, he told her, he pulled the box out from under his bed and posted it to his parents' house near Lublin with no letter, no explanation. Just a box full of scraps. For his few remaining days in Warsaw, waiting for the Russians to come and liberate the city, he had felt as he had when he first arrived there as a young student: unencumbered, free, alone. Ready for a new life to begin.

His parents had, perhaps, opened the box, thinking that it was a gift from the son they scarcely ever saw. Puzzled, they must have riffled through the letters and worn-out ballet shoes, looked at each other and replaced the lid without exchanging a word. Maybe they had thought he would come to collect it.

Sarah had written to the address Jozef had spelt out for her, too weak, by then, to write it for her himself. He hadn't known if any of his family were still there and she hadn't expected a reply. She addressed it to nobody in particular, simply to the

'Wojciech family'. When a letter in a thin envelope with a Polish stamp eventually slid through the letterbox in the street door of the lifeless flat above the Mountain of Light, she had seen it as some kind of salvation.

൭

She wakes and goes down to the kitchen for some water, drinking it at the sink. It is afternoon. The cold filters down to her stomach and sits there so she can almost feel the shape of it.

Through the window she can see movement. Without directly looking she knows that it is a group of three or four shirtless men laying concrete. Marking out areas in metres squared with lengths of wood which they hammer into place with stakes and mallets. She saw them there yesterday, skimming over the top of the soft new surface to level it. Bursts of crouching and sweating concentration were interspersed with smoking and laughter; they would wipe their hands on the fronts of their trousers, the colour of cement, and tighten their shirts which were tied round their waists and light up. Without going over to the window as she did on the first day she was here, drawn by the long gash of light in the cool room, she knows that the concreted area will have grown a little, the rough earth blanketed, sealed up to be impervious to weather. They will have to allow for rain, she thought yesterday. They will have to make it slope into a gully and down to a grid. They will have to make allowances for the weather. Now, staring down at her bare feet on the dark tiles, she remembers thinking this. She stands as still as she can, seeing the window shape of sunlight slanting towards her across the floor.

167

The first day she was here, the day before yesterday, she came into this strange new room and found the window, made it her first point of contact.

'*Proszę,*' Ryszard's grandmother said, nodding encouragement, and she came over to help Sarah with the catch. The first window opened inwards into the room and the second pair creaked outwards, juddering from the force of her unaccustomed touch. One of the workmen saw her and shouted across to her. She wasn't sure how to reply. His words caused the others to raise their eyes from their work and they sauntered over to the window, their voices mingling together, their faces silhouetted in the bright sunlight, so she couldn't see which one was speaking. She shrank from the opening a little then, hoping her plump hostess would fill her space and shift into easy talk. Half hidden, she met their foreign greetings and their proffered handshakes as her arrival, her Englishness, her visit, was briefly explained to them.

And then she sat down at the kitchen table with Ryszard, who had met her at the station just two hours earlier, and his grandmother, and they drank hot, black tea. As his grandmother pulled out some of what she remembered about her lost, much missed brother, Ryszard translated her words for Sarah, so everything that was said took twice as long. But she found comfort in the slowness of it, the necessary precision, and the methodical way in which Ryszard, every now and then, would gently stop his grandmother and repeat what she had said to Sarah so that the balance of telling and understanding was kept more or less constant. As the old woman spoke, Sarah listened to her thready voice, its mysterious cadences and pauses and repetitions, and watched as she carefully stirred a spoonful of cherry jam round and round in her tea until it dissolved.

At one point she became tearful and seemed angry, her voice high and querulous. Ryszard put his hand on her shoulder and left it there. Sarah made to leave the room, feeling that it must be her arrival, her news of Jozef's death, but Ryszard gestured her to stay. When the old lady was calmer and was carefully dabbing her apron into the corners of her eyes and sniffing, Ryszard explained that she wasn't angry with her but with Jozef, her stubborn brother. How like him, she had said, to act as if he were all alone when he had a perfectly good family who would have been overjoyed to see him. He had chosen to go away and leave them. When had he ever spared a thought for what they had gone through here in Poland? There were plenty of people who genuinely didn't have anyone left after the war, and here was this poor girl spending all her time with him as if he had no family at all, feeling sorry for him . . .

The old lady took a deep breath and put her glasses back on – she had been polishing them ferociously with her apron as Ryszard was speaking. Then she looked up at Sarah and reached out to her, touching her cheek softly with the back of her fingers.

She looked across at Ryszard and said something else.

'She says she's sorry for getting upset,' he said, as the old lady rose stiffly from her chair and went to fill the kettle. 'It isn't your fault. She says you are very welcome here.'

Ryszard's grandmother, whom he calls Babcia, last saw her brother in October 1937 when he came to see his family on a brief visit from Warsaw. When their parents died, the house was passed on to her alone because there seemed little point in leaving a share of it to someone who might be dead for all they knew. Once the hope had faded that Jozef might follow the box he had sent, it had lain, more or less forgotten, under the single bed in what his sister continued to refer to as 'Jozef's room'. Years later, her daughter found it as she decorated the room for the son she was carrying. She gave the contents of the box a cursory scan and then found someone to carry it upstairs into one of the attic rooms for her. She stowed it in the bottom of a cupboard, her mind too much on other things to be bothered with dusty memorabilia. When her son, Ryszard, was a child he found it while hiding in the attic cupboard during a tantrum, and thought he had discovered hidden treasure. The tantrum was forgotten entirely, and his grandmother – who had no idea the box existed – and mother had pored over the old letters while Ryszard trailed a long chiffon scarf across the room and played with the Chinese bangle.

This sketchy family story is familiar to Ryszard; he has grown up with it. He scarcely needs his grandmother there to remember the details, she told it to him so many times during his childhood. The blank areas, the gaps, are as substantial now as the facts; somehow the mystery had become a part of his family, weaving itself into them so that it had almost held them together when he was a child. And it had been especially fascinating for him. Hadn't Jozef's old room, closed up for so many years as if waiting for him to come home, been opened up again only when he himself was born? There had always been, in his mind, a connection between the two of them because of this. And he had spent hours poring over the box of letters and photographs. But all in all it had always raised far more questions than it had answered.

When he received the letter from London he had not looked

at the box for more than ten years; his mother and grandmother had long wearied of the blind alleys it led them up and had abandoned their quest. His mother had gone to her grave less than a year ago knowing no more about her mysterious, romantic uncle than she had discovered the day Ryszard had hidden in the cupboard, and his grandmother, he was sure, had all but forgotten about her brother. Even he had tired of it eventually, and had, at some point, put it back in the cupboard in the attic room. But when Sarah's letter arrived, he had run up the stairs two at a time, the letter still clasped in his hand, and pulled the heavy bedstead away from the cupboard door. He took out the box and set it down in the middle of the floor. He decided not to open it until the English girl arrived, for she had known the mysterious recipient of all those letters, the great-uncle he had never met, whom they had all, after so many years, almost stopped wondering about. He felt there was something ceremonious and solemn about all this happening just now, when the house he had grown up in, always full of life and people, or ghosts of people, was suddenly his alone, with only his grandmother left for company.

The kitchen now is silent and empty. Like sand beneath the constant coming and going of a tide, it weathers its peaks and troughs of activity and stillness, the arrangement of its parts shifting as plates move from cupboard to table to draining board, and cutlery is dispersed, laid out, and gathered together again, all forks and knives and dessert spoons jumbled, then segregated in wooden drawer compartments. Ryszard's grandmother as she moves around it preparing breakfast, dinner, supper. Her ease. She is in her element, singing to herself, or along with some tune on the radio which Sarah thinks she must turn on when she is alone. There is something about her oneness with her surroundings that makes Sarah think of Balu in his beloved restaurant and she feels a stab of affection for him. She remembers him waving her off as she walked away towards the bus stop, towards another country, with her rucksack on her back. Just before she rounded the corner she turned and saw him still there, watching her till she was out of sight.

Just like Balu, Babcia's movements in her kitchen are fluid, familiar. As she straightens up from replacing a colander or a pan in a cupboard she closes the door and, knowing that without her intervention it will sag on its hinges and not close properly, she hitches it up a little with her toe and nudges it into place, supporting herself with one hand on the edge of the cooker. Only she, Ryszard says, can cook a perfectly risen sponge cake in the ancient oven. She slams the door and tucks a tea towel round the edges with the blunt blade of a butter knife to seal up the gaps where the rubber has perished. She turns on the taps and a stream of water flows for her obediently. When Sarah tried to fill the kettle on her first morning here the tap hissed and spat, setting off a shuddering and thumping spasm deep within the pipes. Babcia laughed and tapped the side of her nose conspiratorially. She beckoned to her and showed her how to turn it gently, slowly, to coax it into submission. Having divulged one of the many secrets of her domain, the old lady hovered anxiously as Sarah tried again and was rewarded with a silent, steady stream which widened obediently and flowed down the plughole.

'She has never shown me how to do this,' Ryszard announced from the table in his lilting, precise English. 'She tells me I am an intruder in her kitchen. You are a woman. You are different.' He was smiling, happy that his grandmother accepted this thin, questing stranger; welcomed her, as someone long-expected, into her home.

The kitchen now is as it was then, the day before yesterday, when she followed the old woman into its still, silent embrace and stepped across the floor to the window.

When she steps back from the sink she stands absolutely still on the cold, pristine tiles and watches the fading footprints she has left behind, pressing her feet together – they fit exactly into the space of one tile – and feeling the bone against bone of her ankles and knees.

Last night's vodka has left her leaden and exhausted. It is afternoon. Two thirty, maybe three. Babcia is probably out shopping. Ryszard is at work. She has the huge silence of the house to herself. She thinks fleetingly of home; it must be nearing four o'clock. She wonders where Jude is, whether he is still in London or has gone off somewhere. What is he doing? Is he happy, glad to be away from her? Or does he miss her? Does he wish all of this hadn't happened?

၈

Balu tips a teaspoon of salt into the heavy stone mortar and adds a bulb of garlic, unpackaged from its tight layers of papery thin skin and broken into cloves. He cracks them open against the worktop in handfuls with the weight of the *batta*, roughly picks away the red inner skin and throws the fat, bruised flesh in with the salt. The texture and grain of the salt helps him pound it to a creamy, smooth pulp, releasing a heavy, sticky pungency. It is a particularly fresh bulb and the smell is sharp, hitting the back of his palate instantly with a menthol-like punch which brings a film of tears to his eyes.

There's a stillness about the place today, he thinks. He can feel the absence in the flat upstairs. It's more than Sarah being away; it's everything that has changed between these young people he cares so much about. He has never been sure he understands any of them really; of course they have their youth as a unifying thread between them, something which has always excluded him a little, kept him separate from them, and left him unsure of the inferences, the points of reference which they so comfortably share. But now he has a sense that there was no solidity in it after all. That the unity he had sometimes almost envied was chimeric. All at once it cracked apart and their lives veered away in opposite directions.

He is probably worrying too much. Young people have to have their crises, have to find their place in the world. That dreadful evening when Jude left, that unexplained conflict with Hari that he had witnessed on the roof above was past, would become unimportant and be forgotten. The broken panes of glass in the skylight were already replaced. He thinks back to his own passage into the comfort of routine and limited expectation, the relief, really, that comes with the passing of innocent hopefulness. He had been desolate at first, when he discovered his marriage was not to be. He had yearned for a renewal of love, or another love, had seen it as his due. Had been unwilling to believe that the brief shimmer he had felt was all there was going to be. That love was already over. Soon after starting work at the restaurant he had met someone whom he thought might replace his lost wife-to-be. She was the sister of one of the other waiters. Had been here longer than he had, a year or so, even though she was younger, and she had taken pity on him and spent time with him. Innocent hopefulness had not yet left Balu and he had mistaken her pity for something else. One day in the park he had tried to tell her about his burgeoning feelings. She had been very kind, but there had been no more walks in the park.

He reaches for a saucer of chopped ginger next and scrapes it onto the wooden chopping board, deciding that he must chop it a little more finely before tipping it in with the garlic, or it will be too fibrous and spoil the texture of the dish he is preparing. He attacks it with a straight, two-handled knife, anchoring one end with a finger and thumb and rapidly chopping up and down with the other, scraping the little pile together after each flurry of chopping and then going over it again until he is satisfied the pieces are small enough. Then he lifts the board, scrapes it clean over the mortar and begins pounding again.

He feels glad to be away from all the urgency of the young. He watches Hari sometimes as he is working and he doesn't envy him at all. Oh, he knows there's fun to be had, but you have to know how to find it. And there will always be pain and disappointment however much else you can squeeze out of it. All in all, it is so very much easier when you hope for nothing at all and seek a more solid fulfilment elsewhere.

He can feel his shirt sticking to the back of his neck, and his upper lip feels cool with beaded sweat. The garlic and ginger are satisfactorily blended with the salt – he tries a bit with his finger, feeling for lumps, but there are none. He lays the pestle down beside the mortar and has a short rest before continuing. He wishes he was able to do this preparation sitting down, these days, but he has never been able to. Like his mother he has always preferred to stand and it's too late now to change.

He wipes his moist forehead with the back of his hand. He

wonders sometimes whether it's worth it. Having someone. Another person who knows you almost as well as you know yourself. He thinks maybe too much store is set by it, too much time spent searching. After all, he has lived his whole life without that special someone and his life has not been bad. Maybe he was just destined to be self-sufficient.

ॐ

In the empty attic room she finds the fragments of Jozef's life with Ewa scattered as she and Ryszard left them on the carpet when they finally went to bed, just before dawn. She picks her way through them and opens the shutters, suddenly aware of the dust she has caused to circulate in the stifling room. She remembers how, last night, Ryszard had been there with her for nearly an hour before he suddenly jumped up without a word and closed them. Her head has started to swim and she lies down slowly on the stripped bed.

The letter Ryszard read out loud to her, pushed carefully back inside its envelope, is on top of the fat dictionary he had brought up from downstairs at some point during their long night. She leans over and picks up one of the American news-paper cuttings from the floor, remembering her jubilation the previous night at finding something written in English. She reads it again, slowly.

Polish Ballet Sets Crowds Cheering at Fair's Hall of Music
by Burns Mantle

There was a good deal of excitement at the fair last night. The culture group was having an inning at the Hall of

Music and the Polish Ballet was making its first American appearance. Last night's program started with a dance arrangement fitted by Bronislawa Nizinska to the E Minor Concerto of Frederic Chopin, a fine opening as the program suggested for a Polish Ballet. The second number was a colorful romance to do with the wedding of a gay mountain girl which was interrupted by a bold dashing brigand. The brigand, with the help of his followers, abducts the willing bride and carries her off to camp. 'Harnasie' was the title. Here setting, costuming and choreography are vigorous and stirringly alive. The primitive folk dances of the mountaineers, the challenging wild figures of the brigands, set to a lively, interpretive and typically racial score by Karol Szymanowski . . .

Scribbled in the yellowed margin in pencil is '*Daily News*, June 7, 1939'. Is that Jozef's handwriting? She realises that she has never seen his handwriting. The paper is brittle where it has been folded and then smoothed out. If she holds it up to the window she can see pinholes of light. She wonders whether he tore the article out of someone else's paper and folded it into his inside pocket, carrying it around with him all day in New York.

Karol Szymanowski. *Szymanowski*. She practises saying the word as Ryszard has taught her. She enjoys the feel of it in her mouth, angular and sibilant. She stretches out her arm and drops the cutting back onto the floor. She wonders, sleepily, whether she could buy the piece of music when she gets back to London.

She watches dust particles in the air, seeming neither to have been forced up from the mattress when she sat down on it, nor to be in the process of resettling. She thinks of home, of Jude, of Hari and Balu. Her garden. The Mountain of Light. She remembers them now as if she is remembering another, a different, life. This life, here, seems tidy, containable, like a role in a play or a novel, where characters' lives are cushioned within the text, their actions propelled by a series of clearly defined purposes. She has no roots here, no connections, and she is temporarily severed from her usual orbit. She likes the neatness of it, yet she knows it is illusory, that she has not simply walked out of her own life, and that even if she wished to it would never be as simple as just going somewhere else. There are, wherever you go, those threads of history that hang between people in a huge, transparent web. She wonders whether Jude feels this too, or whether he is different and is really able to start again.

But this pared-down feeling of separateness she feels at the moment is refreshing and calming. She finds pleasure in the absence of material possessions which usually weigh her down, pin her to a spot, to an identity. She relishes the spareness of what is contained in the one bag she has brought with her. A few changes of clothes. Basic toiletries. Her passport, a couple of biros, a notebook and *Anna Karenina*.

She lies on the bare mattress, staring up at the ceiling. Dust flecks are still moving above her head, flickering and disappearing as their angles catch the light. It is fiendishly hot. She wonders if it is as hot at home, and then sits up suddenly, remembering the time she and Hari escaped from the heat of her flat into the garden and ended up lying naked in the rain. She feels restless again. She wishes it would rain here. Downstairs she wanders into the high-ceilinged room which seems to be used for 'best'. The room is furnished in an old-fashioned style – lots of lace doilies and antimacassars draped over the chair backs. There is a huge vase of lilies on a small, fussy table in front of one of the windows and the room is filled with their sweet, slightly nauseating scent. The windows are all closed, as if the house is empty, and the air feels thick and heavy. She closes the door again and goes back up to the attic room.

ᏀᎧ

Puffing slightly from the climb up the fire escape, Balu unlocks the flat door and walks into Sarah's kitchen. Sita, who had leapt up from the wall she was sunning herself on and raced up the steps ahead of him and then waited for him at the top, slowly stands and stretches and stalks in behind him. He sits down heavily on one of the kitchen chairs, feeling the veins throbbing in his forehead, his mouth dry and slightly numb. Sita marches up and down in front of him, catching his dangling hand with the tip of her nose, the corner of her mouth and one side of her body on each turn. Balu feels the length of her tail pull through his fingers.

As she eats, he permits himself a quick glance into the living room, telling himself he only wants to check how the skylight looks after its repair. He hasn't been in the flat alone since he lived here and, as he opens the door and remembers that it is someone else's home, he feels something which makes his stomach lurch and all at once he wishes he had never left, had never moved to Enfield, to the soulless house that doesn't feel like home, where he feels he has to ask before he leaves his shoes in the hall or hangs his washing out to dry.

And there's more. Hadn't he promised himself, after the success of the skylight – his idea – that he wouldn't allow himself to be persuaded into doing what others had already decided was best for him? Yet his resolve had weakened at the very first hurdle; he had allowed his brother and Sharmila to frighten him, to use his angina to persuade him that he really oughtn't to be living alone, that he would be much better off living with them.

He feels ungrateful thinking this. It's just that being here reminds him . . . He unfastens the shutters and looks at the garden through the glass. The bright green leaves of the skinny acacia tree brush silently against the window in a stiff breeze which thrills through the fennel fronds, and even the sturdy red geraniums twitch every now and again. He looks at the ground and finds it dancing with lacy shadows. He should water the plants really, Sarah has been away for days and he hasn't done it yet. I'll ask Hari, he thinks. He will do what I cannot manage.

ॐ

Sarah looks up at the tiny, high window. The view of nothing but sky. Wonders if coming here was such a good idea after all. It is just so hot. And she is wary of going out on her own. What else should she do while she is here? She isn't entirely sure why she *is* here. Maybe she should just pack everything into the box, push it back into its cupboard, and go home now. Try to sort things out. Find Jude. But she knows it isn't as simple as that. Somehow, she just needs to be here now. Or at least needs to be somewhere that isn't home. She used Jozef to give her flight a purpose, but she knows that there is more to it than just tying up those ends. There are ends of her own which need to be cauterised, sealed off and made safe, made bearable. But she knows she can't stay here forever. She sits down and slaps the palms of her hands down on the table. On the ceiling a circular shave of light pulsates and shifts from side to side, the water in a forgotten glass from yesterday agitated by her sudden movement.

At six o'clock she hears Ryszard's careful tread on the stairs. His tentative steps as he approaches her. She can smile to herself about the fact that he seems to be a little in awe of her.

He comes into the room and stands just inside the door, closing it without turning away from her, leaving his finger-tips pressed against it behind him, a gesture which makes him appear needlessly deferential. He looks different, older, in his work clothes. He pulls at his tie to loosen it.

'Babcia says you have not eaten today.'

She looks at him and smiles, noticing how anxious he looks at the edge of the room.

'Aren't you going to come in and sit down?'

He relaxes a little at her voice. Funny, she thinks; this is his house and yet he is standing there by the door like a trespasser. She, on the other hand, has spent the entire day in the room and has become acquainted with it. Throughout the morning she has heard people and trams in the street below, and at midday the sun streaming through the window threw a bright rhombus onto the opposite wall. At some point in the afternoon she sat down on the colourless mattress, which was stained yellow in places and sagged in the middle from the weight of bodies that had slept on it, and studied the texture of irregularities in the plaster beneath the wallpaper.

Ryszard is still standing at the door looking at her. She stares down at the rug, noticing the pattern, the colours in it, the worn areas where the weave shows through.

'Would you like something to eat?' he asks, and the kindness which spills out of him with his words makes the tears start in her eyes.

'Thank you. Yes, that would be nice.'

There is something about his quiet practicality which reminds her of Hari, and she likes that. He is looking out for her the way she has sometimes seen Hari look out for Balu, making sure he doesn't take too much on, taking over from him, giving him the opportunity to escape if there is a difficult situation with customers. Ryszard has obviously come home and come straight upstairs to see her without a second thought. She feels pleased he is preoccupied with her wellbeing and can't stop herself from smiling because of it.

'Well, what would you like?' Now that he has seen her smile he sits down on the chair, his shoulders hunching over inside the suit jacket. She doesn't know; she doesn't really want anything, is only being polite. 'Come on. Come with me and see,' he says, joking with her, standing up and holding out his hand to her as if she were a child. She smiles again. 'Come on. Babcia has been shopping. You must help us eat everything. She always buys far too much. Come. No more hiding!' He holds the door open and, her reluctance gone, she stands up and follows him down the stairs.

ॐ

They hadn't been able to make love. It was a Sunday morning and she could remember that six months ago, six weeks ago even, it hadn't been like this.

Before Jude, when Hari finished at the restaurant, she knew instinctively the time to rouse herself from whatever she was doing and listen for his steps juddering on the fire escape, and his cautious, polite knock on the kitchen door. It wasn't a physical rousing – she would stay exactly where she was, would continue languidly reading, stretched lengthways on the sofa, a cushion behind her head, but her immersion would become gradually less profound as she rose from her solitude like a surfacing diver, to the moment of their embrace. And the moment before that when, as she fumbled with the key, she pushed up the blind with her other hand and saw his face distorted through the rippled glass. The last inches of water before she reached the surface and breathed. There had never been any doubt then that he would come. When it ended, it had not ended like that. She had always been sure of him.

Hari had never stayed all night, so Sunday mornings were not something she could connect with him, but she had cherished the silent endlessness of Sunday mornings spent with Jude.

The day she remembers now was no different from any other Sunday to start with. They woke and fell asleep again without being aware of it, let alone of each other. When she turned onto her side away from him he followed and she felt the soft, dry penis warm against her buttocks, and his arm stretched out straight beneath her neck so that, if she opened her eyes, she could look along its length as though she were looking along the barrel of a rifle. His hand was turned palm down against the sheet so the unconscious fingers could not twitch and furl in his sleep. She felt him wake, heard the rise to consciousness in his breathing and wondered if he knew that she, too, was awake. She stayed still, trying not to break through the skin of the day, remembering how, at one time, they had been unable to get enough of each other and would have relished a morning like this. His other arm was resting across her, around her, trapping her arm against her side so that, had she not been so comfortably sleepy she might have felt confined and moved away from him to an area where the sheets were cool against her cheek and her legs and she could turn onto her belly, enclosing herself, clasping her arms somehow at her chest, carefully, like a cat tucking in its feet.

He took a deeper breath and tensed both his arms so that the one beneath her raised her head a little. He brought the outstretched hand of the upper arm to her and pressed it hard against her belly. She felt his penis stir. With two brisk movements she lay on her back. Yes, I'm awake, she thought. Now I'm awake.

There was an inkling of desire, of arousal, which she could feel rise and subside as palpably as if it were a wave of nausea. But in it there was a lethargy which she tried to attribute to being only half awake, but knew that that was not really it. There was something else between them, isolating them, encasing them, something that could not include the other. She didn't know what it was.

She had wanted to make love. The thought of it had appealed. It was the thought of it that caught the waxing of her arousal, but the reality of it, his presence, the close heat from his body making her suddenly too hot, his eager erection, brought about its wane.

It's my bad mood, she had thought. It's me. And they did not make love that morning, though they stayed in bed in each other's arms off and on, passing overlapping shifts of sleep between them, until the afternoon when suddenly he got up from the bed and left the room.

There was no antagonism in their scarcely having spoken all the rest of that grey afternoon. No reason. She had been reading, sitting cross-legged just within the circle of light from the lamp. He had seemed peripheral. She had made him seem so deliberately perhaps. They had both, in a way, spent the day alone, and yet she had been glad that she was not alone.

꩜

She has ventured out alone, to a park Ryszard brought her to the first evening she was here and has dragged her out of the house to every evening since.

She sits down at the edge of the ornamental lake and stares into the sluggish water. It seems viscous, like half-set jelly, and the slight breeze can scarcely move the small rafts of twigs and drinking straws, the ducks' feathers, leaves, and swollen, watery pieces torn from slices of bread which are suspended in the top inches of its surface like dead flies in resin.

Deeper, she catches the sudden, lambent flicker of tiny, silver-coloured fish moving beneath the sun-dazzled surface. Their cool, willow-leaf bodies move together as if they are feathers or nacreous scales on the dorsal ridge of some much larger creature, shimmering as it glides and turns, catching the light. She remembers gazing down through the skylight at home and thinking it was a little like peering into water, giving quick flashes, glimpses of passing shapes, creatures in an underwater world, as they moved silently beneath her. She would sometimes watch until she saw somebody familiar – Balu's rolling, gentle gait as he walked down the restaurant

185

checking that everything was all right, or Hari, deft and assured, his movements never more than they needed to be, never extravagant like Jude's sometimes were. Her thoughts fix on Hari; he wouldn't be able to sit here like this, she thinks. All around her, pigeons are whirring their wings and strutting up and down, murmuring deep in their throats and blinking their expressionless, orange-rimmed eyes at her before they dip their beaks into the water. Hari hates pigeons, hates their whistling, clapping wings and mangled feet. He would have waved them away, or stalked off to sit somewhere else by now.

She has forgotten to wear her watch and as she sits at the water's edge the thick summer afternoon moves seamlessly into evening, the heat unabating. When she feels the numbness of sitting too long in one place she stretches her arms above her head, yawning, and lowers them slowly, flexing her wrists, hearing the bones creak. Her sudden movement sends several pigeons wheeling vertically into the air. She feels the draught from their wings fan her face. Hari would wince at that, she thinks. He would think the air contaminated, like the air that follows a tramp, foetid with the ripe, sweet odour of an unwashed body.

When she blinks she sees the outline of the little shrubby island, around the hem of which she has watched sun-basking ducks drift lazily all afternoon with their heads tucked onto their backs, one reptilian eyelid opening and closing periodically in acknowledgement of the shadows of birds overhead and the beating of their wings breaking the skin of silence.

She has been feeling the press of silence in the empty house. When Babcia is around she follows her like a puppy and they mime conversations with each other, using Ryszard's big dictionary, which Sarah hugs to her chest whenever she goes in search of the old woman, to try to communicate in single words. Babcia laughs girlishly when they are alone together and corrects her pronunciation, and Sarah does the same when Babcia attempts to speak English. One giggly afternoon they learnt the names of everything they could point to in the kitchen in each other's language. But today Babcia had errands to run and Sarah had not spoken all day. Suddenly she jumped up, ran down the stairs, out of the house, and fled into the throb and heat of the peopled park, seeking moisture, the lushness of bankside shrubs, damp, dark earth. She was sick of the dry, papery existence in that room with the yellowed newspapers and letters, and Ryszard's neat English handwriting translating Ewa's words into blue biro. She hated the dust and the awful eviscerated trunk whose contents were spilt shamelessly across the floor.

She stands unsteadily, feeling the dampness in her skirt where it has been tucked behind her knees. She steps over the railings and starts to walk across the grass into the shelter of the trees. She is cooled by the slight draught her motion causes and it feels wonderful. She spreads her fingers wide and runs them through the air, wishing she had thought to come out here earlier, instead of spending most of the day cooped up inside. It is darker among the trees, between the dark solidity of trunks and the earth-smelling paths of deep, perpetual shadow. Her eyes, used to the sharpness of the sun on the water, and the heat beating out from the cracked grey concrete, draw a blind of emerald and aquamarine down over themselves and, momentarily, she can see nothing. She feels a little intoxicated with the heat; her feet feel heavy and dragging, and her head is thumping unpleasantly, but the coolness she has entered is like water. It reminds her of when she was a child. Running in from the garden in her orange bathing suit (with a white pleated skirt round it that made her feel like a ballerina, a daisy) shiny-limbed from jumping into puddles in the grass, sprayed by the watering hose. Her bare feet on the cold kitchen linoleum and the smell of clean-scrubbed wood and stems of lilac in a vase. The kitchen never saw the sun, and she would run in there, roasting, mad for its coolness, and for half a minute she would stand still and just feel the changed air on her skin before running out again into the sunshine.

She walks as slowly as she can between the close-standing trees. In the green-tinged shade of outspread leaves the air is even stiller. She has been so consumed with the box full of Jozef's things she feels she has almost forgotten there is a world outside, which has nothing to do with it. She feels as if the stone which settled inside her when Jozef died and Jude disappeared has dissolved a little. There are people in the park who have nothing to do with what has happened to her; ahead, out in the sunshine beyond the trees, two children are chasing each other, running in giddy circles around their mothers who are sitting together on the grass, laughing. She feels released by them, as if, somehow, permission has been granted for her to start living again. She knows that Ryszard is worried about her; he thinks she is spending too much time alone in the attic room. He insists on taking days off work, has suggested they maybe take a trip somewhere. He tells her it would be silly to come to a whole new country and have nothing to remember but the inside of one bare room when she leaves, and she is starting to see that he might be right.

* * *

She needed to get out of the house, Ryszard could see that, and he was growing impatient with the fact that she couldn't see it too. It was obvious: no good could come from her mooching around the house all day thinking about the boyfriend who had disappeared and going through that box of old stuff over and over again. He was beginning to tire of it, all the loose ends and unfinished business which were keeping her strung as taut as a wire, and was starting to wish the two of them had just met in ordinary circumstances and could get to know each other normally, instead of wading around in the past as if it were so much more valuable than the present.

It was the first thing that occurred to him, to take her to the place where the photograph of Ewa with the swans was taken. Afterwards he wondered whether it was an altogether wise suggestion, what with her being so obsessed with the whole story anyway; this would only make it worse. But it was a lure. He felt that if only she could be got away from spending day after day closeted away in that room she would gain some colour, would start to see him as another person, here and now, not dead, not lost, but right in front of her, alive and eager and . . . The lure was just to get her away. Then they could just be themselves, and perhaps . . .

His idea was to find the pier, the exact place where the picture had been taken, and he would photograph her. He knew that this made their whole trip laden with implication but he couldn't think of anything else, off the top of his head, that would be likely to get her to leave the house, and he was tired of trying to think of ways of tempting her out of herself. Anyway, wasn't the photograph of his great-uncle's dancer surrounded by swans on a beach the one that had always fascinated him the most when he was younger? He could indulge himself too, couldn't he? Especially now, with Sarah's appearance in his home with the missing parts of the family story. It, she, was so unexpected, so utterly enthralling, that he felt a little foolishness was justified. This sort of thing didn't usually happen. And so, if he behaved a little unusually, it was because of the situation. Because it was outside the normal, the expected pattern of things.

It worked; she agreed to go on the night train to Gdańsk and then get another train west to Sopot, the seaside town where Jozef and Ewa had gone, in the days when the rich and famous went there to be seen.

ॐ

Jude wakes up slowly, a creeping deadness working its way through his veins, his body leaden, weighed down with poor sleep. He has spent the whole night in the same position, curled on one side facing the wall, and the protrusion of his hip bone feels bruised, the arm he has been lying on for hours, dead. Without opening his eyes he straightens his legs and shuffles over onto his left side, dragging the thin cocoon of sleeping bag with him, banging his elbow awkwardly on the floor, making the funnybone fizz. His body aches at the movement; it bears the marks of these nomadic nights spent on floors, his knees and each knobble of his spine darkened by a full rainbow of bruises.

Tentatively he blinks his eyes open; he can't remember whose floor he is on – he has spent the night in so many different places since packing his things into the rucksack and army kitbag he had arrived with and walking out of Sarah's flat. He notices something flashing repeatedly, at the outside edge of his vision, and turns to see a video recorder on the floor beside his head. It must have been switched off at some point and the unset time, a row of green zeros, flashes off and on, off and on, irritatingly regular.

The day after tomorrow he won't have seen Sarah for three weeks. He thinks of her now as he last saw her, crouching on the kitchen floor, forking out cat food from a tin. Her closed face turned briefly to him with a curt, 'See you later.' How is she right now? What is she doing? He imagines her in her garden. Sitting there alone, wondering where he is. And then Hari stalks into his head and anchors himself beside her and he has almost physically to shake his head to get rid of him.

He sits up. All of this is stupid, of course. He doesn't even know, really, who he is angry with. But the old man is just an old man and it's easier to hate Hari, easier to imagine that relationship than the other.

The basement room he is in has no curtains and he looks out at the early dawn light in the narrow, overgrown back garden as a train full of commuters rips by, so close he can feel it through the floor, can see the heads of the people inside it as it tears past the backs of row after row of dreary, South London streets.

He's tired of this. Tired of London and dragging himself up from some floor or sofa every morning and washing in an inch of tepid water. He can't do it any more and, suddenly, he feels a powerful urge to be away from here altogether. Away from Sarah and Hari and the old man, who is probably dead by now, and the whole fucking mess and really get away. He wriggles out of the sleeping bag and stands up, swaying slightly as he rummages through the kitbag for his damp towel.

ఌ

It is five thirty in the morning. Sarah sits down on a wooden platform bench, exhausted from the effort of waking up and dressing in a moving train carriage, and waits for Ryszard to tell her what to do. They are soon alone, the train rapidly empties and its sleep-crumpled passengers scuttle off into the encroaching Gdańsk day.

She feels as if she is riveted to the bench. She has no inclination to move, even to turn her head as another train draws up beside the one they have just got off. Shortly, a stream of men in overalls begins to pour down the steps from the footbridge. She watches each of them as they pass, and recognises in the determined steps propelling them forwards their grim forbearance in the face of such a grey, inhospitable morning.

The train to Sopot departs at nine minutes past eight, Ryszard tells her. At seven o'clock a uniformed man opens up a waiting room and gestures, seeing their motionless figures on the bench. Then he disappears, leaving them alone in the cavernous room which doesn't seem much more comfortable than outside. It has a door at either end so that it can be accessed from opposite platforms, and inside there is nothing but long wooden seats like church pews running the length of each of the walls and, in the centre, a double line, back to back. The walls are a dirty beige, unalleviated by advertising posters or timetables, and the floor is an unyielding grey concrete. They perch on a seat, side by side, and wait.

It occurs to her, as she stares out of the window on the little local train as it picks up speed, that the pier might not be there any more. They might be coming all this way and it mightn't even be there. Or it might be so changed that it is unrecognisable. Ryszard has the photograph in an envelope in his bag

. . . She wishes the sun would come out; it would be so much better if their day at the seaside could be bright. But, now that she has woken up properly and the morning is under way, she at least feels a little brighter herself.

‿

At London Bridge he feeds fifteen pounds into the ticket machine and watches it spit out his change and a single ticket to Brighton. He scrabbles them out and pockets the few coins. He'll have to make what he's got last until he's sorted out something cash-in-hand, and somewhere new to sign on.

The train is almost empty; he's travelling against the tide and it's mid-morning, everyone who's going anywhere today is already there, it seems, apart from Jude. He props his bags on two seats and flumps down opposite them, stretching out his legs. An old woman follows him into the carriage, eyes him beadily and sits down out of sight at the far end. He leans his head against the back of the seat and sighs. In one hour his new life will begin. The doors bleep and slide shut. Goodbye, London, he thinks.

When the guard comes to check his ticket he fumbles it from his wallet and sees the photo of Sarah he still has in there. Taken in a passport photo booth, when they were both drunk and happy. She was caught off guard and is looking away from the camera, perhaps at him, scrambling into the tight space beside her in time for the next flash. In semi-profile she looks young and fragile, the skin on her turned neck too white, bleached by the flash, her wide eyes gazing upwards, the hint of a frown creasing their corners, or perhaps it is laughter. He stares at it after the ticket man has gone. Tucked behind it is the next in the sequence – the two of them locked in each other's arms, kissing. He should put these away, he thinks. Better still, he should take them out of his wallet right now and throw them out of the window. But he can't be that brutal. Not yet.

৬৵

The pier is still there after all. There are no swans, but then she hadn't expected there to be. She holds the photograph and stands a little way off, looking from one to the other, glancing across the space of half a century.

There it is, in essence the same, although time and seasons have wrought perceptible changes between past and present. It looks shabbier in real life, less stark and powerful, somehow. She wishes she could make out where exactly Ewa is standing. It is impossible to tell whether the sea is in or out. It doesn't matter, she thinks. It doesn't matter. If I could go and stand in the same spot, what then? Would it mean anything more than this? My feet on the same spot as hers? Those grains of sand might be anywhere, spread across the whole length of the beach. Perhaps, by now, carried to some other beach, or part of the seabed. She would not be standing on the same sand, wherever she stood. Ryszard has walked on ahead and is almost in the shadow of the pier. She goes closer, at the same time thinking, in spite of herself, what time of day was it, did he tell me that? Her mind draws the line of the sea up and down the beach like a blanket in the passing of a night, pulled by turn up to the chin and then thrown down in the restless heat of a dream. If I could remember that. But he probably didn't remember himself.

She catches up with Ryszard and stands beneath the pier, smelling the dampness, the rotting seaweed. In the photograph it is a bright day; the swans' shadows are sharp and black against the sand, their feathers bleached a dazzling white. Everything stands out sharply. Sarah can feel it, the way the sun is shining in Ewa's eyes, making her squint and shield them, and then that sudden relaxation into shade when, for a moment, everything goes darker. The coolness where the sun cannot reach, and the awareness of her bare arms inside the soft woollen cardigan she is wearing over her flowered dress.

Today is quite different. It has warmed up now, but the sun is behind heavy clouds, and there is the same colourless light which Sarah has been watching grow since dawn.

She stands just in front of one of the huge supports, with her back to the sea. She looks down at her feet, imagining Ewa's shoes against the sand, her trained feet turned out unconsciously. She lifts her head and looks across the deserted stretch of sand they have crossed, the wavy line of their footprints. And then she turns slightly and Ryszard is watching her, the camera he has just photographed her with still half upraised in his hands.

He smiles and she feels again the shifting movement, the sense of heaviness lifting, that she felt in the park that day. This trip of Ryszard's was such a good idea; she's glad he insisted they come. She feels a little as if she is returning to an absent self who for a long time she hasn't even realised has been missing. She looks down at her feet again and studies their solidity against the sand. She wiggles her toes, scrunches them and digs them into the sand, enjoying the abrasive feeling of the wet grains pushing between them.

When Ryszard walks towards her she knows that he is going

to kiss her, and that very soon she will probably make love with him in the faded, shabby grandeur of the seafront hotel they have just booked into. In the few steps it takes for him to reach her and pull her to him she sees it all in advance, that all of this will happen: she will love him fiercely and briefly, and then she will go home.

Eclipse

Balu is sitting at an unlaid table poring over his latest book when Hari arrives at the restaurant. He waves at Balu through the window before he reaches the door but when he comes in he sees he is reading so he doesn't speak. There is something about reading which makes him feel excluded; he envies Balu's ability to set himself down anywhere, increasingly now in the restaurant before he opens up, and fall into another world. Sarah too. He had watched her pack her bag before she left for Poland and choose a book to take with her as if it were an integral part of the trip. As if the wrong book might spell disaster, or at the very least overshadow it with a completely different cast. And she handled the book – a thick one, *Anna Karenina* – with ease, with familiarity, intimacy. Such books didn't intimidate her as they would him. He knew he would never read it. He had sat awkwardly with her that last evening before she left, feeling that something had changed for ever. That there was something destructive in her.

Balu has followed him into the kitchen. He holds out a set of keys tied together on a piece of string.

'You take charge of these,' he says.

In the silent flat upstairs Hari feeds Sita, who has made the place her own since Sarah has been away. A corner of the sofa is covered with a fine layer of grey-black hairs. On the kitchen floor he finds the remains of a mouse supper which he scoops up with a piece of kitchen roll and drops over the rail of the fire escape. The living room is stale and dark. He unfastens the shutters and peers out into her garden, remembering lying there naked with her on a blanket they had dragged outside, the fancy skylight beside them, a huge, luminous swelling in the encroaching night. He had rolled onto his belly and raised his head and shoulders up to peer down at the people in the restaurant. He remembers watching a couple he had seen before, regulars; he recognised them even by the tops of their heads, the table they sat at. As they ate their meal and talked and ordered coffee he made love on the roof above them, knowing that tomorrow he would be that waistcoated waiter with slicked-back hair, scribbling notes and scuttling out of sight into the kitchen. He found it curious, rubbing shoulders with so many people in the restaurant week after week, and yet never knowing any of them beyond the surface.

Really, it had always been like that with Sarah. Their close-ness had been something intensely physical, but unexpressed. They had done little more than rub shoulders. Their lives had grazed against each other, nothing more. He remembers how sad he had been when Jude appeared on the scene and eclipsed him entirely. When she told him, with no intention to cause him pain, that she was in love with someone else, he had not felt he knew her well enough to tell her his feelings.

He pulls the windows open and walks out into her garden. There is the skylight he knew first from beneath, not con-sidering, as he bustled round tables, scarcely lifting his head, that he would come to crave this other angle, this other side of it which meant proximity to Sarah. It was never the same, afterwards; it became an inverted talisman, a tangible symbol of her presence whenever he walked beneath it or glanced up into its darkness at night. Now it has changed again. He refuses to acknowledge what he once felt connected him to her, remembering only Jude's ghost-green face, the greedy, madman eyes boring into him, and the night the glass was broken, when Balu had almost had a heart attack. He had gone so ashen, once the restaurant was empty, that Hari had wanted to make sure he arrived home in one piece.

Rearranged around the perimeter of the newly repaired skylight is the jumble of herbs in pots: coriander, curry leaves, parsley, mint. In the corner a spindly bay tree grows from a grey metal mop bucket and a rosemary bush stands rigid in an old ghee tub.

He once handed her a pip from the apple he was eating.

'Plant this.'

It grew. It stands in its pot now, a tiny, sparse-leafed twig, like a pea stick. One day an apple tree.

He lifts the watering can he has filled and douses it with water.

ॐ

Jude stands in front of a mirror in a stark, featureless room and looks at himself, at his eyes, shyly, as if observed and uncomfortable meeting them in another person's presence. His eyes, his mother has always told him, are her eyes, brown and gentle-looking. His brother Tom has his father's – very blue, dark-ringed irises with pupils that seemed small even in dim light. His own pupils, in this bright room – the curtainless window behind him radiating whiteness onto the bare, uncluttered walls, the thin mattress covered over with a worn, pale-coloured counterpane – are as usual large. In the flat above the Mountain of Light they had lit candles and Sarah had pulled him to her and his unruly dark hair had brushed her skin. He had noticed the fallen shape of it, the scattered question marks curling against her shoulder, the bare, thin whiteness of her. She pulled against the back of his neck, wrapping her fingers in his hair, bringing his head lower. She said, smiling, '*Bel uomo.*' In the mirror his hair, longer now, hangs in loose clumps about his face. She had liked that, the way each lock was so wildly independent, so separate from the rest.

He is rigid with tiredness. He knows that he will have to get used to this – to being here on his own. What he feels saddest about is that he will never experience things with Sarah again, that they will never share events like they used to. This place feels so alien, and it seems so wrong to be here without her. He feels a little frightened of it; he has no connections here, no history.

He wonders where she is, what she is doing. She feels too far away from him now, but it has seemed like this for months, even when they were together, with whatever it was that was going on between her and Hari, and then that fucking old man. He cannot bring himself to think his name, although he has heard her say it often. That smug, fucking Polish name. He can't bear to think of him. Or of Hari. And that day, the day before he left, when it had all come spilling out, how he knew she had been sleeping with Hari before they were together, and how, for all he knew, she was still sleeping with him. In fact, of course she was. He had seen their secret looks, had noticed how they crept off to the kitchen to whisper and God knows what else that night the four of them had sat drinking, late into the night, in the restaurant. He had watched her.

He wishes he could unsay everything he said. The instant it was all out, and Sarah had stood looking at him with a shuttered face he hadn't seen before, he wished ardently that he had said none of it, even if it was true. But out it had all come, and once it was said there was no re-entry. That hard expression, shutting him out, wanting him to go. So he had stewed in the flat for a day and then spat it all out at Hari and almost sent him crashing down through the skylight into the restaurant.

He wonders if he'll ever regret leaving, if he'll ever wish he could go back. If things had been different what kind of life might he have made with Sarah, over the Mountain of Light? What friends might Balu and Hari have been?

There isn't any worth in thinking about it; those connections are well and truly severed. And his pride would never let him in any case. But walking into this room for the first time confirmed the finality of it all somehow. It was all so unapologetically dismal and stark. On his left a large oval mirror with bevelled edges hung by a chain. In front of him a single bed was draped with a tatty nylon bedspread. To his right was a bare window with a wide sill and a wicker chair beside it.

He turns slowly from the mirror. He will go out, he thinks. He will get out of this room and then things will seem better. He looks round for his coat and sees it hanging on a hook on the back of the door. He has no recollection of putting it there. He has done it without thinking, his body seeking desperately the small comforts of familiar habits. When he was a small child he would climb onto his father's knee in the evening and rub a small pinch of his office shirt between his finger and thumb, feeling the texture of it, the friction it caused. When he started school, and afterwards, after his father had died, he would insert each hand beneath the jumper cuffs at the opposite wrist and take his own shirt sleeves between finger and thumb, surreptitiously in his lap.

He decides to make for the seafront, and begins striding lengthily, unswerving, along the unfamiliar streets. Once he gets down nearer the town he will know where he is. He has been to Brighton before, with Sarah, but he isn't going to dwell on memories. He is glad to be out of the room. Out of the stale, oppressive silence of it. Glad to be away from an atmosphere which has filled him with a kind of pallid strangeness. At least outside he can walk, and the air is filled with the bright sea light, and the sound of seagulls. He cannot bear to be shut up in a room which seems to be mocking his inability even to begin unpacking the two bags he has stood pathetically in the corner.

He comes to the end of a street and, after a moment's hesitation, turns left. He passes a shop selling second-hand clothes and furniture. A rack of creased and dusty shoes on the pavement is spattered slightly with raindrops. A woman appears from inside as he passes, and peers up at the sky then looks at her watch. Jude looks up, too, at the cloudless, blue expanse. She glances at him and briefly meets his eyes, before turning to straighten a dress, something frivolous from the 1950s, which is hanging from the shop's awning and has been blown awry in one of the sporadic, brisk seaside gusts, so that the pink, gauzy underskirt has flipped up flirtatiously, and become caught.

Jude is hot from walking. He shrugs off the unbuttoned shirt he is wearing over his T-shirt without stopping and carries it over his shoulder.

He could buy a cup of tea. He could find a café with a view of the sea and sit at a table in the window. He looks down a side street and sees a narrow triangle of distant blue beyond a slated rooftop. He turns into the street. Funny, he thinks, how the first glimpse is always a patch far out, on the horizon. As if you see it and it sees you and you race to meet each other at the surf line.

The incline of the street propels him onward and he allows the slope to tip him towards his goal, his spirits reviving noticeably as the patch of ocean disappears momentarily and then widens, suddenly entire before him.

He is surprised at the number of people sitting about on the stony beach. It isn't the weekend. But the shelving expanse of grey chalk-coloured, sea-tossed pebbles is dotted with dark huddles of people. He would have preferred to have the sea to himself.

He walks a little way along the lower promenade, stepping onto the stones when he finds a less populous segment and can weave his way down to the sea edge without coming too close to anybody. His boots crunch the stones together loudly as he walks; each footstep feels weighted down. He slides down a sea-piled bank, sending loose pebbles skittering away, bouncing sharply, cracking against each other in the air. The volume of his progress seems to drown out the possibility of hearing any other sound, filling his head as if he were crunching a hard, boiled sweet in his teeth. For a while it drowns out the presence of the people in his wake. When he is close to the shallow frill of sea which darkens the grey stones and slips away between them, welling up again with each fresh wave, he spreads his shirt out flat and sits on it. He rakes his fingers across the pebbles beside him and picks one up at random; it feels cool and smooth against his palm.

He is unsettled by the numerous encampments behind him. He turns round to look at them, to gain some clue to the reason for their presence, and sees immediately the cardboard spectacles, the cameras, the upraised faces. Of course. In the mess of the past few weeks he had completely forgotten about the eclipse. And, Christ, that evening (he'd drunk a lot, was feeling very bad about everything, spiteful towards Sarah) when he'd cooked up that ridiculous idea to go to Romania to see the eclipse, just to torture Hari, trying to make him agree to something it was clear he had no intention of carrying through.

He narrows his eyes and squints up at the sun through his lashes. It's too bright to see anything and his eyes instantly start to water. He turns away and looks out to sea, trying to blink away the blue sun which hovers in the middle of his line of vision. The day is so clear that, even far out, he can see white-caps. The whole surface seems to shimmer with the thousands of tiny, glinting reflections. He rearranges himself on his shirt so that he is side on to the sea and looks across to the old Victorian pier, standing deserted in black silhouette. The eclipse watchers nearest to him unscrew a hissing plastic bottle of cider which they pass round.

Jude gets up and picks his way back up the shingle. He hears the tinny pop of ringpulls, watches a ball being thrown for a thin dog with a spotted handkerchief round its neck, which gallops after it up the beach, and hands a spare box of matches from his pocket to a girl in cut-off jeans who asks him for a light.

'Bit crap, isn't it?' she says, shaking out the match and dropping it so that it slips between the pebbles and disappears. Jude watches it fall. 'Don't worry, *it's biodegradable*,' she says, as if she thinks he is accusing her of something.

'What?'

'Nothing. What's up with you, anyway? Run away from home, have you?'

She is laughing at him. He must look like shit; he hasn't shaved for days, and his face is greyly translucent, his eyes ringed and heavy.

'Yes, actually,' he says, pulling a half packet of Old Holborn out of his back pocket. The girl is making him nervous and his hands are suddenly itching for something to do.

'Here,' she says, handing him the spliff. She stands watching him curiously as he drags on it, holds the smoke as long as he can and then releases it in a long, steady exhalation. 'By yourself, then?' Her way of speaking is curt, as if she dislikes conversation for its own sake. She is wearing a short vest top which exposes a couple of inches of skin and he notices that she has a silver ring in her belly button. He passes back the spliff after another couple of drags and realises that he is starting to feel better already. She's with a group of people but they seem to have closed their circle more tightly, filling the gap she has left. 'Want to talk about it?'

He doesn't know what talking he can do with her, but he nods anyway and she runs back to her gaggle of friends for something. He wonders if one of them is her boyfriend. There are murmured voices; he's too far away from them to hear what they're saying, but a couple of them lift their heads and look at him. Then she comes back with a bottle of cider and they set off in silence, crunching side by side across the pebbles.

ରୄ

Hari wakes up suddenly, with a jerk, and for a moment can't place himself. He feels knotted and uncomfortable. He can't stretch his legs, and his neck is cricked awkwardly. Then he remembers he is on the sofa in Sarah's flat, and feels suddenly guilty at being there. He is still dressed, covered with the dusty blanket he lay on with her in the garden. The garden windows are wide open and Sita is sitting in a patch of sunlight, just inside the room, carefully washing her ears. He looks at his watch; it is nearly eleven o'clock. He sits up slowly. Nobody knows he is here; he is an intruder. Balu has entrusted him with the keys to the flat because – and he has noticed this himself, Balu has said nothing – exertion has been leaving him rather breathless recently, and he would probably rather not go up and down the fire escape twice a day to feed Sita to remind himself of the fact. Balu, he suspects, is one of those men who is deeply suspicious of doctors. Who would not seek one out unless he were at death's door. And reluctantly even then.

Hari's head is heavy and his mouth sour and thick. He pushes off the blanket and realises he is shivering. Sita, alerted by activity, is at his heels in one fluid movement, chirruping expectantly. He blunders into the kitchen and inexpertly forks out half a tin of Whiskas for her, dropping lumps of it on the floor which Sita haughtily ignores, preferring to eat from the bowl. If Sarah walks in, he thinks, as he rinses the fork and throws the empty tin into the bottom of the bin, knowing full well that she will not, she won't be angry that he has decided he would like to watch the eclipse from the top of the roof. Not her garden, but the real roof, through that ill-fitting hinged rooflight upstairs which leaks every time it rains and which Balu has never got around to fixing. But he feels awkward nonetheless; he is here uninvited.

He sits on one of the kitchen chairs and watches the cat eat, crouching thievishly over her bowl. Last night, after Balu locked up the restaurant and went off home in his taxi, Hari came up to the flat to feed Sita, as he has done every evening since Balu handed him the keys. And somehow, this time, he stayed. First, he thoroughly watered all the plants in Sarah's garden in the dark. The cat, delighting in company, had followed him solemnly, watching his every movement with her serious, dark face. Carefully he replenished the water in dry saucers and soaked the shrunken, crumbly soil around the bases of the lavender, the bay tree and the Japanese maple, lit by the street lamp and the string of outdoor fairy lights Sarah had looped around the wall. Back and forth he went between the garden and the kitchen, with Sita at his heels, silent and curious. When he had finished he sat on the threshold and smoked a cigarette, suddenly flooded with the memory of his brief, intense relationship with her, which she had somehow felt was never real enough. Which had been extinguished utterly when she met Jude. He had liked Jude in many ways, which made it more difficult to resent him or wish him away. But always Sarah had been between them, distancing them from each other, so that they invariably felt awkward together.

After the cigarette he decided to check upstairs, just in case Sita had dragged in a bird and left it to swell and decompose in some warm, airless corner. He crept up the stairs and peered into Sarah's bedroom, smelling her familiar presence although she had been gone for weeks, particles of her scent lingering in the fabric of the room, the bedclothes, her clothes, some strewn on the bed as if discarded at the last moment during her packing. That last evening, when he had come to see her before she left, she had carried her bag down and searched the bookshelves before stuffing in that dog-eared copy of *Anna Karenina* and zipping it closed. Jude was gone, but neither of them mentioned him. He had hugged her quickly, feeling her thin shoulders through her shirt – he had forgotten how thin, how fragile she was – and then he had left.

Last night he resisted the urge to actually go into the room, to lie on her bed and curl into happy, forgetful sleep. But he hadn't been able to leave. Promising that he would replace it, he opened a bottle of wine left in the kitchen, turned on the TV and drank himself to sleep.

The TV is still on, and is now showing live scenes of people in the USA watching the eclipse. He has half a mind to lie back down on the sofa and sleep off his hangover, but why waste the day? He decides not to, and goes in search of the stepladder.

Teetering slightly, he pushes up the rooflight, pokes his head and shoulders out and blinks like a mole. Carefully he passes up Sarah's pile of garden blankets and cushions, the radio from the kitchen and a couple of cold bottles of lager he has found in the fridge. Then he hauls himself through the hole.

Clouds are forecast. He feels in his back pocket for the cardboard spectacles one of the customers gave him last night, rather crumpled after being slept on, and tries them out. The sun is a tiny orange marble. Everything else is black.

He stashes the lagers up against the chimney, and arranges his nest of cushions in its creeping shade. He will open the first one when something starts to happen. He glances at his watch. Forty-four minutes. He wonders if two bottles will be enough, if he oughtn't to go down now for another, but instead he lies, face up, on the bed he has made and closes his eyes. His heart is racing after the effort of getting up onto the roof, his head thumping slightly.

The first sign is a tiny dent at the top, slightly to the right. Barely noticeable. He sits up to open one of the bottles and switch the radio on. There's an excited commentary; cloud predictions and repeated reminders about how long until the moment of nearest totality, interspersed with brief vignettes of pointless interviews with people up on Parliament Hill.

He can't remember whether Sarah will be able to see it at all in Poland. Probably not. He wonders briefly whether Jude is watching somewhere, alone. He leans back against the chimney stack. There are a few people dotted on the rooftops in the next road. One of them sees him looking in their direction and waves at him, whooping hopefully. He raises his bottle in a salute, his grin wide enough for her to see, then, when she turns back to her friends, he switches the radio off and lies back into his bed of cushions. He is already regretting the lager and wishing he had brought up a bottle of water instead. Sita has picked her way suspiciously up the ladder and is sitting bolt upright on the very edge of the trapdoor hole, the curved shelf of her back in profile like a black satin bustle, her feet in a tight row. She is so still that he can see the tiny rocking movement caused by her breathing. Sometimes when he sits that still he feels his heart rocking him; he feels the blood surging through his veins and thinks the movement of his body is visible.

The dent has grown to a curved slice. Maybe Jude went to Romania after all, he thinks.

ൠ

In the restaurant, Balu looks up from the book he is reading. He stretches, yawning widely, cracking his fingers above his head and letting escape a small, voiced sigh, then he gets up and goes to check on the slowly reducing milk in the kitchen. His latest idea is an amaretto *kulfi*. In the oven, inside the heavy cast-iron pot, dried apricots are drinking in the sweet flavours of a mixture of white dessert wine and an amaretto liqueur. The apricots will be sliced as thinly as possible and returned to the steeping juice, which will form the basis of the warm syrup with which he plans to encircle each cone of *kulfi*, like a castle with a moat. When the soft outer shell of the finished dessert is broken into, a core of amaretti pieces and cracked almonds should reveal itself. He has been planning just such a combination of warm and cold, yielding and brittle, for some time.

In the kitchen he remembers, suddenly, why the street is so quiet. He turns down the heat a touch, waiting until the milk responds with a more sluggish bubbling, before he goes out through the kitchen door and onto the lowest flight of the fire escape. He looks up at the sun but, without those silly glasses they've been selling everywhere, he can see nothing at all out of the ordinary. He climbs up a couple of steps of the fire escape, to get a wider view of the sky, feeling the reverberation of his heavy footsteps in the handrail as he grips it. He is breathing heavily, just with the effort of climbing these few steps, and he can feel his heart thumping behind his ribs. He has one more go at looking at the sun and then stomps back down the steps and into the kitchen, blinded blue.

He takes a packet of amaretti out of the cupboard, carefully snips off the corner to let out the air, and crushes the biscuits with a rolling pin. He tips them into a bowl which he covers with a lid, checks the viscosity of the milk again, giving it a gentle stir and adjusting the heat minutely, then wanders back to the book which he has left splayed open on one of the tables in the silent restaurant. As he scans the poem he has just read again, the imprint of the sun flicks across the page with the movement of his eyes.

໑

'Do you think we will come back here ever?' Ryszard says suddenly, breaking into the silence which has enveloped them for nearly an hour as they lie sleepily on the sand. He says 'we' but what he really means is will I come back, she thinks. To this place, this shabby, worn-out old holiday resort. To this country. To him. Will I? She turns her head so that she has one cheek pressed against the dry sand and looks at him.

'I don't know,' she says, already drifting back to the last time she saw Jozef.

'She didn't come back,' he said. He kept on saying it. And she said nothing. When he seemed to have fallen asleep she got a cup of tea from the vending machine she had spotted in the hallway on her way in the first time she came. She carried the hot, plastic cup by its rim, carefully, and went out into the garden. She sat down on a bench with someone's name on it and tried to sip at the too-hot tea. She wanted the dead feeling to wash out but it sat inside her like a stagnant, stinking puddle. She wasn't sure how things would be from now on. Not that there would be very much longer. She blew on the tea. But they had come to the end of the past.

When she returned to the room he was still asleep, and she

stood at the door, taking her silent leave, not wanting to re-enter in case she woke him. She had worked out that Ewa must have left him, but hearing it, hearing him tell it, was much worse than just the suspicion she had had before.

'Sarah?' He was awake. She moved closer, back within his compass, and sat down again. She didn't want to hold his hand any more. She felt suddenly wary of him without knowing why. And anyway, they were OK, the two of them, she thought. They had made it to the present.

She looked at him and said nothing. Looked at him without his story. Seeing him as one sees a person who usually wears glasses, without them. His breathing was heavy and painful. The way he hunched his shoulders forward to hold the pain away.

'Do you want the nurse?' she asked.

He carried on breathing, calculating: in and out, in and out. Waiting for it to subside. His shoulders dropped a little.

'No,' he said. 'No.' And he shook his head slowly, wearily.

She gave him a sip of water. Helped him sit forward and held the glass for him, feeling his hand on hers as he grasped it. She settled him back against his pillows and waited.

'There's no postscript,' he said eventually. 'I don't know what happened to Ewa. I know what I thought then, and what I think now, but I *know* nothing. All I had, all I have ever had, was suspicion, guesswork. Nothing solid. Nothing real and solid and final that I could have been angry or sad about, then accepted, and put behind me. There's no tidy ending. No finish at all.' He paused, tried vainly to still his breath, his chest heaving as if he had just sprinted a hundred metres. He must feel as if he is drowning, she thought. He should stop talking. But he had more to say.

'You see,' he said slowly, 'I couldn't forgive her for not coming home, for not needing me any more. But worse than that was the not knowing. I couldn't bear it. For years I was eaten up with the thought that Hopper had . . . had *prised* her from me, that I had been usurped in her affections. Do you see, Sarah? She left me *incomplete*. I couldn't let her go.' He had a metallic gleam in his eyes and there was a tightness, a dangerous note, to his voice and she noticed that thick, white foam, like cuckoo spit, had collected in the corners of his mouth.

She was close to tears. Knew she could not try to speak without her voice catching and losing its balance.

She sits up.

'I don't know,' she says again, shaking sand from her hair, brushing it from her elbows.

Ryszard has both his hands over his face and for a moment she thinks he is crying. She reaches for one of them and he uncovers his eyes, grinning like an imp. He points up into the sky.

'The sun!' he says. 'The sun has come out!' and she turns to see that, while they have been dozing, the heavy sky has lifted to reveal a soaring, china-blue expanse which makes her feel suddenly, expansively clear and happy and hopeful. She turns back to Ryszard, smiling, her shadow falling across his face, shading his eyes. As he looks up at her, her head seems to be surrounded by an aura, a burning halo of golden-orange hair, radiating out in wispy tendrils and falling down onto her shoulders, the silhouetted moon of her face dark and secret until he reaches out his hand to touch it.

An End

Since returning from the seaside Sarah and Ryszard have spent every available moment together, and when they have not been together, she has wandered in the park alone, sitting by the bathing lake trying, hopelessly, to read, dozing on a blanket on her belly in the wavering shade of the trees or shopping for fruit in the market. Babcia has shown her how to make *piroggi* and *barszcz* during the long afternoons when she has been filling in time until Ryszard's return. She has neglected the box of letters and photographs which so obsessed her when she first arrived, suddenly finding them pathetic, their meaning, their worth suddenly desiccated and expired. Undisturbed, they have gathered a fine, softening layer of dust on the table where, weeks ago, she carefully piled them in chronological order, handling them with quiet reverence. But at points during the past day she has found Jozef's low voice, clear and insistent, with the precise, lilting accent which is so familiar to her, breaking through the interstices of her sudden happiness, reminding her that it is too unreal, too perfect to survive.

For some reason, and she thinks it is possibly a sense of something almost incestuous or gratuitous, she feels slightly embarrassed to think of Jozef now. As if she has somehow changed and skewed things between them by allowing this diversion to step in and distance her from him. As if he were still alive to judge her. And yet there's no reason why he should disapprove of what has grown between her and his great-nephew.

She knows she must leave soon – she has already been away for a month, and is beginning to feel the soporific effects of this place's dislocated, seductive, eternal present. She feels, at times, entirely cut off from her real life, as if she has always been here, reading the same passages of *Anna Karenina* over and over, unable to make progress, walking for hours in the park and lying alongside Ryszard at night.

She leant over Jozef and kissed his forehead before she left that last time. 'I want,' he said, and swallowed with difficulty. She stayed bent low over him, her face hanging above his. 'I want . . . wanted her to come back,' he whispered. 'Wanted the kind of love from her that would risk anything.'

In the park she emerges from the parasol of close-standing trees which enclose her within a cool, tawny-green filtered light into the full glare of the sun. Beneath her feet the soft, mossy ground turns hard-baked and scorched. Bare patches of cracked, flaking earth show through the clumps of yellowed grass.

She feels aimless and unsettled, has a fluttering, shapeless anxiety which won't leave her. She knows she must leave soon. Upstairs in the attic room she sits down heavily in the basketweave chair. She lifts one hand to her forehead and gathers up the loose wisps of hair hanging down and pulls them behind her ears, then leans back in the chair and lets her head drop backwards. She stays like this, immobile save for the pulse in her neck, a flicking shadow, and her eyes blinking up at the ceiling. She knows that it is precisely because it must end that what she has with Ryszard is so perfect, so healing. She holds nothing back for fear of the future. They can just *be* together and nothing more. The projected window of sunlight on the wall inches infinitesimally closer. *Anna Karenina* lies, half-read, on the sill.

She straightens up in the chair, covers her face with both hands and presses them tightly into it, feeling her screwed eyelids, her lashes, trembling against the damp skin of her palms. Despite Ryszard, she is suddenly desperately homesick. She thinks guiltily of her flat, of Sita wandering from room to empty room, and of Jude who, for all she knows, might have come home . . .

The phone is ringing. Hari can only hear it once he has slammed the street door on the heat and brightness of mid-afternoon, the increase in traffic signalling the early start of a stifling, edgy rush hour. In the dark, narrow passage leading to the stairs up to Sarah's flat he stumbles past her bike, his T-shirt catching on the handlebar and pulling the frame away from the wall. It crashes against the facing wall, wedging itself at an angle and barring his way. He swears as he stumbles over it and runs up the stairs three at a time, knowing the ringing will stop before he even reaches the door, key outstretched.

He has just come back from the hospital and feels shaky and nauseous. When he arrived at the restaurant what seems like days ago, although it is less than three hours, Balu was lying in a slick of oil on the kitchen floor, surrounded by a mess of *pakoras*, pale and uncooked. The gas flame was roaring and the air was heavy with greasy heat and the tang of burnt oil.

The ringing stops. He grabs the receiver anyway and listens to the dialling tone, the severed link with whoever was phoning. He knows it was Sarah, prays that she tries again.

For that brief frozen moment in the kitchen doorway he

had believed Balu was dead. But then he had knelt down to him in the pool of oil, and Balu had looked up at him, his eyes filled with a blind terror Hari would never forget. He stood up and phoned for an ambulance, a dark circle of oil on each knee of his jeans, and then knelt back down beside his immobile friend. Tangled in amongst telling him that everything was going to be OK, and that help was on its way, and to keep calm and concentrate on breathing, out had tumbled in a muddle of words, that he loved Sarah, that he had fought with Jude, that it was probably his fault he had gone away so suddenly, and he didn't know how he was going to tell Sarah this, if she ever came home. He didn't know why he had suddenly needed to say it all, at such a precipitous moment. He had just started talking, thinking that so long as he kept going (it didn't matter what he said, anything would do) Balu would be able to hang on until the ambulance arrived. His breath was coming in rapid, shallow gasps and his lips beginning to turn a little bluish. Hari took his sweatshirt from round his waist and put it under his head and stayed there beside Balu in the oil, his words finally dried up, until the ambulance arrived.

The phone starts ringing again.

'Hello?'

'Oh, Hari.'

'I knew it would be you.'

'What are you doing there? I was . . .' hoping Jude had come back, he thinks. You didn't want to hear my voice. He fights the urge to replace the receiver, the sudden, welling disappointment he feels.

'I was feeding Sita,' he says, his voice leaden, suddenly exhausted.

'What's happened? Hari?' She can hear the catch in his voice. Knows instantly that something is wrong.

'Balu's in hospital. He's had a heart attack.' He pauses; she can hear the dry gulp as he swallows. 'I found him. I thought he was dead.'

She waits, listening to his silence, the space between his lips and the receiver. Well, that's it then, she thinks with a jolt. It's time to go home.

ဢ

In the end, the story of his grand love affair, like the affair itself, had just fizzled out. Like all real stories, there was no finale, no tragedy, just regret and uncertainty and the disappointing drift into inconsequence. She found it unbearably sad. Jozef had felt there was something monumental about the love between himself and Ewa, something timeless and fixed. He had believed it would endure, and had been cheated because, like most things between people, it had proved to be fleeting and imperfect.

At some point during those last days he had told her a little about his life after Ewa. The terrible years of hardship in Warsaw during the war had shocked her, and yet life had endured even through such desperate times, with a significant proportion of the population silently immured behind high brick walls.

He had met up again with an old girlfriend – the Magda she dimly remembered him mentioning once before, who had been eclipsed by Ewa's bright star. For a while she had lived with him in his rooms when her home was destroyed. But she hated him for still loving Ewa. Ewa who was a coward, she said. Ewa who had run away. She hated needing to be with him day after day. They couldn't resume their relationship where they had left it before Ewa. They made love selfishly, keeping themselves back, holding on to the comfort they could draw from the act. As if by clinging together they could add another thread to the thin skein of their existence. But it was a joyless union, born of propinquity, nothing more, and as soon as she could she moved on.

Jozef had lost friends, colleagues. People just disappeared. For six years he had lived like a ghost with his memories, hating Ewa for leaving him alone in this desperate, flattened place where they had once loved. Wanting her to come back. And then he had come to London to try to forget, hoping, once again, that a change of place could put right what was wrong.

'I wanted the kind of love from her that would risk anything.' That was one of the last things he had said to her. Until now, she hadn't really understood what he meant.

He had wanted something so absolute that nothing but fantasy could satisfy him. It was reality that had crept up on them so unexpectedly in New York, nothing more. It wasn't George Hopper or the city or Ewa's ambition, her gift, her beauty. Or perhaps it was all of those things. They could all have played their part. But what had happened in New York was that they had really seen each other for the first time. That was all. And each of them had started to build their defences from that point, moving inexorably further away from each other, unable to help themselves.

Sarah thinks of Jude, of how it all started to peel apart between them when he moved into the flat above the Mountain of Light, when he had closed in on her life. Perhaps he wasn't so different from Jozef.

ॐ

220

'Open your eyes.'

For a few seconds more she stands with her eyes closed, his guiding hands still on her shoulders.

'*Teraz*. Open your eyes.'

The room is dotted with candles and tea lights. Ryszard has pulled the dining table into the centre of the room, opened it out fully, and draped a white cloth over it. His hands still on her shoulders, she swivels round to face him.

'Thank you, Ryszard.' She smiles. '*Dziekuję*'

The room seems oddly empty; he has moved the usual arrangement of armchairs and small tables up against the walls so that when he disappears back down to the kitchen and she is sitting alone at the island table, she feels cut adrift as if she is already partly gone.

Babcia is out for the evening at her old people's club. She knows her grandson wants tonight to be just himself and the thin English girl he has fallen in love with, who is leaving tomorrow.

It is a close night but there is a strong breeze and both windows are flung open to the increasingly turbulent air. The net curtains alternately suck outwards and flutter into the room; the bright candle flames lining the mantelpiece and dotted on a table here, a shelf there, flicker and lean until they are almost horizontal. Clear wax runs freely down one side of each of the tall candles on the table in front of her, slowing and clouding as it cools and hardens. On the other side, the hollowed shell of wax is cliffed high, soft and translucent. She thinks of tree trunks and the side that gets the sun, the other, mossier side in shade. She resists the urge to let the wax run onto her finger and harden, imagining the sudden sharp pain and then its cooling, protecting warmth.

He comes back into the room with a tray. He has made pierrogi for her, with cherries bought from the market, each one dipped carefully into the rich batter and laid on grease-proof paper ready to be tipped into boiling water. He would not let her come into the kitchen although she laughed and begged and said she didn't mind helping. She had already packed her few things into her backpack so she went up to the attic room to take her leave of it, carrying a duster and a tin of polish she had pulled from Babcia's cleaning cupboard when Ryszard's back was turned. Carefully she twisted the lid off the tin and wiped a smudge of the yellow wax across the table top, releasing a rich, beeswax scent which seemed to call from another era. She rubbed it in, going right into each corner, and then found an unused part of the duster and buffed the residue away until the surface had a deep lustre. Next she wiped the thin layer of dust from the windowsill and the little table beside the bed, and then she knelt on the mattress, collected more polish on her duster and worked it carefully into the bevels and notches of the headboard.

She did not yet know what she would do with Jozef's memories, all those letters and postcards sent to him from cities around Europe where Ewa had toured with the Balets Polski in the few years before the war. When Ewa was away from Jozef she had loved him, Sarah thought wistfully, picturing Jude, now somewhere far away from her. Picturing Hari all of a sudden, which gave her such a curious feeling that she kept rubbing furiously at the same patch of headboard over and over, finding a strange comfort in the repeated action.

Ryszard had read all the letters and postcards to her, trans-lating as he went along, so she had followed Ewa's discoveries

222

of Paris, Berlin, London, Copenhagen, her voluble accounts of the minutiae only ever shared between lovers.

She put down the duster and moved the box onto the bed, lifted the lid and and peered inside. There, carefully replaced, were the worn-out ballet shoes, the newspaper clippings, the photographs, the theatre programmes, and the mementoes from New York. She shook up the snowstorm, the gift Ewa had never received, once more, and waited for all the flakes of snow to settle again before she placed it inside an upturned felt hat and tucked it beside the photographs. She reached inside and picked out a bundle of postcards she had carefully retied with the string Jozef had first used sixty years earlier. As she loosened the knot and glanced through them one last time, Ryszard crept up behind her and pulled them out of her hands. The one on top was from London, from St Paul's Cathedral. 'I love only you,' he whispered into the back of her neck, like one of the secret mouths close up against the cold plaster of the cathedral's dome, their messages carried round, some to be picked up by other ears. *Mine didn't come back to me,* Ewa had said on the postcard. Her curving whisper had been arced away.

Sarah laughed. 'Go back to your kitchen!' But after he had gone she sat down on the bed and looked through the bundle again. A photograph of Trafalgar Square, with the National Gallery in the background. Ryszard had written out a translation for this one. She unfolded the pale piece of new, lined paper tucked in with the age-yellowed postcards and read the blue biro scrawl:

I went to see the Leonardos. Our guide said I looked like Madonna of the Rocks! I fed pigeons in this square in the photograph; one did its business on my shoulder. Don't worry, the coat is not ruined, it has been sent for cleaning and the weather is so good I have no need of it. Isn't it meant to be good luck? Four days till when I can see you again, my love . . .

He would like to translate everything for her like this. Perhaps he will. But for now she has put everything back into the box and returned it to the cupboard of Ryszard's childhood where it has been for more than half a century. She tends to forget this, that it was all so long ago. That in a few months it will be part of a completed century, an old millennium. Yet another line drawn neatly underneath: finished, boxed, entire.

She closed the lid on it all little more than an hour ago and locked the window in the small, bare room where the polish-tainted air was already returning to that thick, closed-up kind of air only encountered in rooms that are not used. Ryszard was preparing her goodbye meal, clanging pots and pans in the kitchen far below, but she could hear nothing up there in her silent eyrie.

She lines up the cherry stones on the rim of her plate, then looks across at Ryszard's plate and sees he has done the same. Jude always used to make a pile – cherry pits, olive stones, cardamom pods. Hari? She doesn't know. Small differences. She taps each one with the end tine of her fork.

'Tinker tailor soldier sailor rich man poor man beggar man thief tinker tailor soldier sailor rich man poor man beggar man thief *tinker*.' Ryszard widens his eyes.

'*Co?*'

The long net curtains billow suddenly into the room; she

feels the burst of air cool on her face, and the tortured candle flames on the table between them gutter and vanish, leaving two twists of grey which spiral upwards momentarily and then are sucked away as the curtains belly outwards. They hold their strange, pregnant shape for a few seconds, and then another tug of wind slips their tail ends over the sill and they fly like streamers in the night air. Laughing in the faint smell of snuffed candle, Ryszard hauls the flapping escapees in, like a fisherman hauling in his catch. He pulls closed the outer windows which have been clanging and creaking against the wall. Then he turns to face her, his face cliffed in moving shadows in the yellow, far-off light, his eyes grinning, shining.

ഔ

Balu leans back against the pillows the nurse has arranged behind him and reclines, Buddha-like, in new pyjamas. How many men, he thinks, can have a brand new pair of pyjamas, still wrapped in cellophane, waiting in a drawer, ready for an eventuality like this? Old men with fretful wives, perhaps. And unmarried men with doting mothers. These were from his mother, for his last birthday. His forty-seventh. He is still a young man, still sees himself as young. His hair is thick and black, his flesh firm and unwrinkled. He has a good colour. And yet he's here, in a ward full of sick old men. Sick.

If he's truthful, he can't really remember all of what happened, and this frightens him a little. It was yesterday, some time mid-afternoon. It had been a reasonably busy week, but nothing he couldn't manage. Colin was on holiday so he'd had Hari in doing extra hours in the kitchen, but that had left him short of waiters. Jude could sometimes be called upon in emergencies, but he'd disappeared off the face of the earth, and Sarah had gone off who knows where, with some mad idea in her head. And Hari was only half concentrating on his work. Forgetting orders, getting the tables mixed up, and crashing about in the kitchen. Everything had changed recently; suddenly everyone seemed eaten up and strained, and there was only himself, stolidly reliable and unchanging, in the centre.

Hari must have found him slumped on the kitchen floor. Balu raises his hand to his cheek and presses around the sore area gingerly. He must have caught it as he fell. He can't remember. His other hand is bandaged. He had been cooking, he remembers that. He had been waiting for the oil to heat up and he must have upset the fryer. Jayesh had been to the hospital that evening and said not to worry, Hari had cleaned everything up. Balu looks at the white bandage carefully wound round his stubby hand. The stark, clean whiteness against his skin. He has always been healthy. The fingernails on the tips of his protruding fingers are strong and white (his mother used to make him drink a glass of milk every morning when he was a child); he has never had a filling in his teeth, never been plagued by aches and pains, never had a day when he has not been at the restaurant. In the twenty-odd years he has been in this country he has been to the doctor only once. Admittedly, he thinks, looking down at the white curve of his belly underneath the sheet, he could lose a few pounds. But he has always been healthy.

Sometimes he is filled with sadness at the loneliness at the centre of his life. He looks at his brother, Jayesh, often nowadays, watches him with his wife and child, or watches the young couples in the restaurant, stroking each other's hands and eating from each other's plates, and wonders what it feels like not to be alone. And there are times, still, when his prurient curiosity is almost as powerful as that of a schoolboy, his sense of injustice strong, that he has been deprived of the simple, pleasurable experiences others take for granted. But usually he is of the opinion that perhaps some people are just meant to be alone as he is, and he stops daydreaming and goes back to the security of his kitchen and feels the warm comfort of familiarity seeping deep into his bones.

The young nurse smiles at him as she walks past, holding carefully upright a pisspot with a spout. Why do they make those things out of such transparent plastic? He watches as the piss of the emaciated stick man three beds away, looking an unhealthily clouded yellow, is paraded in state down the centre of the ward.

'OK, Balu?' the nurse asks. 'Can I get you anything?' She is young, pretty. She has very yellowish-blonde hair, like a nineteen forties starlet. She pronounces his name with the stress on the 'u' so that he sounds like the fat friendly bear in *Jungle Book*. Maybe that's how she sees him, he thinks, a big, round, brown, half-witted bear. She is called Saffron. He smiles at her and shakes his head. The tea in here is awful – over-stewed and bitter-tasting and never quite hot enough. He is hungry but he doesn't want to ask for something to eat, the ward is a little too quiet, and he feels guilty, anyway: a fat, healthy-looking man asking for a biscuit so soon after lunch, in a ward full of men who can keep nothing, it seems, in their stomachs for more than five minutes.

'No thanks,' he says meekly. 'I'm fine.'

His mother would approve, he thinks – a yellow-haired girl called Saffron. She would like the tidiness, the appropriateness. She had chosen the name Balu for him when he was born because he was so tiny. It is an affectionate, diminutive name;

it means 'small' in his language. He feels a sudden, unexpected stab of longing: for his mother, for the house he was born in, the warmth of the kitchen and his mother's stories as she cooked. He remembered helping, sometimes, breaking up the dough into individual pieces which he would carefully roll into spheres in his small hands and line up along the edge of the low table in the centre of the room, or picking the tiny seeds from cardamom pods. A stab of longing for everything he no longer has – his happy, distant childhood, the love and day-long attention of his mother, the smells which drifted from her cooking pot, by which he could tell the season, the celebration, the day of the week.

He thinks of her as she was last time he saw her, sitting squarely on a low stool in her modernised, fitted kitchen, changing channels on the portable TV with the remote control she keeps in her apron pocket. It is four years since he was last in that kitchen with her. If he were at home, he realises, he would phone her. (And when he thinks the words 'at home' he thinks not of his brother's house in Enfield but of the scruffy, adorable flat above the restaurant where he was so happy.) Of course it's because right now he cannot climb out of bed and phone her – he is on total bed rest until further notice, and isn't even allowed out of bed for a pee without asking first – that he feels the need to hear her voice so strongly.

If he could speak to her right now he would ask her to tell him one of the stories she used to tell him as a child. All those stories; he has no idea where most of them came from, and probably she doesn't either. They were just a mixed-up bag of bits of tales from here and there. Some of them probably heard from her own parents and grandparents as they shaped dough in the middle of the day on the same cool marble slab, others he remembers reading in schoolbooks, or following in the picture books he had before he could read, turning the pages for his mother – Hindu stories, Greek myths of mortals and nymphs being metamorphosed into swans and rams and stags. English and Scottish kings fighting battles, watching spiders, burning cakes. He closes his eyes. It's a warm, late summer day, and the ward is quiet. He relaxes into his pillows and concentrates on the thin stream of blackbird song trickling in through an open window.

It's a pity he won't pass the stories on, he thinks, sleepily. He should start telling them to the baby, perhaps, if Sharmila will let him. Now he has been in hospital she will be bossier than ever. Will make him relax dutifully on the leather sofa all day and forbid every passing thought about the restaurant.

He misses his friends, he realises. He still has Hari, of course. Hari, the closest he will ever come to having a son – someone to worry about, nurse hopes for, care for. He wants Hari to be happy, wishes, sometimes, that he would do something more with his life. Hopes beyond any realm of possibility that he might, some day, take on the Mountain of Light. But Hari will go his own way, just as they all have. Burning bridges – doing it out of spite for the lives they can't quite control or understand – and moving on. Always leaving.

But Sarah is coming home – Hari has told him. Sarah is coming home to the Mountain of Light, and perhaps they will all be happy again after all . . .

ॐ

She is flying back to London. The coach would have taken three days and, anyway, since she hadn't booked a return date she would have had to wait for a seat. Ryszard went with her to Warsaw and lent her enough for the fare. Said repay it when you can. It doesn't matter. Now go. And she had walked away from him.

They are flying over cloud at the moment, great, fluffy whipped-cream piles of it, towering upwards in the distance like the quirky, insubstantial turrets of dream castles and spreading outwards in every direction in an empty, hummocky, perfect white landscape. The sky up here is an unblemished blue, the sun sharp and bright, slicing in through the tiny portholes, making the cabin seem dark and gloomy. Some passengers have half pulled their blinds to shade their faces as they doze, but Sarah has again abandoned *Anna Karenina*, drawn to the serenity of this privileged view. Periodically the cloud changes, flattens, and for miles seems more like a still sea than land. When holes appear she peers down into the deep chasms at the brown, patchy world below, and it seems to be crawling by so slowly.

In the state of sleepy limbo induced by flying she finds herself thinking about Hari, about how guarded they were in that strange, intense time of sleeping together, how reality never had a chance to hit, it was such a self-contained and short-lived thing, just like her brief relationship with Ryszard. Would it have soured too, she wonders, like her and Jude? Like Jozef and Ewa? Was there no other ending? Or did you just have to put your trust in people and see what happened?

He will be at Heathrow waiting for her. She has never been met by a man at an airport before. The thought makes her smile. She wonders whether she will be relieved to see him. Whether she will spot him in the crowd and run to him and be glad that it is Hari there and not Jude or Ryszard or anyone else. Just Hari. She feels a twinge of anxiety in her stomach. She is going home but, in a way, it feels as if she is flying somewhere entirely new, into a different, unpredictable, untested life.